"Do you ever fe___ ___ be out there wa___ __ you?"

Keely asked abruptly.

Sam straightened at that remark. "Why would you ask that?"

Keely suddenly felt very silly asking the question. "Fanciful imagination, I guess," she said lightly. "Maybe it's all those books I've read about monsters in the woods."

Sam sensed there was more to her question than she seemed able to admit to just yet. A strange feeling was running around deep in his stomach. He didn't like this feeling. Every time he had it, something bad happened.

Keely started for the door, with Sam following her at a more leisurely pace. Just before he stepped inside, he looked over his shoulder toward the nearby woods.

Could someone have been out there tonight?

Dear Reader,

I'm not going to waste any time before I give you the good news: This month begins with a book I know you've all been waiting for. *Nighthawk* is the latest in Rachel Lee's ultrapopular CONARD COUNTY miniseries. Craig Nighthawk has never quite overcome the stigma of the false accusations that have dogged his steps, and now he might not live to get the chance. Because in setting himself up as reclusive Esther Jackson's protector— and lover—he's putting himself right in harm's way.

Amnesia is the theme of Linda Randall Wisdom's *In Memory's Shadow*. Sometimes you *can* go home again—if you're willing to face the danger. Luckily for Keely Harper, Sam Barkley comes as part of the package. Two more favorite authors are back—Doreen Roberts with the suspenseful *Every Waking Moment*, and Kay David with *And Daddy Makes Three*, a book to touch your heart. And welcome a couple of new names, too. Though each has written elsewhere, Maggie Simpson and Wendy Haley make their Intimate Moments debuts with *McCain's Memories* (oh, those cowboys!) and *Gabriel Is No Angel* (expect to laugh), respectively.

So that's it for this time around, but be sure to come back next month for more of the best romance reading around, right here in Silhouette Intimate Moments.

Yours,

Leslie Wainger

Leslie Wainger
Senior Editor and Editorial Coordinator

Please address questions and book requests to:
Silhouette Reader Service
U.S.: 3010 Walden Ave., P.O. Box 1325, Buffalo, NY 14269
Canadian: P.O. Box 609, Fort Erie, Ont. L2A 5X3

IN MEMORY'S SHADOW

LINDA RANDALL WISDOM

Silhouette®
INTIMATE™MOMENTS®

Published by Silhouette Books

America's Publisher of Contemporary Romance

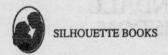

SILHOUETTE BOOKS

ISBN 0-373-07782-3

IN MEMORY'S SHADOW

Printed in U.S.A.

Books by Linda Randall Wisdom

Silhouette Intimate Moments

No More Secrets #640
No More Mister Nice Guy #741
In Memory's Shadow #782

Previously published under the pseudonym of Linda Wisdom

Silhouette Romance

Dancer in the Shadows #49
Fourteen Karat Beauty #95
Bright Tomorrow #132
Dreams from the Past #166
Snow Queen #241

Silhouette Special Edition

A Man with Doubts #27
Unspoken Past #74
Island Rogue #160
Business as Usual #190
A World of Their Own #220

LINDA RANDALL WISDOM

first sold to Silhouette Books on her wedding anniversary in 1979 and hasn't stopped since! She loves looking for the unusual when she comes up with an idea, and only hopes her readers enjoy reading her stories as much as she enjoys writing them.

A native Californian, she is married and has two dogs, five parrots and a tortoise, so life is never boring—or quiet—in the Wisdom household. When she isn't writing, she enjoys going to the movies, reading, making jewelry and fabric painting.

For Lynne Smith,
good buddy and fellow volcano climber,
who also enjoys anything that goes bump in the night.

Prologue

Echo Ridge, California, thirty years ago

The loud voices raised in argument didn't wake her. But the startling sound of her mother screaming did.

"Mommy," she whimpered, sitting up in bed and rubbing her eyes with her tiny fists. She raised her voice. "Mommy." She huddled under her fluffy pink blanket, hugging her much loved and very battered stuffed dog against her chest to keep her nighttime terrors at bay as the loud voices echoed in her room. Her parents never argued, so she didn't understand what was going on. She could hear music. It was one of her mom's favorite songs. She couldn't understand why a song said that darkness was an old friend. She didn't like it when it was dark. But it was the raised voices that frightened her now.

When the voices didn't stop, she climbed out of bed and carefully reached for her slippers. They were pink and fuzzy just like her blanket; Santa gave them to her last Christmas and she liked the way they kept her feet warm.

She wondered if they were watching a scary movie. Mommy was screaming the same way she did when she found a spider in the linen closet. She carefully opened her bedroom door and peeked out. Why did it look so scary out there? And how come the night-light wasn't on? She didn't like to have to get up and go to the bathroom unless the night-light was on.

"Mommy?" she whispered, feeling more and more scared. She was afraid to raise her voice. After all, she was supposed to be asleep. She tried to tell herself that Mommy and Daddy were just watching a scary movie. That's why Mommy was screaming, she told herself as she crept toward the stairs.

She should go back to her room so Mommy and Daddy wouldn't know she was awake, but she wanted to know why Mommy was screaming and why Daddy was now yelling and saying a lot of bad words. She dropped to her knees when she reached the stair's railing and curled her fingers around the bars as she pressed her face between them. From past experience she knew she could see downstairs from here.

Her tiny brow furrowed as she watched her parents standing near the front door. The man who took care of their garden and did other stuff around the house was there, too. She knew who the man was. She thought he was nice. He would even growl and pretend to be a big bad lion, which made her laugh and shriek as if she were frightened. And he'd fixed her playhouse yesterday. Why did he look so mad now? She hadn't done anything bad. At dinner, Mommy told her what a good girl she had been lately and how she was going to take her to see the new cartoon movie tomorrow.

"You're crazy!" Her daddy shouted, pointing his finger at the man.

"Don't you call me crazy, you son of a—" the man said in a low voice that was so chilling, goose bumps traveled up her spine. She shrank back at the fury in the man's voice. She wanted to cry out and demand to know why he was acting so mean? Why did he make her mommy cry?

She wanted to call out and ask them what was wrong, but something held her back. She wasn't sure what, maybe it was because she wasn't supposed to be out of bed, but she remained silent.

Her mommy and daddy looked surprised when he pulled a gun out of his jacket pocket. Her mommy put her hands to her throat and backed away while her dad shouted, "You bastard!" and leapt for the gun.

The sound was deafening and caused her to jump. Her eyes were glued to the scene below.

Her daddy fell against the wall and sat on the floor. It looked as if her finger paints were splashed on his shirt and there was a weird look on his face. Mommy screamed and knelt on the floor, reaching for Daddy.

"What have you done?" she screamed at the man. "He's dead! You killed him!"

But he didn't answer. Instead, there was another loud noise and her mommy fell down beside her daddy.

She couldn't move as she watched the mean man touch both her mommy and daddy. Something told her she should go back to bed before he saw her. She carefully released her fingers from the railing and inched her way backward by sliding on her bottom and her hands until she reached her door. She crept inside and carefully closed the door before she ran back to her bed and jumped in. She didn't even bother to take off her slippers. She lay there, tightly hugging her toy dog as if he could protect her from the evil out there. She could hear music still playing, this time about a white rabbit and how pills can make you big or small. Her mommy once smiled when she asked her if it was a song about *Alice in Wonderland.* Now, the song just sounded scary.

A few minutes later, she heard her bedroom door ease open. She kept her eyes shut tight, breathing softly just as she would do when Mommy came in to make sure she was asleep. It seemed like a very long time before the door closed again.

She didn't know how long she lay there. She didn't get out of bed again even though a tiny voice in her head told her Mommy wouldn't be coming in to make sure she was asleep tonight.

Chapter 1

Woodland Hills, California, thirty years later

"You know this running away to Hicksville, U.S.A., won't solve anything."

Keely turned slowly at the sound of her ex-husband's voice. She stared at his golden, tanned good looks and wondered why she had never before noticed the slight weakness in the chin and the arrogance in the eyes. She couldn't say all their years together were a waste. She had a wonderful daughter as a result. But the thought of her ex-husband left a very bitter taste in her mouth. She didn't mourn the loss of him, but she did mourn the loss of a marriage she had thought would last forever.

"I'm not running away, Jay," she said as calmly as was possible after she tamped down her first reaction—to deck him and hurt his pretty face. "I decided it was time to

make some changes in my life. This was one of them."
She waved her hand in the direction of the movers, who
were busy loading furniture and boxes onto the van.

His brilliant blue eyes slid sideways toward a teenage
girl who was chattering away with two other girls.

"What about her?"

Now Keely really wanted to plant her fist in his weak
jaw.

"*Steffie,*" she said, stressing their daughter's name,
"doesn't like the idea of leaving her friends, but she's
willing to give it a try. After all, her father doesn't seem
to give a damn she'll be moving several hundred miles
away."

He flushed. "I just thought I'd ask," he said sullenly.

"You bastard," she snarled, making sure to keep her
voice low. She wasn't about to let their daughter know just
what a jerk her father was. "Why are you even asking
now? You never cared before."

"I'm not the one taking her hundreds of miles away
from the only home she's ever known." He was gentleman
enough to keep his voice low so he wouldn't be overheard.

"And I wasn't the one who had an affair that stirred up
this whole mess," she retorted. Keely's fingers curled
tightly into her palms. For a moment, she seriously thought
about punching the man. "I realize she might be a perfect
image of you, but every day I thank God she didn't get
your personality." She stepped back and took a deep
breath. "Forget it. I promised myself I wouldn't fight with
you."

Jay turned his head and stared at his daughter. Steffie's
shoulder-length tresses were a darker shade of blonde than
his own sun-gold coloring and her eyes a darker blue that
turned cobalt when she wore any shade of blue. He never
seemed to notice that, though. All he saw was that her jaw
betrayed the same stubborn vein as her mother's and her

temper as heated as her mother's. When news of his affair had come out, Steffie hadn't lost any time in telling her father exactly what she thought of him. He first blamed Keely for telling their daughter, but Steffie had overheard their argument and let it be known that a so-called good friend of hers had told her what she overheard her parents talking about. When Jay lost his wife, he had lost his daughter, too. Jay's guilt would have forced him to disown his flesh and blood, but his daughter had already taken care of that.

"Hey, Mom, are we going now or what?" Steffie called from the truck. She didn't look at or acknowledge her father by word.

Jay held out his hand. "I hope everything goes well for you, Keely," he said formally, as if speaking to an acquaintance instead of the woman he had been married to for close to fourteen years. "Although, I still can't imagine you wanting to go back to that hick town. It's not as if you grew up there. You left there when you were five years old, for heaven's sake. There's nothing up there for you."

"Right now, Jay, a nice quiet life sounds like exactly what I need. I plan to fix up my parents' house and settle in there." She started toward the utility vehicle she'd bought for the trip. Even with the extra room, the back was piled high with things Steffie didn't feel she could live without until the movers arrived with the rest of their belongings.

"Bye, Jay," Steffie said breezily, climbing into the passenger side. She smiled sweetly at her mother's knowing look.

"If you have any problems, you call me," he told Keely.

She thought about telling him she hadn't called him before when she had problems, so why should she bother now? Instead, she gave a curt nod as she climbed into the truck.

Jay shook his head as he studied the four-wheel-drive vehicle. "I can't see you driving one of these."

"Max will be perfect up there," Steffie spoke up.

He grimaced. He'd never understood why Keely felt the need to name her vehicles.

"His name is from the *Mad Max* movie," Steffie explained.

"Appropriate," he muttered, stepping back.

"Bye, Jay, have a good life." Keely started up the engine and backed down the driveway.

"Did he give you the speech about watching out for bears and tigers in the woods?" Steffie asked. "Or did he tell you that Echo Ridge probably still hasn't gotten running water in their houses yet and you'll have to go outside and chop wood so we'll have heat? And all the men will call you 'little lady.'"

Keely burst out laughing. "You are an impossible child."

"Yes, but you love me anyway because I'm just like you."

"How true. Steffie, we are going to have the time of our lives up there," she announced.

The young girl immediately turned on the radio, pushing buttons until she got the rock station she wanted.

As Keely drove onto the freeway, she felt a strange ticklish feeling creep along her backbone.

Her parents had died in a traffic accident when Keely was five. Keely had been gravely ill with pneumonia and she was told her grandmother had come over to take care of her that day. Not long after Keely recovered from her illness, her grandmother moved the two of them south to San Diego.

When Keely was young, she always felt as if a part of

her life had abruptly ended with the death of her parents. As if something had been left unfinished. It also bothered her that she couldn't remember them. She had stopped asking her grandmother after she saw how upset her queries made her. But she never forgot the questions that she always hoped she'd find answers for. That part of her life had been effectively wiped from her memory. But there were times she wished she knew why she remembered so little before moving to San Diego.

It was only recently that Keely had felt a strong need to return to her roots. While cleaning out a box of papers, she'd found the paperwork for the family home in Echo Ridge. The property had been left to Keely and even when young, she'd insisted her grandmother never sell the house. So it had always been a rental. For the past couple years, it had been unoccupied, so Keely thought this was the time to move up there. She'd contacted the Realtor who'd managed the house for her. Since it was currently uninhabitable, she arranged to rent a house until she could fix hers up.

Keely thought of the nightmare that had plagued her last night. Voices. Music from the late sixties and a terror that had her waking up in a cold sweat. She eventually put it down to the movie she had watched before going to bed and lay back down, but it was a long time before she was able to fall asleep again. It seemed all too real.

None of it mattered now. Keely was looking for a new life and she felt Echo Ridge would give it to her. Her work as a graphic designer could be done anywhere, thanks to computer modems and fax machines. For now, she would just concentrate on making this a true adventure for herself and her daughter.

"What do you think, Steff?" With her hands on hips, her face smudged with dirt, dressed in grubby denim cutoffs and a faded pink T-shirt, Keely looked more like her fifteen-year-old daughter's older sister than her mother.

Steffie looked around the living room. She looked as unkempt as her mother in a pair of faded gray shorts and a blue T-shirt although her curly dark blond hair had been pulled up in a ponytail. The movers had obligingly moved pieces of furniture until Keely and Steffie could agree where they wanted them, and boxes were piled up against walls. But it was the floor to ceiling expanse of glass that attracted her attention and the side door that opened out onto the deck overlooking the woods. They stood there looking at the lush trees that lined the large backyard.

"You do realize that in a horror book there'd be some ugly ole mountain man or monster in those woods watching us all the time and wanting to carry us off to their cave," Steffie said, turning to her mother. "Which one do you think we're lucky enough to have? And is there any chance he could look like Brad Pitt or Christian Slater?"

Keely shuddered. "You know very well we'd end up with someone who looked like a very old tree. I wish you'd quit reading those books!"

Steffie widened her eyes in mock innocence. "But Mom, you told me I can read anything I find in the young adult section!"

"I was thinking more along the lines of *Nancy Drew* or *The Babysitter's Club*."

She rolled her eyes. "Give me a break, Mom. I outgrew those years ago."

Keely looked at her daughter and wondered if she would survive the next few years with her sanity intact.

"Let's concentrate on unpacking the necessary stuff now and we'll worry about the rest tomorrow."

"What about dinner? I'm starving."

"If we're lucky, someone around here delivers."

Steffie peered closely out the living room window. All

she could see were trees. "I don't know about you, but it doesn't look as if we'll find something close by. But it looks like there's another house not far from here."

Keely went into the kitchen and searched for the box she'd marked To Be Opened Immediately. She had packed a little of everything in one box so she wouldn't have to spend days hunting for anything they might need right away.

"I thought I saw a house up there when we went too far trying to find this driveway. Do you want to find the phone book for me?"

Steffie twirled her ponytail around her finger as she walked in the kitchen and searched cabinets until she found the phone books. "Hm." She thumbed through. "We're in luck. There are a few places that deliver. Chinese or pizza?"

"Anything. I'm starving and—"

"And you don't want to cook!" Steffie teased, picking up the cordless phone and punching out numbers. "Okay, then it's Chinese and we're going all out because I'm starved. I just hope they make good lemon chicken."

As Keely emptied the box and thought about the many changes in her life in the past few months, she listened to her daughter ask questions about certain dishes and briskly place their order. She kept wondering if she'd made the right decision about the move. She hadn't thought Steffie would be willing to leave school with only a few months remaining in the present school year, but the teen had patiently explained to her mother that it was for the best because she'd have a chance to get acquainted with other kids before summer. And Keely knew if anyone could settle in to a new situation and make new friends with remarkable ease it was her daughter.

"We are set!" Steffie announced with her usual exuberance. "They actually have bacon wrapped shrimp, so I ordered that, too."

Keely grinned. "I guess that means we can stay."

"You got it." Steffie pulled a can of soda out of the refrigerator. "How long do you think it will take to fix up your house?"

She shrugged. "I won't know until we go over there and take a look. The Realtor was supposed to keep up any major repairs so it should only need painting and new carpeting. The roof was replaced last year, so hopefully that means there won't be any water damage."

"It's nice and quiet up here and the roads look great for in-line skating." Steffie popped the tab and drank deeply. "I'm all for that."

Keely shook her head and chuckled at her daughter's reasoning.

Steffie set the can on the counter and looked at her mother with a gaze that looked vaguely troubled. "Does it bother you? Coming back here after all this time?"

Keely took the time to study her emotions and gauge the feelings that had been running through her since they arrived in Echo Ridge. There had been a faint sense of unease when she drove through the small mountain town, but she put it down to the reason why she'd left here close to thirty years ago. There was still that heavy curtain hiding a part of her life she knew she would never recover. More than one doctor had told her not to worry about it. A bad case of pneumonia after her parents' deaths had left a little girl's memory blank.

"No," she said finally. 'It doesn't bother me."

Steffie studied her mother's face, but she didn't look reassured.

Later, Keely wasn't sure what woke her up in the middle of the night. She got up and headed for the window to see if an animal was prowling around and its cry might have awakened her. She didn't see any need to worry about the human kind. She had heard the crime rate up here was almost nonexistent thanks to a sheriff who cracked down on lawbreakers. As she looked out into the darkness all she saw was a pinpoint of light in the distance. At that moment, an animal's howl sounded far away. At least, she hoped it was far away.

"Welcome to the real world, Keely," she murmured, going back to bed.

Keely and Steffie went into town the next day to pick up groceries and do some exploring.

Keely looked around the small town with fascination as she and her daughter noticed the old buildings blending with the new. Steffie was more fascinated with the drugstore that still sold a little of everything.

"Wow," Steffie breathed, picking up a bottle of tonic bearing a label explaining it was for "lady's complaints." "You mean they knew about PMS even back then?"

Keely looked at the bottle that stated the tonic had been manufactured since the late eighteen hundreds. "I'm sure this is a surprise to you, but that was a bit before my time."

"Hi!"

They turned to find a girl of about Steffie's age looking at them with a bright expectant expression on her face.

"You're the Harpers, aren't you?" she said, looking from one to the other, her gaze lingering on Steffie. "I'm Lisa Barkley. Actually, I live up the road from you. We heard you'd just moved in."

"I'm Steffie Harper, the more interesting member of the family, and my mom's Keely," the girl explained, sending her mother a teasing look. "Are you in the tenth grade?"

Lisa nodded.

"How are the teachers up here?"

"Some great, some make you work."

"How terrible for you kids!" Keely laughed. She looked around the store. "Is your mother here with you?"

Lisa shook her head. "I just have my dad," she explained. "He's around somewhere."

Steffie looked at her mother. "Is it okay if Lisa shows me around?"

"Wouldn't it be nicer if Lisa volunteered?"

"I'd love to!" Lisa looked around then waved at someone. "Hey, there's my dad."

"Well, Lisa, you sure didn't waste any time, did you?" The male voice was slow and husky to the ear.

Keely turned around and found she had to tip her head back. She was tall, almost five feet nine inches, but this man was easily taller. She gauged he had to be close to six-two. Graying brown hair was cut short, as if the owner preferred minimum care; he had brown eyes that she'd bet didn't miss a thing and a nose that looked as if it had been broken once or twice. Chiseled lines in his face showed every month of his forty-something years, which told her time had not always been kind to this man. The khaki shirt covering his chest and the worn jeans that didn't go with it seemed to suit him. Her gaze fastened on the star pinned to his chest. No wonder. Lisa's father was the town sheriff.

"Dad, this is Steffie Harper and her mom, Keely. And this is my dad, Sam Barkley." Lisa practically bounced with her enthusiasm, as she added unnecessarily, "They moved into the Reynolds' house. Is it okay if I show Steffie around?"

Sheriff Sam Barkley kept his attention focused on Keely's face. "If it's all right with her mother."

"How do you expect to get back home?" Keely asked Steffie.

"I'll be around the rest of the day. Either myself or one

of my deputies can run them home when they're ready," Sam offered.

"How many people can say they have the town law for chauffeur service?" Steffie asked her mother.

"Don't get her started," she said with a sigh. "All right." She barely had the words out when her daughter and new friend had taken off.

"They'll be fine," Sam assured her. "We're still pretty much a small town around here and Lisa knows if she tries anything she shouldn't, someone will be on the phone in thirty seconds tops to tell me what she did."

"I guess some things don't change," Keely smiled.

He glanced around. "Well, I better get back to work. Don't worry about your daughter. She'll be home as soon as Lisa makes sure she sees everything and meets everyone." He smiled, tipped his hat and walked away.

Keely turned to watch him walk out of the store.

"Don't be offended. While Sam's the best sheriff a town could have, he's never been known for his social skills."

The man appeared to be in his late forties with a smile that said he knew just how charming he was. His white pharmacist's jacket set off his deeply tanned skin and dark hair heavily threaded with silver. She sensed he knew just how well the white jacket suited his dark good looks.

"John Harris." He held out his hand. "And you're Keely Harper, who's decided to return to the fold. Although, why you'd want to come back here is beyond me. Not much goes on around here."

"That's fine with me," she replied. "I'm looking for some peace and quiet."

She didn't like the way he held on to her hand longer than necessary or the intense way he looked at her, as if she were a specimen under a microscope. She reminded herself that lechers were everywhere, even in small towns.

Not to mention she saw him as someone honestly too old for her. She kept her smile intact as she slid her hand from his grasp.

"Well, I carry pretty much anything you can find in the big city," he assured her. "And quite a few things you might not find there. If you need anything I don't have, I'll be only too happy to order it for you."

"Thank you." She kept her smile firmly fastened on her lips even as her unease grew. She couldn't pin her feelings down, but there was something about the man that bothered her. "If you'll excuse me, I still have several errands to run."

"Come by anytime." His smile grew broader.

"Thank you." She nodded at him and quickly left, pushing the glass door with a bit more force than necessary.

"I hate to think he hits on every woman who goes in there," she muttered, tossing her packages in the back of her Blazer.

As Keely continued her errands, she noted she was receiving discreet but decidedly curious stares as she wandered through the town's bookstore in search of reading material. She put it down to typical small-town curiosity and quickly escaped to the shelves promoting recent bestsellers.

"Don't mind the gawkers. It's a small town and good manners are usually forgotten. As for me, I've never considered good manners all that much fun, so I'll be crass and just approach you. You must be Keely Harper."

Keely turned to the speaker. She looked to be about Keely's age, dressed in navy blue leggings, navy leather flats and a red-and-navy geometric print, hip-length cotton shirt. For a moment Keely could swear even her eyes matched her outfit.

The woman laughed. "I'm Chloe Webster, owner and

general slave of Echo Ridge's bookshop. Don't be surprised I figured out who you were. We don't get a lot of newcomers in town and besides, Sheila over at the Realtor's is one of my best customers and loves to brag about her new clients."

Keely smiled. "Did you hear anything else about me that I might find interesting? I always enjoy hearing what people think about me."

"You're divorced, you have a teenage daughter, you lived here thirty years ago, you're now leasing the Reynolds' house until you can get yours ready for habitation and you're a graphic designer." She ticked off on her fingers. "Have I left anything out?"

Keely chuckled. "At least no one talked about the alien I keep locked up in the hall closet. I'd hate for that bit of gossip to get out."

"I'm sure that little tidbit will come up in the next day or so," Chloe assured her, her dark blue eyes dancing with laughter. "So, what kind of trash reading are you looking for?"

"What do you suggest?"

"I'm what you call a book slut. I read a little of everything." Chloe picked up several paperbacks and handed them to Keely. "You can't go wrong with these." She turned her head as someone called out her name and asked a question. "Tell Amy I sold the last copy yesterday, but I did reorder it. It should be here by Thursday." She looked at Keely. "Come by either Tuesday or Thursday. Those are my slowest days and we can sit in the back and have coffee. If you're a wonderful person you'll bring something filled with sugar, preferably chocolate, and I'll be your friend forever."

"I'll remember that." Keely hefted the books in her hand and headed for the checkout counter. She turned around to ask a question but said nothing when she noticed an odd look flash across Chloe's face. If she didn't know any better she'd swear it was pity. She managed to give the woman a bright smile that indicated she hadn't seen her expression and she hurried to the register. In the end, she dismissed it as perhaps Chloe's being unable to imagine why someone who had spent so many years in Los Angeles would want to come back here.

As she wandered through the grocery store stocking up on staples and anything that looked good, she was aware of more curious glances thrown her way. She expected that. After all, Echo Ridge wasn't that large a town. But what she couldn't understand was some of the expressions on the faces of the older residents. She was almost sure she saw sadness there before they hastily turned away. She never felt so glad as when she finished her grocery shopping and was ready to return to the house.

As Keely's bright red Blazer headed for the outskirts of town, quite a few people watched her. And all had their own views about her.

"I was surprised to hear she was willing to come back here after what had happened," a silver-haired woman confided in one of her Tuesday afternoon bridge partners. "Do you think she remembers what happened that night?"

"She sure doesn't act like it. She was very ill after the incident and some say she lost her memory of what happened. She still might not know the truth. I can't imagine her grandmother ever told her. Evelyn was pretty broken up afterward, if you remember."

A third woman joined the conversation. "I know I wouldn't want to remember something like that. My Barney still has nightmares about that night. I still remember him coming home after he was at the crime scene. He said he had to take a shower. But I heard him in the bathroom and he was sick as a dog. He told me the room looked like the inside of a meat-packing plant. Willis should have gone to the chair for what he had done to them instead of living in prison for the rest of his life."

"I heard she's fixing up her parents' house and plans to live there. Maybe her ex-husband ended up with everything and she had no choice but to come back here."

"I heard she has her own business. She asked if there would be a problem if she had four phone lines installed. Now, what does a woman need with four phone lines?"

"Maybe it has to do with her business. You know, their deaths was something we all kept quiet for about the short time she was here before Evelyn moved her away. I always thought a lot of Evelyn. She was a good woman who helped out anyone who was in need. I'm sure not going to say anything about it."

It wasn't just the women who wondered about Echo Ridge's newest resident. Men standing around the gas station had their own opinions to offer.

"I'm surprised Evelyn let her come back here."

"The woman is an adult, so it's not as if she had any say in it. I was always surprised Evelyn hadn't sold the house years ago."

One man lit up a cigarette and drew on it deeply. "With that kind of history, do you think she could have sold it? I know I wouldn't want to live in a house where such a horrible murder happened. I have to say she grew up into a fine-looking woman. Someone looking like her won't be single for long. Too bad she's got that kind of history on her plate. It could make a man think twice, even if it had nothing to do with her."

They all shook their heads in sympathy. Even thirty years later, the unspoken vow taken back then still held— the townspeople would never bring up the terrible murder of Keely's parents.

Not all felt sympathetic toward Keely. One had watched her, feeling the hate build up inside like a bitter bile. That witch had ruined lives thirty years ago, by breaking up a family and eventually sending innocent children into foster care. If she intended to stick around, she would soon find out what payback meant.

"Lisa's really nice," Steffie informed her mother as they ate dinner in the early evening. "She's lived here all her life."

"All those years," Keely said dryly. "The poor dear."

Steffie wrinkled her nose. "Give me a break, Mom. Her mom died when she was nine and her dad became sheriff when his dad retired. She says he's not as geeky as he looks."

"I don't think Sheriff Barkley looks geeky," she said absently.

Steffie's blue eyes took on a dangerous gleam at her mother's statement. "I didn't think so either. Lisa said she'll take me around at school and introduce me to everybody." She toyed with her green beans.

Keely resisted the urge to be a mother and say she was glad her little girl was making friends and all sorts of mom statements like that.

"I'm glad the two of you hit it off. She seems like a nice girl."

"I told her if she was that open and nice at my old school, she'd be blackballed before homeroom was over."

"That's right dear, don't hold things back. Tell the truth." Keely shook her head at her daughter's blunt words. "And she's still talking to you?"

"Sure, she believes in telling the truth, too."

Keely inwardly shuddered at the thought of another Steffie wandering around. The girl frowned at her mother, catching the meaning of her action.

"You don't mind if she comes over day after tomorrow, do you? I thought we'd have lunch."

"That's fine with me. I'll probably still be setting up my office. I want to get that artwork off to Mainwaring Engineering. Although I also want to go over to the house and see what needs to be done first," she said. "All I ask is you don't try to cook something complicated that leaves the kitchen looking like a war zone."

"Come on, Mom, give me some credit." Her next statement warned Keely to prepare herself for a shock. "I'm going to be fifteen and a half in two months."

She peered closely at her daughter's face. "Yes, I can see the crow's-feet already beginning to form. Perhaps we should find a good antiwrinkle cream for you."

She shot her mother a "get real" look. "Ha, ha, very funny. I'll be able to get my driver's permit then and before you know it, my driver's license."

Keely shuddered at the thought of her baby behind the wheel of the truck. Racing down the road. It was enough to give a mother nightmares.

Steffie looked off into space. "What kind of car do you think I should get?"

"A Big Wheel sounds perfect."

Keely was glad Steffie had met someone so quickly since it helped her adjust to her new life. While she knew she didn't need to worry about the girl, she did. She felt guilty for taking her away from her friends and familiar surroundings, but when she had broached the idea of moving up here, Steffie was all for it. Deep down, she knew if her grandmother had been alive, she would have vehemently protested Keely's idea and probably tried to persuade her to move to San Diego.

Keely could never understand her grandmother's vehemence about the town, although she'd spoken fondly of old friends. She had never questioned her grandmother's opinion because one thing the older woman had always been very tight-lipped about was anything to do with the town of Keely's birth and the time of her parents' deaths. Keely, as a child, decided it hurt her grandmother too much to talk about her only daughter's death so she stopped asking. The adult Keely wished she hadn't stopped. Perhaps she would have learned something by now.

Keely was busy hooking up her computer equipment when Lisa arrived. The girl greeted her with a bright smile and loped off with Steffie to the latter's bedroom. Within moments, rock music vibrated throughout the house.

"I'm sure it could be worse," Keely murmured, as she returned to setting up her office.

Keely wasn't too sure about the idea when the two girls volunteered to make lunch until she realized they had planned on not making anything more demanding than grilled cheese sandwiches. She didn't know about Lisa's cooking skills, but Steffie's were minimal at best.

"I heard Mike Palmer's coming out to see you," Lisa announced to Keely as they ate their sandwiches.

"Why would he want to see me?"

"He works for our local paper." She made a face. "He thinks he's really hot stuff because he used to work in Sacramento and once interviewed the governor. Some say he got fired because he was caught in bed with his boss's wife." She giggled. "He's been divorced twice and he's dated every single woman in town."

"He doesn't sound all that difficult to resist," Keely commented.

"She's been out with some real jerks," Steffie confided to her new friend. "I told Mom at least she got it out of her system first thing."

Keely rolled her eyes. "Am I to have no secrets?"

"Not a one," Steffie cheerfully declared, popping a potato chip in her mouth and crunching down. "Maybe now you'll find some nice guy.'' She shared a sly glance with Lisa.

"I just figured I'd warn you about Mike,'' Lisa said. "Last year, everyone was talking about Chloe Webster's affair with Mike. Some of the women were so nasty to Chloe she almost cried. Dad got so mad, he told them if they didn't knock it off, he'd see if the old statute about women being publicly dragged through the town for malicious mischief was still on the books. That really shut them up.'' She giggled again.

"Your father sounds as if he doesn't put up with anything or anyone,'' Keely commented, finding herself curious to know more about the taciturn man in khaki.

"He doesn't. He said he was made sheriff to protect everybody and he intends to do that. Old Mrs. Stone says he's supposed to protect the good people.'' She made a face. "He told her not to worry. That he'll protect the old biddies the same as anyone else. She didn't like that. She thinks she's the real leader in this town, but everyone knows it's Miz Nan who knows everyone's secrets and if anyone gets out of line she puts them back real fast. She used to be a teacher.''

"So Mrs. Stone thinks she needs to watch over the morals of the townspeople?'' Keely asked, fascinated with the gossip that probably traveled through the small town as fast as the speed of light.

"Her husband was a minister. Dad said he probably died just to get away from her nagging.''

Keely choked on her drink and hastily put down her glass. She shook her head and stood up. "And on that note, I do believe I will return to setting up my office,'' she announced.

Just at that moment, the doorbell chimed.

Lisa ran over to the front window and peeked

out. "Mike's Porsche is parked out front. He'll be doing his welcome to the community speech."

"You girls finish eating. I'll take care of the welcoming committee." Keely shook her head as she walked to the front door. "What I wouldn't give for a few hours of peace and meditation."

The door chimes echoed through the house again.

"Damn," Keely muttered. "So much for peace and meditation."

Chapter 2

Keely quickly noticed Mike Palmer turned out to be everything Lisa had said. And more.

She opened the door to find a man lounging on the doorstep. She assumed he was dressing the part of the renegade reporter in jeans and a tweed wool blazer topping a cotton shirt with the collar left open. His designer sunglasses were ostentatiously tucked into the front pocket of his jacket. She privately decided he felt the demeanor went with the snazzy black Porsche parked in full view behind him. She just bet he spent his weekend mornings patiently hand-waxing the shiny exterior.

"Keely Harper?" He flashed a lady killing smile. "I'm Mike Palmer." He held out his hand. "I'm with the *Echo Ridge Pilot*. I wanted to welcome you to the community and see if I could do a quick interview for our paper."

Keely had never liked a man with smooth hands. It told her he didn't deign to get his hands dirty. Mike's hands were not only smooth, but a bit soft, and the nails professionally manicured. What irritated her even more was the way he looked her up and down in that thoroughly masculine way. For the first time, she didn't mind a good-looking man catching her in her rattiest jeans, a T-shirt that hung loosely down to her hips and her hair pulled back in an untidy ponytail.

"Is that all right with you?" he asked when she didn't answer him right away.

"Why would you want to do a story on me?" she returned.

He looked confused by her blunt question but quickly recovered. "Why not?" He flashed his killer smile again. "Not too many women want to return to a small town when they've had a taste of the big city. And I would think someone who looks like you would prefer the nightlife instead of wildlife."

"You moved out here." She knew she was rude by not inviting him in, but she sensed if she had invited him in, he'd be next to impossible to usher out.

He shook his head. "I've been here only for the past six years. I wanted a change of pace from big-city reporting, and the freedom of working on this paper means I have more time to work on my book. So, how about it? Any chance in my getting to know all about you?" He lowered his voice to an intimate murmur.

"I think if you wanted to know all about me, you'd be better off talking to my daughter," Keely said pleasantly. "Steffie's the one who knows all my secrets. Steffie!" She raised her voice. "How do you feel about being interviewed for the local paper?"

Steffie, with Lisa right behind her, appeared behind Keely.

"Newspaper?" she asked with wide-eyed innocence. "Really?"

Keely wasn't fooled by her daughter's look of naiveté. She had to give her credit for putting on such a good act.

Mike looked disgruntled but quickly recovered. "Sure, maybe the kid can tell me a few of your innermost secrets." He chuckled.

Keely swallowed her laughter. There was nothing Steffie hated more than being called a kid. She was positive the girl would do her best to put on a good show.

"Perhaps she'll find out a few of yours," she countered.

He stopped just before he stepped over the threshold. "You're not the cream puff I thought you were," he said with a trace of admiration. "How about dinner some night?"

She wondered if he'd accept her rejection if she explained she could be starving and she wouldn't go out with him. "Let me get back to you."

He nodded, as if there was no doubt she'd call him with a suggestion they take off for the weekend. He glanced down at his watch.

"Wow, I had no idea it was so late," he said with studied surprise. "I'm sorry, but I guess I'll have to talk to your daughter another day."

"Fine with me," Steffie piped up.

He managed a smile and nodded. "I'll call you." He flashed his polished smile at Keely and ambled back down the steps to his waiting Porsche.

"Egocentric jerk," Keely muttered, carefully closing the door after him even though she really longed to slam it.

"What a putz!" Steffie said, storming into the room with an astonished Lisa on her heels. "Sheesh, Mom, the guy acted as if he expected you to jump his bones any second." She rolled her eyes with typical teen disdain.

"If he's hoping to get lucky he better not hold his

breath." Keely managed a wan smile at Lisa. "You poor thing, you probably didn't expect all this."

"Are you kidding? I got to see Mike Palmer put in his place," Lisa enthused, eyes shining. "Dad said he'd get his one day and I'm just glad I got to see it."

"With someone like him it's not usually over so easily," Keely said.

"But you basically told him 'Thanks, but no thanks,'" Steffie argued.

"Which means he thinks I was playing hard to get and he'll be back for more."

Lisa looked at Keely with open admiration. "How do you know that?"

"I asked her that once and she told me it came with the years," Steffie pronounced.

Keely looked properly affronted at that. "I am not over the hill just yet."

Steffie jumped up. "Come on, let's dig through my makeup collection. I went to school with a couple girls whose moms were on the soaps. They always shared the makeup they got from the makeup artists. I've got tons of stuff," she bragged.

Keely thought of the box Steffie had packed so carefully. "Tons is a good word for it," she murmured, not even wanting to think what the girls would end up looking like.

Sam's favorite time of day was the evenings when he sat on the back deck with a beer and cigarette, although he was cutting down on the latter. He enjoyed this time because he could reflect on problems that had cropped up during the day and sometimes even solve them. This evening was no different. Except the problem he mulled over didn't come from the station, but lived right up the road and had the kind of smile that warmed a man's insides.

"You shouldn't be sitting out here by yourself," Lisa scolded, walking outside and settling in the chair next to him. She wrinkled her nose at his bottle of beer and cigarette. "Not healthy, Dad."

"Yeah, but neither is chocolate and I remember you scarfing that stuff down only five minutes ago."

She haughtily ignored his teasing statement and looked off in the distance where she could see what he did—pinpoint lights twinkling from Keely and Steffie's house.

"Keely is really nice, isn't she?"

Sam's internal radar sounded a warning at his daughter's all-too-casual question. "She seems to be."

"Steffie says even with her heavy work schedule Keely always made sure to get to anything going on at Steffie's school. And she goes in-line skating with her." Lisa's enthusiasm grew with each word. "Isn't that neat? I don't know any moms who would do that."

"In line?"

"Rollerblades."

Sam shuddered at the thought of rolling on skates not that much more reliable in his eyes than ice skates. Lisa had been asking for a pair and he had been able to put her off so far. He feared if her new friend had a pair, it wouldn't be so easy to deny her from now on.

"Daddy." A small hand wiggled its way into his.

He set his beer bottle on the ground and transferred his cigarette to the other hand so he could keep her hand in his. "The last time you called me that you wanted me to allow you to go to the movies with Richard Lamb. You're not going to ask if you can bleach your hair blonde or something equally disgusting, are you?"

"No." She prudently remained quiet a few moments. "I just thought we could have them over for dinner some night. I mean, they're new in town and everything."

"Honey, I don't think we have to worry about their

being alone for long. I wouldn't be surprised if Mrs. Harper's social schedule was be filled in no time," he said with a wry twist of the lips.

"Not if she tells all the creeps off the way she told Mike Palmer." She giggled, then proceeded to tell her dad about the aborted interview.

Sam had to chuckle at that. "It just goes to show there are some women who can't be charmed by a snake."

As he sat in the darkness with his daughter curled up beside him, Sam thought about the years that loomed ahead of him. He knew Lisa was growing up so fast. Before he knew it, he would be spending these evenings alone while wondering what boy was daring to debauch his daughter and plotting what he'd do with the kid. Along with those thoughts were more than a few about the lady living up the road. If he was even half as cocky as Mike, he'd be on the phone asking her out for dinner. Except Sam never liked rejection and if he wanted to be honest, he doubted he was even close to the type of man Keely Harper liked. After all, what woman wanted a small-town sheriff who wasn't into bright lights and parties?

"Are you sure you don't want me to drive you in for your first day?" Keely asked Steffie over breakfast.

The girl shot her mother her patented "Get real, Mom" look.

"Lisa said her dad will take us today although she usually takes the bus," she explained a little too patiently. "It will look more normal that way. I won't look like the new kid in school."

"You're right, it's entirely normal for a child to arrive in a sheriff's car." Keely poured herself a cup of coffee. She decided not having to get up at four in the morning was a definite plus. "And whether you like it or not, you are the new kid."

"Not if I don't act like one. Which means I can't have my mother driving me to school my first day." Steffie displayed composure Keely was certain the girl had been born with. "What about you? You're not going to turn into one of those moms who cleans the house until it's sterile and bakes cookies, are you?"

"Someone must have crept into the house years ago and stolen my real daughter, replacing her with a perky little robot. Surely by now, you know that will never be me."

"Little? I'll have you know I'm almost an A cup!" Steffie thrust out her chest. She glanced at the clock and yelped. "I've got to get my stuff together before Lisa and her dad show up!"

Keely chuckled as she settled back in her chair and sipped her coffee.

"So, what are you going to do today?" Steffie shouted from her room.

"I thought I'd invite Mel Gibson over for a quickie."

"Ha! If you had Mel Gibson over you'd make sure he'd never leave the house and that I could never get back in!" Steffie bounced back into the kitchen, carrying a knapsack that held notebooks. "There they are." She ran for the front door at the same time she heard a horn. "See ya later."

Keely followed at a slower pace. She doubted she looked all that attractive with her hair barely combed and no makeup, but she could see the two girls were rapidly turning into good friends and figured Lisa's father might as well see her at her worst. Hopefully, he wouldn't run off screaming.

By the time she reached the outside, Steffie had already climbed into the back seat with Lisa.

"Are you sure you want to do this?" Keely asked, greeting Sam with a broad smile.

His grin split his craggy features and almost softened

them. "Two is usually easier than one. Plus, they can't get into any trouble back there."

"I like the way you have the screen dividing the front seat from the back," she commented, then turned on her mother persona. "I think I'll see if they can do that with my Blazer. It could come in handy sometime. Steffie said the bus would bring her home."

He nodded. "It drops them off around three forty-five. Although either I or one of my deputies pick Lisa up when the weather's bad. I can do the same for Steffie if you'd like."

"That's very nice of you, but—"

"No, it's just my way of keeping them safe," he interrupted what he knew to be a protest. "And none of my men mind helping out. We're a small town and we all do what we can for each other."

"Since I work at home I'm more than willing to share carpool duties," she offered.

He nodded and grinned. "Sure, if you want to be that brave." With a wave he started off.

Keely winced as she heard her daughter's voice through the open car window as the truck rolled down the driveway.

"I can't believe Mom had the nerve to come out here without any makeup on! Believe me, she usually doesn't look so bad."

"She used to be such a sweet baby," she complained, going back into the house.

When Keely later drove into town to pick up her mail, she found a hand-printed envelope in her mailbox. Once she was seated in the Blazer, she used her thumbnail to slit the envelope open.

Keely;
You ruined too many lives to be allowed to go un-

punished. The time is coming when you will understand just what you will have to do to atone for such terrible sins.

"Welcome to small-town America," she said to herself, tossing it to one side. For a moment, she wondered how the writer had gotten her post office box number, not to mention what the letter even meant. Right now, she wouldn't put it past Jay to send her the letter as a sick joke.

Keely put the letter out of her mind as she returned home and performed chores around the house before retiring to her office after lunch. Except, as she sat before her computer, the words from the letter haunted her. When she realized there wasn't any way she could design a cheery logo for a baby clothing store, she turned off the computer and went into her bedroom. It didn't take her long to change into an old pair of jeans and T-shirt. Perhaps poking around the house would keep her mind off the letter.

"Mom, where are you?"

Keely looked out of her bedroom. "What are you doing home so early?" she asked, glancing at the clock. "It's only one-thirty."

"Isn't it great? They only have a half day every other Thursday," Steffie explained, pulling off her backpack and setting it down. "What are you up to?"

"How was school?"

She shrugged. "Not too bad. Pretty much like my old school, except most of the kids with a driver's license don't have a BMW. Pickup trucks are the vehicle of choice around here."

"Thank heavens for small favors," Keely said under her breath. "I thought I'd go over to the house and make a list of what needed to be done, so I know what I need to hire someone to do and what I can do myself.''

Steffie's eyes lit up. "Can I come along?"

"Sure. An extra pair of hands is always useful. You better change into something you don't mind getting dirty."

Steffie changed her clothes in record time and they were off.

Keely felt the first stirring of something foreboding as Steffie read the directions to the house and Keely began driving. She could feel her palms grow moist and slide along the perimeter of the steering wheel, although the air in the truck was comfortably cool. A tiny knot began twisting its way through the lowest part of her stomach and she felt as if her lunch had turned into a large disagreeable ball.

"Turn left here," Steffie instructed, unaware of her mother's distress.

Keely's hands slipped on the steering wheel as she turned it. She quickly wiped one palm then the other on her legs as she drove slowly down the side road. Towering trees hid the house from view but something in the back of her mind told her that there was a time the trees weren't that high. She stopped the Blazer in front of the two-story house and just stared at the building.

The wood exterior was appropriately faded and weathered and the stone along the sides made to look as if the house had been built around old boulders. A bay window dominated the front while upstairs several windows were bare of any covering. There was a hexagon-shaped window at one end. There was nothing threatening about the house, so why did Keely feel so uncomfortable the longer she stared at it?

"Wow, this looks really nice." Steffie pushed open her door and jumped out. "Do you have the key?" She jogged up the steps and cupped her hands around her face as she peered in the bay window. "No furniture."

"The house was always rented out unfurnished," Keely said in a low voice. Her pace was much slower as she climbed the five steps. Why did the house bother her so much? She reached inside her jeans pocket and pulled out a key. She could have sworn it suddenly turned white-hot in her hand.

She cleared her throat. "Let's take a look, shall we?" She inserted the key in the lock and slowly turned it to one side.

Steffie stood close to her side, eager to go inside and explore.

Keely pushed the door open. There was no creak as it effortlessly swung back to one side. The interior was dark and she blinked to adjust her eyesight.

Steffie had already gone inside and searched for a light switch. "No electricity," she announced, flipping the switch up and down.

"I guess I'll have to arrange to have it turned on," Keely said in a faint voice. She couldn't step inside! Her legs seemed to refuse to move. She finally ordered one foot to move forward and it did. As she stepped into the entryway, she happened to look at the stairs before her. Without any thought, her gaze lifted to the top of the stairs and the railing that looked down. She swayed slightly. A roaring sound filled her head and brightly colored spots danced in front of her eyes. She felt as if she were listening to screams from far away. Screams and cries and other loud noises rang in her ears, deafening her to anything else. She dropped to her knees, slapping her hands over her ears to drown out the sounds, but they refused to stop.

"Mom? Mom!" Steffie's voice turned to alarm. "Mom!"

Keely was beyond hearing anything but the roaring going on in her head. Her stomach began roiling and she quickly jumped to her feet and ran outside just in time to become violently ill.

"Mom, what's wrong?" Steffie cried out, fast on her heels.

Keely couldn't answer as she collapsed on the bottom step.

"I'm calling for help," Steffie insisted, pulling Keely's cell phone out of her purse.

"I'll be fine," she whispered.

But Steffie wasn't listening.

Keely had no concept of time as she sat there, breathing deeply and trying to calm the insane emotions racing through her body and echoes of screams in her head. The sound of a vehicle pulling in behind her truck faintly registered in her mind as did the sound of a man's quiet voice and Steffie's agitated one.

With her face still resting against her knees she saw a pair of khaki-clad legs ending in highly polished brown cowboy boots before the legs bent slightly and a warm broad hand lingered on top of her head.

"Hey." Sam's rusty-sounding voice was a welcome balm to her tattered emotions.

Keely noticed a strip of silver in her line of vision. She gratefully accepted the stick of gum he held out. She pulled off the wrapper and bit down, savoring the burst of peppermint in her mouth.

"Does that help?" Sam asked quietly.

She nodded, glad he hadn't asked if she felt better, because she doubted she could feel any worse.

"She walked inside and just looked really sick," Steffie explained. The girl stood back, her face white with fear. "I thought she was going to faint or something."

"Steffie tends to exaggerate things," Keely said feebly, starting to stand up. Sam held out his hand and she placed hers inside the warm palm, allowing him to pull her to her feet. "I guess lunch disagreed with me."

Sam didn't look as if he agreed with her explanation. He looked past her at the door that stood open. The darkness beyond was uninviting.

"Checking out the house?" he asked.

Keely nodded. She didn't look over her shoulder. "Maybe there isn't enough air in there or something."

Steffie opened her mouth to argue, but a motion from Sam silenced her. Keely envied the ease he had in hushing her. Keely never had that kind of luck. She made a mental note to find out his secret.

"Why don't I take a look around for you?" he offered.

"Thank you." She didn't protest. At that moment, she didn't care if she ever went inside again.

Sam walked up the steps and disappeared inside. In her mind's eye, Keely could see him walking through every room, then climbing the stairs to the second story and checking out the five bedrooms. She swallowed the bile that started to rise up her throat again. Steffie hovered nearby as if fearing her mother would topple over at any moment.

"Steffie, why don't you sit down?" she suggested. "I'm fine."

She wasn't convinced.

Keely shook her head. "Why did you call the sheriff?"

"You were really sick and you looked so scared. I knew he could make things better," she explained.

Keely took a deep breath. "Steffie, you can't just call up the town's sheriff any time I look as if I'm going to toss my cookies."

"You didn't just look as if you were going to toss 'em, you did," she reminded her.

"Well, no matter, you can't call a man whose job is to

protect people from criminals just because your mother happened to..."

"Freak out?" she supplied the description.

"Allow her imagination to take over," Keely corrected.

"I found a lot of dust and it looks as if some mice took up residence in the kitchen," Sam said as he walked outside. "But there's no sign anyone's broken in," he concluded.

Keely smiled her thanks, but she could feel her facial muscles working overtime.

Sam peered closely at her. "You okay?" he asked.

She nodded. "I guess I should stop watching those horror films about empty houses in the middle of woods."

He still didn't look convinced. "Why don't I follow you back to your house."

"I need to go through the house and make notes on what needs to be done," she protested, although the last thing she wanted to do was step inside there again.

Luckily, Sam overrode her protest. "I think you'd better make it another day. If you want, I'll even go in with you."

"No, I'll be fine," she lied yet again.

Sam's smile was slow in coming and warmed his brown eyes.

"I'll still follow you home."

Sensing he wasn't leaving until she did, Keely climbed back into her truck while Steffie bounced around to the other side.

As she drove down the main road, she was aware of the sheriff's Bronco close behind. Sam honked twice when Keely turned onto the road leading to her house.

"He's very nice," Steffie commented as Keely pulled into the garage.

Keely had no trouble guessing the direction of her thoughts. "Steffie?"

"What?" She gave her mother her most guileless look.
"No."

"What?" Innocence coated the word.

"You know very well what." Keely climbed out and headed for the back door.

"What? Because I said he's nice? But he is! And he's not really old, either. Well, maybe a little older than you, but is that so bad?" Steffie followed her mother inside.

"I have enough complications in my life, thank you very much." Keely dropped her purse on the kitchen counter and walked straight to the refrigerator. She wanted nothing more than a glass of ice water.

"I'd just like to remind you that you're not getting any younger," she went on. "And a nice man is hard to find."

Steffie made sure to escape to her bedroom before her mother could go after her.

"With her arguing skills, she'll make a wonderful attorney," Keely muttered, sipping her water. She was determined to put that episode at the house out of her mind and chalk it up to erratic hormones or something. She'd go back to the house tomorrow and step inside and everything would be just fine. She knew it would.

It was in those eerie hours of the night when anything can happen that the ugly dream crept in to destroy her sleep.

Chapter 3

Keely was asleep. She had to be dreaming. So why did the child's whimpers she heard seem so real? One tiny part of her mind told her she was dreaming and to just fall back fully asleep. But the whimpers in her mind refused to stop. The cries that seemed to come from a distance were those of a frightened adult. The picture in her sleeping mind was hazy, but she imagined she could see the vague outline of a child climbing out of a bed. Searching for slippers, putting them on and heading for the door. Her tiny hand covered the knob and slowly turned it. She shouldn't go out there. If she did, she'd never be the same again. It was as if someone screamed the warning in her head.

Keely shot up in bed. Her body felt clammy from the sweat coating her skin and her heart pounded so hard she feared it would burst out of her chest. When she raised her hand to wipe her face, she noticed it shook violently and that her face was slick with sweat. Since Steffie hadn't burst in to find out what was wrong she had to assume she hadn't cried out as she thought she had. She collapsed back against the pillows, forcing herself to breathe in and out in a steady rhythm to calm her racing pulse.

She wanted to turn on a light to banish the horrors from her nightmare. She didn't want to turn on a light because she feared what she might find. Instead, she focused on the moonlight spilling in the room. She decided the shadows streaking the room were safer than full light.

As Keely lay there, she thought back to her nightmare. She hadn't eaten anything that evening to cause one. She hadn't watched a scary movie, either. Not even a suspense. So why did she dream something so powerful that it scared the hell out of her?

"Next time I'll eat a jar of sour pickles before bed," she muttered, turning her pillow over and punching it into a desired shape.

It was still a long time before she fell back asleep.

Keely wasn't sure when the feeling of something wrong started to invade her bones. For the next few days at odd times a strange prickling sensation would travel up her spine and she'd catch herself looking out the window as if she thought someone was out there watching her.

"Expecting company?" Steffie asked one evening as Keely fingered the drape to look outside although it was too dark to see much of anything.

She jumped, still holding on to the edge of the drape she now wished she'd closed earlier.

"I guess I'm still not used to all the peace and quiet." She jumped again when an animal howled in the distance.

"Oh, yeah, real quiet," Steffie drawled, dropping into a chair and draping her legs over one of the arms. "I've never heard so many bugs and all sorts of critters in my life. I guess it's better than car horns and noisy neighbors, but you'd think they'd get tired of chirping and whatever else they do all night. How can they call country living quiet with all that going on?''

"Homework done?''

She nodded. "Will you double-check my math for me please? Some of those problems are so weird! I don't know why the teachers bother with something we'll never use in real life.''

"I'm not sure you're doing any better asking me. English was my stronger subject.''

Steffie examined her nails. "I could call Sam and ask him about the problems. Lisa said he's really good in math. He helps her all the time.''

"Sam? You mean Sheriff Barkley.''

"He said I can call him Sam. Just like the deputy who's sometimes driven us home said I can call him by his first name.'' She wrinkled her nose. "Although, I really think somebody should bring Rick up to date about women's issues. He is such a chauvinist pig. We heard him talking to one of the other deputies once about this woman he dated and he actually rated her performance in bed!''

Keely was stunned. "Do you mean to say he was discussing sex in front of you girls?''

"Not exactly. He was obtuse enough to think we two dumb little girls wouldn't understand all those guy words,'' she said, rolling her eyes.

Keely smiled at her daughter's sarcasm.

"I mean, like we wouldn't know what he's talking about.'' She threw up her hands. "The guy is so lame!''

Keely broke into a coughing fit. She groped for the back of the couch and dropped onto the cushion.

"Steffie, I am too young to die because my daughter sent me into shock about her knowledge of sexual situations,'' she wheezed. "And please, keep it to theory only for a very long time. Say for another twenty or thirty years.''

''Mom, I know there are a lot of fifteen-year-old girls having sex, but I don't plan to be one of them,'' she informed her mother with a resigned air. ''Personally, I don't think it's all that it's cracked up to be.''

Keely decided this wasn't the time to tell Steffie it was *more* than what it was cracked up to be when a woman was with the right man. No, she'd wait and explain it to her in five or ten years.

''As if I know what the right man is,'' she muttered to herself, heading for her office. She booted up her computer, prepared to finish the updated logo for a fledgling clothing boutique.

''Mom, what would you think of my getting a 300 ZX?'' Steffie called out.

''We'll visit the toy store this weekend to see if they have any available,'' she called back in what she called her sweet mother's voice. ''One of those nice models you can build yourself, so you can feel it's your very own.''

''Ha, ha, ha. Very funny.''

Keely fingered the door key to her family home. For the past week she had put off going back there. Every time she thought about driving over, her stomach began churning and the roaring sound began in her head again. Just as it did this time. She released a deep sigh and hooked the key back on the key rack set up near the back door. She started to reach for it again when the phone rang.

''Hello?''

''Keely? It's Sam Barkley.'' His low mellow voice seemed to wash over her like a warm spring rain.

She smiled. ''And to what do I owe the honor of this call?'' she teased.

His grave tone should have been her first warning. "It's Steffie."

She gripped the receiver. "What about Steffie?" she demanded. For some reason the memory of the unsigned note she had received popped into her head. All she could remember were rambling words about families. Not her baby. She couldn't stand it if anything happened to her Steffie!

"It was an accident at school. Now she's fine," he hastily assured her. "But she had to be taken to our clinic. I'll be by to pick you up."

"Where is it?" she demanded. "I can drive myself."

"I think it would be better if I drove. I'll be there in less than three minutes."

Keely counted off the seconds as she made sure her medical insurance card was in her wallet. She was out front waiting when Sam's Bronco skidded to a stop.

"What happened?" she asked the moment she climbed into the passenger's seat.

Sam put the truck in gear and took off.

"An accident during her gym class," he replied.

"Why didn't they call me?" Her question came out more like a wheeze.

Sam looked over and noticed she was holding on to her purse strap with a death grip. "They tried but couldn't get through for some reason. Lisa told them to call me," he continued. "I tried you by phone first as I drove over there. We have a small-town mentality here, Keely. Neighbors help each other."

She looked out the window, blind and deaf to everything but her imagination.

By the time Sam stopped in front of a two-story white framed building with a sign in front indicating it was a medical clinic, Keely had imagined the absolute worst. She quickly stumbled out of the vehicle and ran up to the door.

"Stephanie Harper," she panted to the woman standing behind the waist-high counter. "I'm her mother."

"Oh, Mrs. Harper, yes." The woman smiled. "Your daughter is fine. Sheriff." She nodded at Sam.

"Fine." She took several breaths to slow her racing pulse. Fear was rapidly overshadowed by anger at the woman's calm reply. "I find out my daughter has had an accident so serious she had to be taken to the doctor and you dare to stand there and tell me she's *fine?*"

"Allison, you're scaring people again." A slender woman wearing jeans, cotton shirt and a white lab coat walked out. "Mrs. Harper, I'm Dr. Rogers." She held out her hand. "Why don't you come on back and take a minute to calm down before you see your daughter? Sam, I'm glad to see you were able to find her for us. Go ahead and have a seat."

He nodded and took a chair in the waiting area.

"What happened to her?" Keely followed her down a hallway. She vaguely noted people in several of the examination rooms, looking out with curious eyes.

The doctor gestured for Keely to enter the end room which was her office.

"Steffie had an accident during her gymnastics class," Dr. Rogers explained. "She fell off the balance beam and got the wind knocked out of her, along with cutting her chin open. I had to put four stitches in it."

Keely felt queasy and feared her face had turned an unattractive shade of green. Her one weakness was her daughter's health. When Steffie was sick, Keely was too. Blood and Steffie did not mix well in Keely's stomach. She blinked several times to clear the dancing lights in front of her eyes.

"Sit down." A pair of hands planted themselves on her shoulders and pushed her into a chair. "Put your head between your knees. Take several deep breaths."

"I once fell and ended up with a chunk of glass in my hand," Keely wheezed. "Six stitches and I didn't turn a hair. I passed out when Steffie was a baby and had her first shots." She straightened up. "Otherwise, she's all right?"

The woman smiled. "The only thing she was upset about was that she couldn't ask me questions while I stitched her up."

Keely managed a wan smile. "That sounds like Steffie. When she had her tonsils out the doctor was positive she was trying to talk to him. I was surprised she didn't ask him to videotape the procedure for her."

"Well, she won't have much fun talking for a while." She leaned against her desk. "Are you sure you're all right?"

Keely nodded. "Other than wanting to crawl into bed and pull the covers over my head, I'm fine. On second thought, I'm dragging Steffie in there with me too."

She smiled. "Keely, I think I'm going to like you. I'm Melanie."

Keely stood up. She was relieved the nausea had left and her world felt balanced again. "Melanie, would you like me to get my daughter out of here before the pain medication wears off and she vies for the Academy Award for major injuries? She can act the part of an ailing patient like no one you've ever seen before."

"Sure, Allison has the paperwork. As a precaution I'd advise you keep her home about a week, but there's no reason why she can't go back after that." Melanie picked up a prescription pad and scribbled on it. "She can take these when the pain gets too much. They're like a heavy-duty aspirin." She tore the sheet off and handed it to Keely. "Bring her back in a week to have the stitches out. I don't think it will even leave a scar, although your daughter did assure me that she didn't mind if it did. That it might even add character."

Keely chuckled. "That's my Steffie." She studied the woman and gauged her to be several years old than her.

"Have you lived here all your life?"

Melanie shook her head. "Only for the past few years. My husband had a dream of opening a medical clinic that he could run his way. He put the word out and Echo Ridge was willing to go halfway." Her smile looked wistful. "Unfortunately, he was diagnosed with an inoperable brain tumor a year after we moved here."

"I'm sorry."

She shrugged. "It's gotten easier. What I wanted to say was, if you ever want to sit back and down a bottle of wine, give me a call." She picked up a business card and jotted down a number on the back before handing it to Keely. "I can usually be found here. I live over the clinic."

"Sounds good to me. I'm always open to making new friends."

"Such as good-looking single sheriffs?" Melanie raised an eyebrow.

"I'm not in the market for a new man," Keely explained. "Right now I'm going to concentrate on getting my graphic arts business on track and making sure my daughter doesn't hurt herself anymore."

"Well, if I were you, I wouldn't keep myself closed off so much that I find myself locked away without a chance of getting out."

Afterward, Melanie directed Keely to a room down the hall. Steffie was lying on her stomach on the examination table while reading a book. She looked up as Keely entered the room.

"Hi, Mom." Her words were garbled as if she'd just had dental surgery. "I did it up good."

Keely winced at the red dots of blood dotting Steffie's shirt and the black thread marring her chin. She took several deep breaths. The last thing she wanted to do was pass out in front of her daughter.

"I thought your strength was the balance beam?"

She used her finger to hold her place in her book as she sat up, crossing her legs in front of her. "It is, but I don't know what happened. First I was doing this great split on the beam, next I was rolling on the floor."

"Maybe if you knew what this did to me, you wouldn't put me through all of this hell." She picked up Steffie's knapsack. "C'mon kiddo, I'm bailing you out."

As they walked out to the waiting room, Keely observed that Steffie's usual bouncy walk was more subdued than usual.

When they approached the waiting area, Keely noticed Allison was deep in a low-voiced conversation with Sam.

"I can't believe she doesn't remem—" she quickly broke off when she noticed Keely approaching them. She conjured up a bright smile that looked just a trifle strained.

"All ready?" she said brightly, bustling back to her desk and shuffling through paperwork before pulling out the required forms for Keely. "Since the accident was on school property, they're handling the medical bills. But you'll need to sign here for her release to confirm that you understand any instructions given to you."

Keely nodded and quickly scribbled her name where indicated. "Thank you."

"I guess you'll have to be more careful when running around on that beam," Sam teased Steffie as they walked out to his truck.

She started to grimace then changed her mind when the stitches in her chin reminded her that her movements would be curtailed for a while.

"These stitches really pull," Steffie muttered, climbing

into the back seat. She sank into the scarred vinyl uphol-
stery.

"I need to stop by the pharmacy and get this prescription filled for her," Keely told Sam.

"No problem." He drove toward the center of town.

Steffie closed her eyes. "Please tell him to fill it fast. I
think that shot the doctor gave me is wearing off."

"I'll stay here with her while you go in,'" Sam offered
as Keely hesitated. She nodded jerkily and jumped out.

John looked up from his position in the rear of the store
when she stepped inside. "Well, hello, Keely, is there anything I can help you with?"

"I need a prescription filled for my daughter." She
walked back to the pharmacy counter and handed him the
paper.

He scanned it and nodded. "Tell you what. I can take
this out to you within the hour. That way you don't have
to wait around and you can get Steffie into her bed."

"Sheriff Barkley brought us over," she explained. "So
I can wait if it won't take too long."

Since she was looking toward the window where the
sheriff's vehicle was parked, she didn't see the dark expression cross the pharmacist's face.

"Did your daughter have an accident or something?"
he asked, stepping back to the shelves holding various
drugs. "I see it's for a painkiller and an antibiotic."

"She had an accident at school and cut her chin open,"
Keely replied, walking over to the bath products aisle and
studying various bath salts. She settled for a citrus fragrance.

John shook his head, clucking under his tongue. "Kids
can really do a job on themselves, can't they? But I guess
you're grateful it wasn't anything worse."

"Actually, I consider her lucky this time. She usually
breaks a bone." Keely set the bath salts on the counter

along with a variety of teen magazines in hopes they would occupy her easily bored daughter until she turned into a human being again. Keely was the first to admit her darling child wasn't the best of patients.

"So, are you and the sheriff seeing each other?"

John's casual question and curious expression set warning bells off in Keely's head.

"He was just kind enough to drive me to the medical clinic," she replied.

"Then maybe you'd be interested in going out for a meal and movie some evening," he suggested.

"I'm afraid my time is going to be tied up for a while between getting my house set up and catching up on my workload." She hoped to let him down carefully without coming right out and saying she'd rather eat dirt than date him.

"Some other time then." He took it as her giving him a rain check.

Keely didn't correct him. She wrote out a check and accepted the small white paper bag he handed her. When she returned to the truck, she found Steffie curled up on the back seat while Sam was half turned in his so he could talk to the girl easier.

"Are we going home now?" Steffie whined, shifting in her seat.

"Yes, sweetheart, we are." Keely buckled up.

"Hey, slugger, you'll be back to yourself in no time," Sam assured Steffie.

"Oh, sure, just as soon as Mom gives me my pills," she moaned.

Keely and Sam shared a smile that only parents could understand.

"She'll be playing the role of the suffering saint for a few days," Keely said in a low voice. "She'll alternate between that of the dying heroine and the stoic woman who can bear anything.''

Sam grinned. ''Lisa's good at that, too.'' He realized Keely's exotic fragrance would probably linger in his vehicle for several days. Each time he climbed in, he would be reminded of her. His daughter had been hinting he should ask Keely out. But he hadn't missed the Keep Off signs the lady had posted the few times he was around her.

''Can Lisa come over?'' Steffie asked when Sam pulled in front of their house.

''I thought you felt terrible and just wanted to collapse in bed,'' Keely reminded her as Sam helped her, and then Steffie out of the truck.

She wore her most morose face. ''Yeah, but she could cheer me up and make me forget about my pain.''

''If your mother doesn't mind, I can drop Lisa off after school.'' Sam looked to Keely for confirmation.

She gazed into his eyes and wondered why she had never thought all that much of brown eyes before. She was used to people wanting to look unusual by having brilliant green eyes, blue, aqua or even lavender. They would opt for colored contact lenses if necessary. But there was something about Sam's steady gaze that seemed to reach out to her. To give her the peace she hadn't felt since she first heard about Steffie's accident.

''That's very nice of you,'' she said softly.

His face split in that grin that Keely was finding unsettling to her mental balance. ''It's either that or they'll be tying up our phones for hours.''

''And she won't drive me crazy every five minutes wanting something.''

''M-o-m!'' Steffie wailed, hopping up and down by the front door.

''There are days when I hate that name,'' she told Sam. ''Obviously, she's forgotten she has her own door key.''

"The name *Dad* can be just as bad sometimes," he said.

"Parents with these inside jokes are so lame," Steffie huffed.

Keely started for the door. She wished the pain shot Steffie had been given had lasted longer. She waved as Sam drove off. She wondered if she should ask Sam and Lisa to stay to dinner; then she hoped she had something appropriate in the house to offer them.

Once inside, she urged Steffie to lie down while she fixed her tea.

"Do we have any straws?" the girl asked, snuggling under the rose-blue-and-green afghan one of Keely's co-workers had made and given her for her birthday one year. "It really hurts to move my jaw."

"How sad. You won't be able to talk," Keely murmured, setting a cup in the microwave and punching buttons. "I think we have some. Anything else you want, madame?"

"Didn't the doctor say I should use an ice pack to take down the swelling?"

Keely thought of the list of instructions Allison had handed her. "I'm sure she did. I'll fix one for you."

She settled Steffie down with warm tea and a straw dangling out of the cup before she handed her some medication.

The girl examined the pill, then looked up. "Don't I get water?"

"Why?"

"To take the pill!"

"You have tea. It's a liquid and will work very nicely."

She screwed up her face. "I can't take a pill with tea! I need water, Mom. Please?"

Keely walked into the kitchen, pulled a glass out of the cabinet and turned on the tap.

"Can't I have some of the lime seltzer water instead?" Steffie called out.

"I thought you wanted *real* water."

"It's water!"

"My fifteen-year-old daughter just regressed back to age six," she muttered, using more force than necessary to open the refrigerator door.

When Lisa arrived a few hours later, the girl was overwhelmed by Keely's enthusiastic welcome.

By the time Sam showed up, Keely was already showing signs of strain.

"You're invited to dinner," she stated without preamble when she threw open the door.

"I wouldn't want to put you out," he said, stunned by the glazed look in her eyes.

"You're not putting me out. In fact, you're doing me a favor because as long as your daughter is here, my daughter acts almost human and I don't want to throttle her." She grabbed his arm and almost pulled him off his feet as she dragged him inside. "In fact, I may not allow Lisa to leave until Steffie is feeling better."

"Hi, Dad." Lisa appeared at the end of the hallway. "Keely, Steffie wants some more tea."

"Sure. More caffeine on top of the pain pills. Just what every teenager needs," she grumbled, gesturing Sam toward the kitchen.

Sam stopped to examine the painting propped against the wall. He gathered the bold colors were supposed to be some kind of flower although he wasn't positive about it. While he had never proported to be a fan of modern art, he found himself liking what he saw. He decided it suited Keely's energy. Maybe that was why he liked it.

"I finally found my hammer so I can hang it," she admitted, coming up behind him. "I found it at an art fair in Laguna Beach. To this day, I have no idea why I like it, but when I look at it I always feel as if I've just gotten a shot of energy."

Sam nodded. That, he could understand. "Tell you what. Get the hammer and hooks and I can hang it for you now," he offered.

"I didn't ask you over here to hang paintings," she protested.

He looked at her over his shoulder. "I know that. But there's no use in my not doing something that's probably easier for me to handle than for you. That's a pretty big painting."

"With my token protest over, I'll get the hammer and hooks." Keely disappeared into the kitchen and reappeared with the necessary tools.

She stood back and offered a comment only when he asked if it was where she wanted it.

As Keely watched Sam stretch upward to hammer the nails into the wall, her gaze kept drifting downward to where the khaki pants tightened across his rear. Her mouth suddenly grew dry as she wondered what he did to keep his body in such good shape. She couldn't imagine him going to a health club on a daily basis. She continued to stare at him as he picked up the painting and laid the wire across the hooks. She had to shake herself back to normal when he turned around.

"It looks great. Thank you," she managed to say as she led him into the kitchen. "Ah, would you like something to drink? Tea or something stronger? I have beer and wine."

"Beer is fine." He took the chair she pointed him toward.

She nodded and pulled a can out of the refrigerator as she popped a water-filled mug into the microwave.

"Unfortunately, when Steffie was younger I worked outside the home and I wasn't able to be home with her when she was sick," she said, pausing to open the oven and check the contents of a large casserole dish. "We had a wonderful housekeeper at the time, but the woman always prayed vigorously every time Steffie was sick. Now I know why. It wasn't that she wanted Steffie to get better. She didn't want her to get sick again!"

Sam nodded. "Lisa had the measles when she was ten and in the beginning she was so sick she just wanted to be left alone, but when she started feeling better, she had me hopping. I was worn out by the time she was well enough to go back to school." He chuckled, popping the tab on the beer can.

"Didn't Echo Ridge feel unprotected while you played nurse?" Keely teased.

He looked down at his hands cupping the can. "I wasn't working up here then." He looked up at her. A hint of pain clouded his gaze. "When I graduated from high school, I attended college in Sacramento and went to work for the police department there. I worked my way up to detective and spent several years in Homicide. A few years after my wife died, I moved back up here. I felt both Lisa and I needed a change of scenery and a slower way of life. My dad wanted to retire and said I'd be the perfect replacement for him."

"Ah, connections," Keely murmured with a teasing grin.

He grinned sheepishly and shrugged.

Keely ignored the microwave's insistent beeping in the background.

"How did your wife die?"

At first, he didn't seem to hear her soft-spoken question. When he did speak, his raspy voice was so quiet, Keely couldn't hear him at first.

"At the age of thirty-two, my wife, who belonged to a health club and religiously worked out four times a week and ate so much of that health food that I used to accuse her of turning into a plant, just keeled over. The autopsy showed she'd had a massive heart attack. It was so sudden she didn't have a chance. At least, that's what the doctors told me. Even they couldn't figure it out, but they say it sometimes just happens. At least it's not genetic, so I don't have to worry about Lisa.''

Keely couldn't ignore anyone's pain. She dropped her hand on his shoulder and pressed her fingers into it. She didn't speak the words, but Sam knew them all the same.

''I hope you don't mind casseroles,'' she spoke in a neutral tone. ''I find they're handy when you need something in a hurry. I made an old standby that Steffie's always liked. It's like lasagna but it's composed of layers of chicken, salsa, corn tortilla pieces and grated cheese.''

Sam was grateful for that normalcy and for the fact that Keely didn't offer comfort at a time when he had worked his way past that point. He took those minutes to bring himself back under control.

''It sounds like a lot of work.''

She shook her head. ''Not really.'' She poured herself a glass of wine and sat down across from him.

''You've fixed this place up nice,'' Sam said, pointing his thumb toward the whimsical plaques decorating one wall. ''Your philosophy?''

She turned around to look at them. ''Pretty much, although I feel 'So this isn't Home Sweet Home, Adjust' describes me the best.''

Sam braced his arms on the table and studied Keely with an even stare she returned.

''Do I pass whatever test you're giving me?'' she asked with an impish grin.

''I just wonder if you're going to be able to settle down up here after all the bright lights and entertainment you've been used to,'' he said honestly.

"Believe me, the quiet life is just what I want," she said fervently. "As far as I'm concerned, the world can keep L.A. I'll take Echo Ridge, thank you very much."

Sam's smile was slow in coming but when it did Keely felt as if it created magic. And she felt that slow warming deep inside her that told her she might not have *completely* sworn off men....

Chapter 4

Keely stared at the computer monitor as if it held all of life's answers. She studied the intricate design she'd created to grace announcements for a specialty boutique's private sale. Once she had the design the way she wanted, she would write the copy and soon have a camera-ready sheet for the printer.

She resisted the urge to rub the sand she was confident had been poured into her eyes. Catching up had never been easy, and with Steffie home her time had been even more limited. She also had the sneaky suspicion that before too long she was going to need glasses while working.

"That looks really pretty," Steffie said, setting a glass of iced tea on the desk within Keely's reach and remaining there to peer over her mother's shoulder. "Too bad we don't live close enough to take in the sale. They have such hot clothes."

"Considering it's a lingerie boutique that's just fine with me." Pleased with the results, she tapped the Save key.

"There's nothing wrong with you having a sexy night-gown for those special evenings," the girl commented with a sly smile.

"Considering I can't imagine a special evening requir-ing a sexy nightgown, I'd say there's nothing wrong with what I wear now."

Steffie wrinkled her nose. "Trust me, Mom, you wouldn't get a man's interest in what you wear."

"Since I don't care to snag a man I guess it means I can wear any old thing I want to to bed," she said lightly, looking down at her ragged shorts and T-shirt. "Not to mention any other time."

"Old is right," Steffie observed, dropping onto the floor and seating herself in a cross-legged position. "You wear stuff even *I* wouldn't be caught dead in."

Keely spun her chair around. "Are you hinting for a shopping trip?"

She shook her head. "Not for me, Mom. For you. It's just that you really should consider how you look. You don't want men to perceive you as a woman who doesn't care about her looks, do you?"

"*Perceive* me?" she repeated. "Amazing you would come up with that specific word. And is there any man in particular you're thinking of?"

Steffie looked up as if the answer just might be written on the ceiling. "Not exactly," she said in a vague voice, "but you never can tell who might just happen to walk into your life. You should want to be ready." She fingered the bright pink yarn she'd used to tie up her ponytail and wound it around her finger.

Keely smothered the sigh threatening to crawl up her throat. "Honey, unfortunately you know the divorce wasn't exactly friendly. Right now I'm not looking for another relationship. I'm more interested in spending my free time with my darling daughter," she cooed.

Steffie adopted a haughty pose. "Excuse me, but I am a teenager and the last thing a teenage girl wants is her mother around."

"I should be insulted by that crack!" Keely teased. She turned back to her computer and shut her system down. She took her disk and returned it to the box. "Is the invalid up to helping me make lunch?"

Steffie jumped to her feet. "It only takes one hand to spread mustard," she said loftily, heading for the kitchen.

It was while they were eating their sandwiches that they heard the doorbell chime.

Keely headed for the door and swung it open. She smiled uncertainly at the man facing her.

"John, what a surprise." She didn't move from the doorway. "Is there a problem?"

He shook his head as he held out a bouquet of flowers. "I just thought I'd stop by and see how Steffie was doing. For the young lady," he added.

She immediately felt guilty that she had acted so uninviting. "She'll be thrilled." She stepped back. "We're just finishing up lunch." She led him toward the back of the house.

"Oh, hi, Mr. Harris." Steffie's look of expectancy faded when she identified their visitor.

"Hello, Steffie, I hope you're feeling better." He handed her the green paper-wrapped bouquet. "I thought some flowers would help your recovery."

She smiled and accepted the gift with a murmured "Thank you."

"I'll find a vase," Keely offered. "Would you like to sit down, John? Perhaps something to drink?" She ignored the frantic hand signals Steffie sent her behind the man's back.

He eyed the two glasses already sitting on the table as he took one of the chairs. "Iced tea sounds fine to me."

Keely poured a glass for him and set it on the table before she sat back down. "How were you able to escape the pharmacy?"

"I insisted no one could need any medication for at least an hour." He smiled charmingly.

Steffie rolled her eyes and dramatically stuck her finger down her throat as she walked behind the man to reach her chair. Keely could do nothing but smile at John who naturally smiled back. His gaze flickered over Steffie as if expecting her to make her excuses and leave the room. The girl smiled brightly and settled down in her chair.

"I guess living in a small town means you know everyone's dirty secrets," Steffie spoke up, blatantly ignoring her mother's embarrassed "Stefanie!" "So, who has the worst?"

Luckily, John didn't bat an eyelash. "The pharmacist code doesn't allow me to divulge my clients' secrets," he said solemnly. "Although I can tell you that Mrs. Hawthorne does buy condoms for her son."

Steffie's eyes widened as she burst into delighted laughter.

John leaned forward to further confide, "Mrs. Hawthorne's son is sixty-four."

Keely could feel her lips quivering and her throat tickle with laughter. "Obviously, she is a very concerned mother."

"Or a hopeful one since Ralph Hawthorne's last date was forty-seven years ago. His prom date ran off with the captain of the basketball team. He never got over the disappointment."

"Sheesh, you'd think he'd realize he might have gotten off lucky," Steffie declared. "She could have turned out to be a real dud." She paused, intrigued by John's expression. "She did turn into a dud, didn't she?"

"Actually, she's a news producer for one of the big

networks," he replied. "But the basketball captain only ended up owning a string of fast-food restaurants in the Midwest."

Steffie expelled a loud snort of disgust. "There was no justice there."

"Once you meet Ralph you'll understand why." John turned to Keely. "I was wondering if you might like to go out to dinner one evening soon."

Her smile froze. This was just what she had feared when she first sensed his interest in her. She wasn't sure why she didn't want to go out with John. Perhaps it was because he was quite a bit older. Or something else she wasn't about to ponder on just yet.

"To be honest, John, I'm just now getting back into the swing of my work what with the move and all," she said, hoping she could come up with the right words. The last thing she wanted to do was hurt his feelings, but she wasn't going to go out with him just because she wasn't sure what to say. "I have a heavy backlog and right now I can't think of much else but getting caught up. I have quite a few clients who have been very patient with me while I went through the move and got settled here, but I need to get back to work. The least I can do in appreciation is to finish their projects as soon as possible."

"Mom has a very impressive list of clients," Steffie said with the pride a mother might use in discussing her beloved child. "Thanks to their recommendations she's always picking up new clients."

"She still needs to learn to take time out for herself," John told her as he pushed himself away from the table and stood up. "I guess I should get back to the pharmacy."

"Thank you for the flowers," Steffie piped up in a polite voice.

Keely shot her daughter a subtle warning look not to hurry their guest along too quickly even as she stood up.

She walked John to the door and stood there offering a wave as he drove away. She closed the door with a sigh of relief and returned to the kitchen to find her daughter already starting to clear their lunch dishes.

"Man, can't he get a date his own age?" Steffie muttered, as she carried the plates to the sink.

"A woman is always flattered when an older man is interested in her," Keely countered.

"He's a pharmacist, not a doctor," she reminded her. "Any woman knows she shoots for a doctor."

"Just remember that when you get old enough to find the right man." Keely playfully pulled on her ponytail.

Sam hated inactivity. Admittedly, he liked it when things were quiet and there were times in the town when the worst crime to crop up was jaywalking. He enjoyed that kind of peace after the dark frenzy of working Vice and later Homicide, in Sacramento.

For now, he sat behind his desk, leaning back in his chair with his booted feet propped on top of his desk. A cup of coffee was cradled in his hands, which rested comfortably on his flat belly.

It was easy to think about Keely Harper. Except when he did think about her he sometimes also remembered Keely Davis. Five-year-old Keely Davis with her oh-so-large eyes filled with pain and confusion as she held tightly on to a stuffed animal as her life fell down around her.

"The girl says Willis killed them."

"Always knew that bastard was an animal. And to think that poor little baby saw it all."

"No way she can tell someone what really happened."

"One of the deputies said she told him the man who fixed her playhouse hurt her mommy and daddy. He said she sounded so sure of herself there's no doubt she's not making it up or somehow dreamed it."

He never realized those old memories would intrude. With his father being sheriff back then, Sam had been aware of everything that happened at that time. His father hadn't liked discussing any of his cases, but this one had affected him deeply. It was the first murder in Echo Ridge in more than fifty years and the fact that a five-year-old girl had witnessed it only made it more heinous.

Sam remembered lying awake at night, hearing his father talk to his mother about the rare composure the young Keely showed as she answered any question put to her. And during the trial, her clear concise answers sealed a man's fate. No one in the court could deny the little girl knew exactly what she talked about.

But at what cost? Only a few days after Edgar Willis was sentenced to prison for his crime did Keely collapse and have to be hospitalized. After she regained consciousness it became evident that she'd lost all memory of her parents' deaths. The last thing she remembered was the day before when she had played with her dolls and looked forward to a day out with her mother.

The town's citizens, as a whole, had performed a rare act at that time. By unspoken agreement, the murder was not discussed. Keely's amnesia was also not discussed so it would not reach any media ears. The little girl had gone through enough already, no matter how much shielding her grandmother and the town had given her. But her grandmother was in too much pain to remain there. She'd packed up Keely and moved south where she wouldn't have to contend with memories. Sam now recalled that it had been hinted they had moved to the San Diego area, but Evelyn Stuart hadn't maintained contact with any of her old friends, so no one knew for sure.

Sam thought of the little girl, then the picture blurred and he saw the woman in her place. He knew if Keely had any idea of the real reason behind her grandmother's taking her away from Echo Ridge, she wouldn't have returned.

He wasn't surprised by her violent reaction when she entered the house of her birth. Obviously, her subconscious remembered what her mind refused to acknowledge. Now he had to fear the day the past would flood back. He only hoped he could be close by.

The thing was, when Sam was around Keely Harper it wasn't easy to think like a cop. He was sure no man could be around her and not see her as a very desirable woman. He sure saw her as a woman.

"Glad to see you're working hard." A plump woman in her fifties bustled in and plopped herself down in the visitor's chair. She lifted her reading glasses, which hung on a pearl-dotted chain around her neck, and tipped them onto her nose. "Have you bothered to read any of your messages today?"

He shrugged. "Was there a reason why I'd want to read them, Fredda?"

"It is part of your job," the office clerk-dispatcher reminded him.

"It's only part of my job if there's anything good there."

She sorted through the small pile of pink message slips. "Maida is convinced Ernie is watching her through his binoculars. She wants us to take care of that 'dirty ole pervert'—her words." She looked up. "Or would you like something a little more intense, such as Rory Landers sneaking out after curfew every night. He's dating Cindy Parker," she clarified.

He frowned. "I thought she was going out with Scott Kinsey."

Fredda waved her hand in dismissal. "That was over months ago. Honestly, Samuel, where have you been? Get with the times, boy. Scott's seeing Beth Donaldson now."

"I'm too damn old for all of this," he complained. "What did you tell Maida?"

"That if she'd close her blinds at night, Ernie couldn't see anything. I told her she's nothing more than a tease and she should be ashamed of herself."

Sam smothered his sigh. Which meant he'd be hearing from a furious Maida before the day was out. Unless Fredda made sure her calls didn't get through to him.

"And I told Felicity Landers if the worst thing Scott is doing is sneaking out, she should be grateful he's doing it in a small town where he can't get away with too much without half the population knowing about it."

"How come I'm the sheriff and you're not?" he asked, amused by her blunt declarations.

"Because this town is still so damn chauvinistic I can't see us having a female sheriff in the next hundred years." Fredda leaned forward and set the message slips down. She sat back and eyed Sam. "I heard John Harris closed up the pharmacy counter for an hour so he could go out to see Keely Harper. He bought a bouquet of flowers at Vern's flower shop."

"Maybe Keely called in a refill for Steffie and he delivered it. She still might be having problems with her arm," he said amiably, even though he didn't like the idea of John sniffing around Keely. Dammit, the man was too old for her!

But then, Sam had no right to think anything. He wasn't exactly a prize for any woman.

"You're not going to let him get away with that, are you?" Fredda demanded.

Sam studied the woman who had worked for his father then stayed on after his retirement explaining to Sam he needed her. And dammit, she was better than any of his deputies when it came to dealing with the public.

"I have a daughter."

"Amazing. So does she. And they're even the same age." She held her reading glasses in her hand, pointing them at him. "I also heard they're fast becoming good friends. Convenient, isn't it?"

"Keely's not interested in any kind of relationship and if she was, she wouldn't be interested in someone like me," he said bluntly.

Fredda continued staring at him with that pained expression that said loud and clear she thought he was an idiot. "Someone like you. And what, pray tell, is wrong with you?"

"She's beautiful and grew up in the bright lights of the big city which she'll undoubtably miss the minute the snow falls around here," he explained. "I'll bet she'll be out of here by the first snowfall."

"You're not exactly roadkill," Fredda replied bluntly. "And she doesn't look like someone who will run at the sight of the first snowflake. There's nothing for you to worry about, Samuel."

Sam grinned. No matter what went on in the world he knew he could count on Fredda to tell him the truth no matter how much it hurt.

"Put on your glasses, Fredda. I'm too tall, have hands that are too big and there's days I'm as awkward as hell."

Her retort was decidedly off-color, which made Sam only laugh.

"Go do some work," he ordered, even though he didn't sound as if he meant it.

Fredda levered herself out of her chair. "It's easier to get my work done on time when your boys turn in their work on time. Rick still hasn't written up last week's reports. I told him if I don't have them by the end of shift today he's not seeing his paycheck until he gets them done."

"You should have been a teacher, Fredda. You would have been hell on wheels."

"Glad you think so, because I need some paperwork from you, too," she said as she left the office. "No paperwork, no paycheck."

Sam thought about his end of month report that hadn't even been started and he groaned. He knew the older woman well enough to know she would make sure none of them found their paychecks until she got what she wanted. Fredda never issued a threat she didn't mean to follow through. He couldn't even use the excuse of having a child to feed. She'd only smartly insist Lisa was more than welcome to have dinner at her house. Sam would not be invited since she considered him dumb enough not to do his paperwork when it was due.

Still, for a moment he wondered if Keely Harper might be tenderhearted enough to feed him.

It was a thought.

"So, how is it going?" Chloe asked as she poured coffee for Keely and herself, in the bookstore.

"The boxes are finally unpacked, although I'm positive there were twice as many as we originally packed," she said ruefully.

Keely had decided to take the morning off for some grocery shopping and stopped by to see Chloe, who immediately suggested she sit down and have a cup of coffee. A plate of delectable pastries sat on the table between them. Keely glanced around and noticed familiar faces. John smiled and waved as he perused popular fiction while Allison, the nurse from the medical center, was engrossed in the romance section.

Chloe nodded, understanding. "They clone themselves during the night." She studied the pastries and finally chose a raspberry one. "When I opened the bookstore I couldn't believe the number of boxes I unpacked. It seemed for every one I unpacked, two more would appear.'' She dusted powdered sugar off her black pants. "When do you plan to move into your parents' house?"

Keely thought back to the day she'd entered it. The cold that streamed through her blood. The fear that she felt that day came back with a vengeance. She noticed her hand was shaking slightly as she put down her coffee cup. Even looking at the pastries left her feeling slightly nauseous.

"I haven't given myself a strict deadline," she murmured, surprised her voice sounded so composed when she felt so strange inside. "I thought I'd worry more about getting Steffie settled in school and my work going first since I knew the house would need some major repairs."

"Home ownership can be a bitch, can't it?" Chloe laughed throatily. "Last winter I replaced the furnace, the hot water heater and my dishwasher. By then I was ready to sell the house for fifty cents to anyone who was crazy enough to take it. But then I figured the day someone would offer to buy it we'd have the major earthquake that would leave my house as the only casualty."

Keely relaxed under the humor that effectively dispelled the unease running through her mind. She leaned forward and picked out a glazed donut.

"What, no bears and wildcats in the woods?"

Chloe leaned forward and whispered, "Only if you count the cute ones wearing khaki and a badge. You know the kind who just happens to have a daughter the same age as yours."

"Do you mean Sheriff Barkley?"

"He's the only cute one around I know of." Chloe sipped her coffee and eyed her speculatively. "You are going to do something about him, aren't you?"

"Men are not at the top of my list," she protested.

"Honey, when a woman is single and as nice-looking

as you, men are always at the top of the list." She chuckled.

Keely started to protest even further when a song from the sixties came out over the radio. The moment she heard the haunting voice sing about the white rabbit she felt icy shivers travel down her spine and her mind went completely blank. Fear wrapped around her like an arctic blanket.

"Keely. Keely!"

She blinked several times and stared at Chloe, whose expression was worried at best.

"What happened?" Chloe demanded. "You suddenly turned as white as a sheet." Even she looked uneasy. "I was afraid you were going to faint."

Keely tried to dig down deep within her soul. She wanted to know why she felt so afraid and what could have brought it on, but nothing came to mind. She slowly shook her head.

"I don't know," she said in a low voice.

They said she still didn't remember, but that damn song affected her. The same song that was playing while the Davises died. She must have heard it even though she was upstairs. Maybe because she's back up here she's starting to remember everything. Now it's a question as to when she'll remember everything. It would be perfect if she remembers everything just before she dies.

She shouldn't have been allowed to live that night. Too many people suffered through hell because of her. But that's all right. I'll make sure she suffers a very personal hell before she dies.

Chapter 5

"He's looking at you."

"He is not looking at me."

"Yes, he is. No, don't look. You don't want him to see you noticing he's seeing you."

Keely expelled a deep breath. "Steffie, while you might be in high school, I am not. So we will not sit here and discuss Sam as if he were the football captain and I was the head cheerleader hoping he'd stop by and ask me to the prom."

Steffie threw up her hands in disgust. She leaned across the scarred dark red Formica table in the town's favorite hangout.

"He's out there looking at you. I can't see what else he'd be looking at but you. What's so wrong with that?"

"He's looking at the window deciding it's time for lunch and nothing more," Keely argued.

Sissy's Diner was known for its greasy hamburgers, crispy french fries, spicy chili, thick malts and towering hot fudge sundaes. Cholesterol and fat grams were bliss-fully ignored here and the customers happily filled the booths during the rush hours.

Keely had suggested they stop here for lunch after a trip to the library so Steffie could pick up books for a school project due in a week.

"Frowns make wrinkles, Stef," Keely teased. "And just because you're in a snit because your teacher said all of you had to do your research manually instead of over the Internet doesn't mean you can try to run my life."

"That wouldn't be too easy since you don't have a life."

"One more nasty little comment and no dessert," Keely said with a broad smile.

Steffie arched an eyebrow. "That threat hasn't worked since I was in the sixth grade." She sat back and drummed her fingers on the tabletop as she glanced out the window. She immediately brightened up and straightened her posture. "It looks as if he and Lisa are coming in here for lunch." She smirked at her mother.

Keely could figure that out for herself as she watched Sam and Lisa walk into the diner. She felt a distinct drop in the pit of her stomach as he came across the room. What was there about him that affected her so strongly? She certainly couldn't say he was drop-dead gorgeous the way Jay was. But there was something about the man that hit her at a level very different from the way Jay had affected her in the beginning.

Maybe she was affected by him *because* he seemed so different from Jay. One smooth-talking gorgeous man was enough in her life, thank you very much.

Now she knew why Steffie suggested she wear her blue chambray sleeveless top edged with red-and-white ging-ham and gingham shorts. Her daughter had magnanimously offered her mother her precious red leather sandals and even offered to French braid her hair.

"Well, hi," Lisa greeted them with patently false surprise. She glanced over her shoulder and up at her father with that same look of incredulity. "Look Dad, Keely and Steffie are here."

Sam's slow smile told Keely he easily saw through the ruse. "Don't worry, Lisa, I don't need glasses yet."

"Why don't you sit with us?" Steffie asked as if the idea had just occurred to her.

"Dad?" Lisa acted as if it would be up to him.

"I think we should leave it up to Keely," he drawled, still standing.

Keely was so engrossed in the very nice male package of khaki shirt and jeans that she almost lost track of the conversation. "It's fine with me. We just ordered." She shot Steffie a telling look ordering her to scoot over to this side of the booth. Steffie ignored it and suggested Lisa sit next to her. Which left Sam sliding into the booth next to Keely.

"Do you want your usual, Dad?" Lisa asked.

"That's fine."

"I'll go up and tell Sissy then."

"I'll go with you," Steffie offered, quickly following her.

Sam glanced at Keely, noting the faint rose color in her cheeks that had nothing to do with makeup.

"Do you think they wanted to leave us alone?" he mused.

"I think my daughter will have to listen to a very stern lecture when we get home," she said softly.

Sam shifted a little more so he could see her better. He was right. The last person she wanted to be around was him. "I'm sorry if they've embarrassed you."

"I should think if anyone would feel uneasy, it would

be you." She glanced at him under lowered lashes. "The fast woman from the big city chasing after the poor sheriff. My my, what fodder for the gossips."

He grinned. "Gossip is the best sustenance for a small town. There are some very sweet little old ladies who know a lot of people's dirty laundry."

"Maybe it's a good thing I didn't grow up here. I was a pretty wild teenager," she confided. "Smoking on the sly, trying beer because it was the thing to do, staying out late."

"My dad was sheriff and believe me, no one got away with anything around here," he told her.

"Not even you?"

"Especially not me. I was the perfect one to hold up as an example to the others."

Keely nodded. "Is that why you became a cop?"

"Actually, I'd thought about becoming a lawyer, but it didn't take long to discover I wasn't in the mood for more school," he admitted. He glanced up and smiled as a waitress deposited a cup of coffee in front of him. "I took a lot of courses while I was with the force and soon realized I was more cut out for bringing in the criminals than defending or prosecuting them."

Keely smiled. "Somehow I can't see you wearing a three-piece suit and pontificating at great length before an awed jury."

Sam chuckled. "Truth be told, I can't see myself doing that either. I'm happy here."

"In a town where there's little privacy and everyone knows everyone else?"

He nodded. "Exactly."

Keely was already aware of the interest directed their way. She silently cursed the two girls who still hadn't returned to the booth. She privately resolved to have a good long talk with Steffie once they got home. Why couldn't the girl realize the last thing she needed was a man in her life! Even more so, she had trouble believing someone so solid and down to earth as Sam would be interested in her. She hated to believe that her self-esteem took a battering during the divorce, but what woman could handle the idea her husband was doing more than working late with his secretary? Or working late with his new partner? Not to mention his other partner's administrative assistant.

"Is there a reason you're curling your lip or should I be crass and ask you if you've had your distemper shots lately?"

Keely grimaced. "Sorry, bad memories."

"Ex-husband?" he guessed.

"I'd love to say 'May he rest in peace,' but that means he'd have to be dead and I haven't been that lucky yet," she murmured.

Sam drew back a few inches. "Bloodthirsty lady, aren't you? That part of you must be hard to keep from Steffie."

"I keep it to myself only because I want to be the better person, but Steffie knows more about her father than I'd like her to know."

His brown eyes softened with sympathy. It wasn't hard to guess that Keely had been the injured party in the marriage and she still carried a few scars.

"Is that why the move?"

"Partly. We both wanted a change of pace and moving into my old house seemed like a good idea." A memory of her family house sent chills skittering along her spine.

Sam noted Keely's haunted expression and easily guessed its source. How could he explain to her that he knew why it upset her? He sensed that the memories were starting to return.

The townspeople's unspoken agreement not to mention the truth about the Davis family to Keely held even to this day, but now he wondered if that was a good idea. He dreaded to think what her reaction would be when the truth materialized in her mind. He only hoped she wouldn't be alone when that happened.

He had to grin when Keely looked toward the counter.

"Steffie, Lisa, why don't you two come over and join us?" she said pleasantly, but it was clearly an order rather than a request.

"I'm impressed," he admitted as he watched the girls climb off their stools and head in their direction.

"It's a gift," Keely said haughtily. "Mothers have this inborn way of getting their daughters to behave."

"No offense to you two, but we wanted to have lunch by ourselves," Steffie informed her mother as she slid into the booth.

"And deny us your company?" Keely shook her head, making a tsking sound. "We can't allow that." She smiled at Lisa. "So tell me, Lisa, what horrible things about me has my daughter told you?"

"Oh, Steffie never says anything about you." The girl looked horrified. "I mean…"

"I know what you mean." Keely immediately took pity on her and reached across to pat her hand. "I just know Steffie. When she was six she told her teacher her father came from another planet and that we would move back there when she turned ten and would be considered an adult."

"M-o-m." Steffie screwed up her face and wiggled in her seat.

Sam nodded. "Lisa liked to tell her friends that I was a spy and there were hidden cameras all over our house. I used to come upon these kids with their noses practically stuck to the walls as they tried to find those fictional cameras."

"This is really sick," Lisa moaned.

"Sick? This is disgusting," Steffie told her. She glanced

up when their plates were deposited in front of them. She reached across her mother to grab the bottle of ketchup and promptly drowned her French fries in a pool of red. "Next thing you know they'll be dragging out our baby pictures and arguing over who looked cuter naked," she confided to her friend.

Lisa was equally horrified at the idea. She looked up at her father who, catching on to Keely's game, just smiled at her.

"There is that one picture when you were about eighteen months old and we had gone camping," he teased. "You looked so damn cute in that droopy diaper."

Lisa moaned piteously and buried her nose in her cheeseburger.

"I'm so glad you suggested our sharing a booth, Steffie." Keely picked up her BLT and bit into it.

"They love to psyche us out," Steffie said to Lisa.

"Yeah, but you don't have a dad who keeps muttering he remembers what it was like when he was my age and the boys better watch out," she replied.

"And at your age I was dating those boys so it's a wonderful idea your father is so conscious of looking out for your well-being," Keely told her with the pious smile only a mother can bestow on a child.

"Amazing how we're supposed to feel so grateful for their experiences back in the Dark Ages," Steffie lamented.

Keely shared a smile with Sam, and she couldn't help the warmth spreading throughout her body at his slow answering smile. She picked up her glass of iced tea but it didn't help cool her all that much.

She was glad Sam didn't argue with her after he tried to pay for their lunch and she insisted on paying for hers and Steffie's.

"And now on to the hardware store," Keely announced, looping her purse strap over her shoulder.

"Mom has decided we need the proper small tools for home repairs," Steffie explained.

"Go to Rainey's Hardware on the outskirts of town," Sam advised. "He carries a little bit of everything in that barn of his and he'll get you all fixed up if you tell him you're looking for a basic fix-it set," Sam told Keely.

"Thank you, I'll do that," she said as she headed for her truck.

Sam followed her, holding the door as she climbed inside and fastened her seat belt. He paused a moment before closing it.

"Lisa and I are barbecuing steaks this Saturday night," he told her. "We thought you and Steffie might like to come over."

Keely silently admitted it wasn't the most graceful of invitations, but she was curious to see where the man lived.

"We'd like that, thank you." She smiled.

He nodded. "About six?"

"Anything I can bring?"

"I'll leave that up to you."

Keely grinned. "Good. I like surprises."

For a very brief moment heat flared up in Sam's eyes. Just as quickly, it was masked and he looked as calm and solid as he had before.

"Don't let Rainey's gruffness put you off," he advised as he stepped back.

Keely nodded her head in a jerky movement and quickly backed out. Luckily, she had her wits about her enough to double-check there was no oncoming traffic as she straightened the truck.

"Well, that was fascinating," Steffie said sarcastically. "You two really need to learn how to communicate."

Keely hid her smile and her relief that her daughter

hadn't picked up on the vibrations zinging between them. Steffie might be growing up, but she wasn't growing up too fast.

When Sam had referred to Rainey's Hardware as being an old barn, Keely hadn't realized he meant it literally. The weather-beaten wooden structure looked as if it needed a face-lift, but she noticed it didn't lack for customers, if she could gauge by the number of pickup trucks and utility vehicles parked in front and along the side.

"They even sell saddles and tack," Steffie commented, gesturing toward one side of the building. She wrinkled her nose. "It smells like a dirty cow in here."

"It might have something to do with the clientele," she replied, glancing at more than one pair of boots encrusted with what she doubted was mud.

After a clerk pointed them in the direction of tools, Keely and Steffie were lost among every tool known to man. And many unknown to many women.

"This is nuts," Steffie moaned, picking up a mallet, staring at it and putting it back down. "Why can't we hire a handyman when something goes wrong?"

"Because it's not always possible," Keely replied, staring at more screwdrivers than she thought possible. Why did there have to be so many different kinds?

"You look confused." A gruff voice intruded on their inspection.

Keely turned to face a man who was probably in his late sixties. Iron gray hair stuck out at odd angles on his head and a heavy beard highlighted deep lines around his eyes that seemed to bore into her soul. His faded blue plaid shirtsleeves were rolled to the elbows, revealing stringy arms, and faded coveralls covered the rest of his rangy body. Dark eyes blazed at her as he looked her up and down then turned his gaze toward Steffie.

"She don't look much like you," he told Keely, jerking his head in Steffie's direction.

"Hey!" Steffie stepped forward but Keely's upraised hand stopped her.

"You must be Rainey."

"I know who I am and I know who you are. What are you doing here?"

Keely chose to ignore his rudeness. "We came in to buy some tools. I didn't realize there were so many types of hammers and screwdrivers and everything else." She held her hands up. "I just want to pick up enough tools to have something on hand for emergencies."

He made a face that could only be described as rude. "Women and tools don't mix."

"Really?" Keely murmured. Nothing raised her hackles more than a patronizing male. Even if he was one who had lived a majority of his years in a world where women were considered second-class citizens. But with this man, she felt something different emanating from him. And whatever it was wasn't pleasant. "Still, I hope you'll be willing to advise me on what tools to buy," she said in the pleasantest voice she could muster.

He brushed past her and picked up a screwdriver. "Your girl better get a basket from the front," he said brusquely. "You're going to be spending a lot of money today."

Steffie shared a speaking look with her mother before taking off for the front of the store.

Rainey still held the screwdriver as he stared at Keely so long and hard she felt uncomfortable. She also noticed that there wasn't anyone close by. With all those cars and trucks parked out front wouldn't there be at least one person in this aisle? Didn't tools have to be replaced on a fairly regular basis?

"Why'd you want to come back here?" he demanded.

She blinked at his sudden question. "I own property here."

She almost backed up when he started toward her.

"I'll send David back here to set you up," he said, thrusting the screwdriver at her.

Keely took several deep breaths as she spun around and watched him walk down the aisle with a peculiar rolling gait, as if one leg were a bit shorter than the other.

Her own movements were jerky as she replaced the screwdriver in the bin. She wasn't sure why, but she refused to buy anything he had touched.

Chapter 6

"You two aren't going to act like parents and embarrass us, are you?" Steffie asked as she and Keely walked up to the Barkley front door. Steffie carried a plate while Keely held a covered bowl.

"But we are parents," she argued as she pushed the doorbell.

"That doesn't mean you have to act like a parent." Steffie eyed her mother's outfit with approval. "At least you chose something nice to wear."

Keely had selected a calf-length dress that looked like two pieces, with a softly gathered red cotton daisy print skirt and a denim vest. She wore a multibeaded choker with it and matching earrings that dangled down against her cheeks. Simple denim flats finished her outfit.

"Thank you for the compliment. As for the parent part, sorry, it's just part of the job," she said cheerfully as the door opened.

Sam in his khaki uniform was imposing. Sam in faded jeans and a dusty green T-shirt was even more unsettling.

He eyed the plate and bowl. "I know I said you didn't have to go to any trouble, but I'm glad you did. Cooking anything remotely complicated is way beyond me." He stepped back and gestured them to enter.

"What do you consider complicated?" Keely asked, stepping inside and handing him the bowl.

"Pretty much any kind of salad other than lettuce and a couple tomatoes and anything that doesn't come out of a box. The kitchen is this way." He guided them down a hallway toward the rear of the house.

Along the way, Keely glanced into what had to be the living room housing a blue-and-mauve print couch that looked as if it wasn't used very much. She didn't miss the hurried dusting job on the coffee table and other pieces of furniture or the newspapers peeking out from an ajar closet door. She also noticed photographs lining the hallway wall and paused to inspect a few. She noticed most of them were of Lisa, from what looked like moments after her birth to her latest school photo, along with many candid shots. Others were of a younger Sam standing with his arm around a woman who was clearly Lisa's mother. Mother and daughter shared the same smile. She also couldn't miss the love and pride and Sam's smile as he looked down at his wife. She felt a tiny tug in the vicinity of her heart. This was a couple who still would have been married today if his wife hadn't died. And she doubted either would have thought of straying. She quickly turned away from the photos.

"At least you don't embarrass me this way," Steffie declared, twisting her face in sympathy for her friend as she gazed at one candid photo where a baby-faced Lisa was licking an ice-cream cone but had more ice cream on her face than on the cone.

"I'm sure we could find an appropriate wall for all the

pictures we've taken of you over the years," Keely commented.

"Not if I hide them first."

"Wow, what did you bring?" Lisa hopped from foot to the other as she stood in the kitchen doorway.

"Texas Brownies and a pasta salad," Steffie announced, moving toward her friend. "I'm afraid Mom's looking at the pictures of you."

Lisa grimaced. "At least this wall doesn't have my growth chart on it, too. Hi, Keely."

"Hi, Lisa. I think this is a great idea for all those pictures we tend to either stick in a box or a photo album that's in the back of a bookcase." Keely walked into the kitchen.

Sam stood at a counter basting steaks with barbecue sauce. "I can't miss when I grill," he told Keely with a slight grin on his lips.

"Believe me, Dad's cooking is much better than it used to be," Lisa assured them. "He used to burn some of the meat so bad we might as well have been eating charcoal."

"Charcoal is good for the digestion," he told her. "I bet no other kid in your class had the good digestion you had."

Steffie rolled her eyes. "Oh, yeah, real important. I'm sure some people would consider that child abuse."

"That's what she used to say when I made her eat her peas," Keely told Sam.

"Why don't you two girls go do whatever will make you happy until dinnertime," he suggested.

"Great idea," Lisa said, promptly dragging Steffie off after snagging two sodas.

"Something to drink?" Sam asked Keely.

"Iced tea is fine." She leaned against the table so she could look around the room without appearing too obvious.

The room showed use but few special touches. The towels were ulitarian white; there was a shade at the window instead of curtains. The appliances showed a recent wipe down and the pans sitting on the stove were blackened on the outside.

Sam poured her a glass of tea and pulled a bottle of beer out of the refrigerator for himself.

"So, what great crimes did you solve today?" she asked lightly.

He cocked his head to one side in thought. "Let's see. Harvey down at the video store discovered kids were putting X-rated tapes in the PG tape cases so they could rent them. They didn't realize the bar code was on the tape, not the box, so they were busted the minute the tape was scanned. I had a talk with a few sets of parents on that. A couple didn't see anything wrong with it. Others thought Harvey shouldn't be renting them out, period. He keeps them in the back room where kids aren't allowed, but they managed to sneak back there anyway."

"Very serious," she said gravely.

He nodded in agreement. "Then Emily Walker called to complain they were playing disgusting music in the supermarket. She didn't feel they should play anything that was produced after 1947. Today's canned music seemed to be from the disco era."

Keely made a face. "It's supposed to be dead."

"Tell that to Louis, who's the store manager. He's positive that music will make a big comeback any day now."

Keely chuckled. "And they say small towns are boring. You might not have any major crimes, but you have your share of interesting ones."

For a second Sam's eyes were shadowed. He tilted the bottle up and drank deeply.

Keely felt her laughter drying up as she watched his

Adam's apple convulse as the beer flowed down his throat. She coughed to cover up her feelings of confusion.

"What can I do to help?" she asked, straightening up.

Sam set his bottle down on the counter. "It looks as if Lisa forgot to get the plates out, so you can get them out of that cabinet by the refrigerator. How do you like your steak?"

"Medium well for me, well-done for Steffie."

He nodded. "That's easy."

Keely uncovered the salad bowl and restirred the contents. She began to wonder if she'd been without a man for too long if she could stare at Sam like a lovesick puppy. She hadn't missed it before. So why would it come up now? She quickly pulled down plates and rummaged through drawers for silverware. It wasn't long before the fragrant aroma of cooking meat wafted through the open window.

"Girls!" she called out. "Do you think you can tear yourselves away from whatever you're doing and come out here for dinner?"

"I'm braiding Lisa's hair," Steffie sang out.

"You can finish it after we eat."

Aware of her mother's tone of voice, Steffie walked into the kitchen with Lisa a few minutes later. Half of Lisa's hair hung straight around her shoulders while the other half was pulled up into an intricate braid.

"I would have been finished in another ten minutes," Steffie groused.

"You can finish it just as easily after dinner." Keely placed the plates in her hands and handed Lisa napkins and silverware. "Why don't you set the table while I get out everything else."

"I thought barbecues meant there wasn't a lot of work," Steffie uttered with a dramatic sigh.

Keely couldn't help but notice how the girls made sure

she and Sam sat next to each other at the redwood picnic table outside. She admitted at least they gave them the side with the view. And what a view.

The woods stood not far from the house and the night sounds were clearly audible but nothing she found threatening.

Not like the nights she stood at her bedroom window and looked out at another section of these woods and sometimes felt as if something, or someone, stood just within the trees where she could be seen and they couldn't. She usually shrugged it off as nothing more than a fanciful imagination. Except there were times she had to wonder why her imagination also conjured up the faint aroma of cigar smoke that seemed to float through the air in her direction.

For now, she would concentrate on her steak and baked potato and pasta salad.

"So are you feeling more settled in yet?" Sam asked.

"I always feel settled in when I get back to my work," she replied.

"Especially since I can now go back to school and I'm not around to disturb her concentration," Steffie chimed in. "I don't even know how she thinks I disturb her since she works so hard a bomb could go off and she wouldn't notice it."

"Self-defense," Keely said, as she cut into her steak.

"Were you a graphic artist during your marriage?" Sam asked.

She nodded. "I started out with an advertising agency right out of college. I was more a gofer than an artist then. I thought I'd be allowed to be in the thick of things. Help design memorable campaigns, but it seemed all I did was color pictures and carry the finished work down to production. I began to wonder if I'd have to wait for someone to die or retire before I could show what I could really do.''

"And what happened?'' he asked.

She grinned. "Someone retired and I was finally given my chance to show them what I can do.''

Sam chuckled. "At least it didn't take someone dying.''

"Even then I had to fight to be given a chance.''

As the two talked, they were unaware of their daughters exchanging significant looks and even more significant smiles.

Sam found himself enjoying just talking to Keely without any awareness of time passing. He had no idea how long they might have still been out there talking if he hadn't noticed her shivering slightly. He started, realizing that the meal was finished and that the girls had obviously cleared the table, thoughtfully leaving the plate of brownies on the table between them.

"No wonder you're cold. I hadn't realized how late it was getting,'' he apologized, more mad at himself than anything else.

"I'm fine,'' she assured him as she got up and walked over to the deck railing. She leaned her arms on the top rail and looked out. "I'm still not used to all this clear air,'' she said.

He followed her. "What got me was all the sounds at night,'' he admitted. "They talk about how quiet it is out here, and compared to what I was used to, this would be considered quiet.''

"Except there are birds and insects and the rustle of leaves in the breeze,'' Keely said.

Sam nodded. "A wild night in town is when the guys get too rowdy during a pool game at Tug's Tavern instead of a drive-by shooting or a holdup at the corner liquor store.''

Keely exhaled a soft sigh. "Sometimes I wonder if I did the right thing moving Steffie away from all her friends."

Sam turned to lean sideways against the rail. "She seems to have settled in just fine."

She continued looking at the dark outline of trees and bushes. "Do you ever feel someone could be out there watching you?" she asked abruptly.

He straightened up at that remark. "Why would you ask that?"

Keely suddenly felt very silly asking the question. She shrugged. "Fanciful imagination, I guess," she said lightly. "Maybe it's all those books I've read about monsters in the woods. I think Bigfoot will walk out at any moment."

"I think he's living further north now." He kept his words in the same light vein as hers but he still sensed that there was more to her question than she seemed to want to admit just yet. He wondered if he shouldn't ask one of the deputies to do an occasional drive-by during the night to make sure everything was all right.

A strange feeling was running around deep in his stomach. He didn't like this feeling. Anytime he had it, something bad happened. He'd hate to think Keely would be the victim this time.

Keely glanced at her watch. "We really should be going," she murmured. "I thought I'd go over to my parents' house tomorrow and do some cleaning."

Sam frowned. "Are you sure it's a good idea for you to go alone?" He wanted nothing more than to tell her why the house upset her so much, but he knew he couldn't. If Keely was meant to remember what happened there, she would have to do it on her own.

"Steffie made me promise to wait until after school so she could go along." She pushed herself away from the railing. "Thank you for dinner."

"Thanks for bringing the salad and brownies. After Lisa's last stint in home ec, we get very few treats. She doesn't do well with ovens except to cause fires." He grinned. "Of course, I'm not any better."

"Steffie tended to forget to set the timer and get on the phone with a friend," Keely told him. "She'd forget all about whatever she was baking until she could smell it burning. I'm surprised her attempts at baking didn't wear out the battery in the smoke alarm." She started for the door with Sam following her at a more leisurely pace. Just before he stepped inside, he looked over his shoulder toward the nearby woods.

Could someone have been out there tonight? Was that why he felt uneasy?

"Why don't I follow you home?" he suggested. "Just to make sure everything's all right."

She slanted him a look filled with amusement. "Small towns are safe, remember? Besides, I left lights on. Steffie!" She raised her voice. "Time to go."

Furtive whispers warned them the girls were coming. Lisa's hair was now completely braided and her bangs had also been trimmed to feather across her forehead.

"Very nice," Sam complimented. "But you're still not dating," he added, sending her smug grin downward.

"Don't worry," Steffie commiserated with her friend. "Mom said I won't be dating until I'm thirty-five."

"At least I only have to wait until I'm thirty."

"Don't be so eager to grow up," Keely chided as they moved toward the front door. "Before you know it, you'll be wishing to return to these days."

Sam and Lisa walked outside with them and waited as Keely and Steffie climbed into the Blazer.

"Thank you for a lovely evening," Keely said softly.

He smiled. "I enjoyed it, too."

"We'll have to do it again, but next time at our house," Steffie suggested.

Keely didn't say anything other than to thank Sam again before driving off.

"They are so nice," Lisa commented as they walked back into the house.

"Lisa, no matchmaking," he advised.

She sighed but didn't make any promises.

"They have a really nice house, don't they?" Steffie said during the drive home.

"Very nice."

"Sam's not like any cop I've ever seen before. He's, well, he's nice and almost sweet."

"Steffie." There was no mistaking the warning tone in Keely's voice. She glanced up when a speck of light caught her eye. Not so far back was the unmistakable glint of headlights. Since the road wasn't all that heavily traveled, she was surprised to see headlights but she knew there were others who lived along this way. She dismissed the lights from her thoughts.

Except Keely soon noticed that the lights didn't come any closer but seemed to prefer to keep a safe distance behind them. Her hands tightened on the steering wheel and she carefully pressed her foot down further on the accelerator.

When she sped up, the vehicle behind her sped up. She wished she hadn't left her cellular phone on the charger at home. Having that little piece of security would make her feel much better.

"Mom, is everything okay?"

Keely exhaled a quick breath. "Everything's fine, honey. I guess I was just daydreaming."

"About a certain sheriff," she teased.

She managed a stiff smile. "No, about what needs to be done tomorrow."

She had already made up her mind if when they came to their road the headlights were still there, she would make an excuse and head straight for town. Now she wished she'd allowed Sam to follow her home. The thought echoed in her head. That was it! He had decided to follow her home anyway to make sure everything was all right. She breathed a sigh of relief as she pulled onto their driveway and drove up to the garage. She noticed the vehicle passed by their house. She wondered why he didn't stop.

As they stepped inside, the phone was ringing.

"Hi, Keely," Sam greeted her the moment she said hello. "I forgot to give you your bowl. At least the girls washed it."

Keely's face froze.

Now that she knew it wasn't Sam, she had to wonder just who was driving behind her. She feared her unknown follower had something to do with the letter she'd received, but she didn't want to bring it up to Sam until she was sure.

Chapter 7

Keely didn't need many hints to tell her it wasn't her day. She couldn't find an important file in her computer and hated to think it was lost. Steffie had borrowed, without permission, her favorite pale blue blouse and promptly spilled orange juice on it at breakfast. Then Keely ruefully noticed there was a suspicious leak under the commode.

"It may as well be Friday the thirteenth," she groaned, sorting through her clothing for her oldest jeans and then discovering they were in the hamper. She shrugged and slipped them on. "Oh, well, they'll just get dirtier anyway."

She loaded cleaning supplies into the back of the Blazer and drove out to the school to pick up Steffie.

"I was going to ask Lisa if she wanted to come out and help," her daughter told her as she climbed into the car, "but she has glee club practice."

"I'm sure she would enjoy that a great deal more than cleaning a filthy old house," Keely said dryly as she drove away from the school grounds.

"Think we can do some in-line skating this weekend?" Steffie asked as she scrunched down in her seat and pulled off her shirt. She quickly pulled on a shirt her mother had brought for her.

"Sure. I need the exercise," Keely replied as the car sped down the road until they reached the side road leading to her family home. As she drove up the winding lane, she felt that same disquiet she'd felt the other time. She deliberately tamped down her feelings and shored up any uneasiness that threatened to creep in.

The house didn't look different. Just a house that needed painting, landscaping and some tender loving care. So why did she feel as if something horrible would happen to her the moment she stepped inside?

Keely swallowed the bitterness creeping up her throat as she climbed out of the truck. She walked around to the back to pull out the cleaning supplies and met Steffie who came around from the other side.

"Wouldn't it be easier to just sell this place and buy the house we're leasing?" Steffie asked, grabbing a mop and bucket filled with bottles of household cleaners and floor wax. "Think of all the work we'd save ourselves. A lot of new owners love a fixer-upper."

"The owner of the house we're leasing doesn't want to sell." Keely took another bucket and cleaning rags.

"Aha! You had thought of it, too!" Steffie laughed as she made her way up to the front porch. She stopped and tipped her head back in order to look up. "Such a sad house," she murmured.

Keely stopped short at her daughter's comment. "Why would you say that?"

Steffie turned around at the sharp note in Keely's voice. "I don't know. Maybe it's vibrations or something, but it just feels so sad inside. Do you think someone who'd rented the house since your parents lived here had something unhappy happen here?''

"I don't know." She straightened her shoulders and headed for the door. "And speculating about the former tenants won't get the job done."

"Oh, boy, she's launching into her big-bad-boss routine," Steffie muttered with a teasing smile as she picked up her supplies and waited while Keely unlocked the door and pushed it open.

The soft creak as the door swung open grated on Keely's nerves. She stepped inside and immediately felt that smothering sensation try to overtake her. She refused to give in to the weakness and instantly turned to her left.

"I'll start with the kitchen," she announced. "Why don't you start dust mopping the floors in the living room?" She didn't stop to think why she didn't even want to look inside that room.

Steffie nodded and pulled out the necessary tools.

Keely walked into the kitchen and pulled up the shade in order to have a better look around the small room. After thirty years, she didn't expect to remember anything. She stared at faded wallpaper that needed to be replaced, appliances that were sadly out-of-date and probably didn't work and scarred cabinet doors. She walked over to the sink and wrinkled her nose at the rust stains marring the white porcelain.

"Mom, should I have memories of here?" she whispered, looking around her as if she might see the ghost of her mother standing nearby.

For a moment her vision wavered and she was positive she could smell the spicy aroma of freshly baked gingerbread and hear a woman's voice. As quickly as the impression emerged, it disappeared.

Keely gripped the counter because she was afraid her legs couldn't hold her up. A second later, she heard the raucous sounds from Steffie's portable stereo. Anything she might have been able to dredge up dissipated under the everyday sounds.

She turned on the water to fill the bucket and with gritted teeth she began scrubbing cabinets and counters. The entire time she worked she felt a cold sensation along her shoulder blades, as if someone was watching her. She tried to ignore the feelings until it got so strong she'd look up and around, even going so far as to glance out the window and open the back door, but each time there was nothing. Even that assurance didn't ease her mind. Not when she was positive she could detect a faint aroma of cigar smoke coming from outside. For the rest of the time she worked in the kitchen she kept looking over her shoulder.

"I don't have to clean out the fireplace, do I?" Steffie shouted. "It's disgusting and I wouldn't be surprised if there are spiders and bats living in the chimney."

"Don't worry, I'll have a professional come out to clean that," Keely assured her, relieved to have a reason to leave the kitchen. She walked through the house to the living room and looked around. "You have done a great job!"

Steffie picked up a dustmop that was black with dirt. "This is only a fraction of the crud I got up. Didn't anyone ever clean around here?" She grimaced as she wiped her grimy hands on her shorts.

"Not for the past few years." Keely frowned as she glanced toward the stairs. Why did they make her feel uneasy? As if they were the basis behind something horrible. The only conclusion she could come to was that she might have fallen down them as a child and had been afraid of them after that.

As it was, she had no desire to climb them to check out the second floor. She knew she would have to conquer this fear sooner or later; right now, she'd prefer it be later.

"Mom." Steffie moved toward the window. "It's starting to get dark."

Keely had already uneasily noticed that the room was growing dimmer. And she hadn't thought to bring any flashlights.

"Why don't we pack up?" she suggested. "We'll stop in town and pick up a pizza on the way home."

"Sounds good to me." Steffie hurriedly piled supplies in the bucket. "And garlic bread."

"Naturally."

Keely likewise hurried. She couldn't help but wonder— if she felt so apprehensive about the house now, how would she be able to live in it?

The little girl was afraid. She hated to hear the loud voices coming from below. She didn't want to leave her bed, but she wanted her mommy even more. Her stuffed dog helped her feel braver as she climbed out of bed and crept toward the door. Where was the night-light? Why was it so dark? It wasn't supposed to be dark like this. It wasn't dark before, was it?

She made her way to the top of the stairs. From there, she could see everything. No! It was dark down there. She could hear the angry voices but couldn't see anyone down there. Were there ghosts or monsters making all the noise? She was afraid to look. Afraid of what she might see. And the lady's song about the white rabbit was so clear, as if she were on the stairs with her.

Then the screams began.

Keely bolted upright in bed. Her heart pounded so violently she wasn't aware of her nightgown sticking to her sweat-slick skin. She drew up her legs and rested her forehead against her knees. Her mouth was open as she struggled to draw much needed air into her lungs.

"What does it mean?" she whispered. "Why do I dream of a small child crying?"

At that exact second the telephone rang. She jumped, covering her mouth to stifle a cry. She leaned over and snagged the receiver before it could ring a second time.

"Hello?" she said softly, wondering if she was letting herself in for a crank call.

Instead of a voice, the soft strains of a song came over the receiver. The same song from her nightmare. Keely moaned and quickly replaced the receiver. She backed up until she was plastered against the headboard and her arms looped around her drawn-up knees as she stared at the phone. It wasn't until dawn before she felt brave enough to allow herself to fall back asleep and even then she didn't relax her defensive pose. She feared she'd only dreamed the phone call. Even if it didn't feel like a dream.

"At least we don't have to worry about a lot of traffic here," Steffie said as she sat on the Blazer's tailgate and pulled on her Rollerblades. She busied herself with her helmet, knee and elbow pads next.

"Or you gawking at the boys playing volleyball when we go to the beach," Keely teased, as she tucked her ponytail up under her helmet. "Or if we're at the park."

"Okay, okay, I get the message," Steffie groused, as she secured the protective padding. "But I noticed there were times when you watched a few guys, too."

"Of course I did. I may be over thirty, but I'm not dead," Keely said cheerfully, standing up. After Steffie stood up, Keely pushed up the truck's tailgate and made sure it was locked. "We still should keep our ears and eyes open for traffic."

Steffie nodded then pushed off. Keely quickly followed. Mother and daughter had spent many a weekend in-line skating either at a nearby park or at the beach and enjoyed the exhilaration the speed afforded them.

Keely had always enjoyed the fresh bite of salt air and the breeze the ocean gave them. Out here, they had the fresh air, but instead of smooth concrete they had a rougher surface to navigate and potholes to avoid as they rolled over the roads.

Since the night she had dreamed of the crying child and the phone call that could have been a dream for all she knew at this point, Keely hadn't been sleeping well. She hoped the exercise would tire her out enough to get a decent night's sleep.

She could see Steffie racing ahead of her, the girl laughing as she spun around.

"Such great hills," she shouted, bending her knees slightly as she sped up.

"Just keep an eye out for cars," Keely shouted back.

They skated until they both felt pleasantly tired and had to stop to take a rest, each taking half of a large boulder set just off the road.

"We need to do this more often," Steffie said. "I told Lisa I'd teach her to skate. Maybe her dad would like to learn, too." She gave her mother a sly smile.

"Oh, sure, the good sheriff can catch criminals as he rolls down the sidewalk." Keely drank from her water bottle. "I don't think this is his style for exercise."

Steffie rolled her eyes. "Okay. smart guy, what do you think is his idea of exercise?"

Bed pillows tossed to the floor. Sheets pulled back. Keely abruptly shook her head to dispel the picture forming in her mind.

"Something a little more he-man than in-line skating," she answered, pushing herself off the boulder. "Come on. We should get back. We're going to be sore enough as it is since we haven't done this for a while, and there are more hills here."

"After all the hard labor you've put me through, this was nothing," Steffie scoffed, pushing off.

Keely was content to follow behind Steffie and enjoy the pull of tired muscles. It wasn't until Steffie half turned around and a look of horror crossed her face that she had an inkling something might be wrong. Steffie braked to a quick stop and made wild motions with her hands.

"Mom, be careful!" she yelled.

At that moment Keely realized there was something behind her. By then, it was too late. A large truck sped past her so close she promptly lost her balance and fell head over heels. She heard Steffie's screams as she finally landed on her back.

"Mom! Mom!" Steffie kneeled by her prone form. "Are you all right?" Her hands fluttered over her as if she were afraid to touch her.

Keely closed her eyes for a moment as she took inventory. "You never realize just how hard the ground is until you've landed on it," she groaned, slowly sitting up.

Her daughter's face darkened with fury. "The idiot never stopped. You could have been killed!" As she looked at her mother, her eyes filled with tears. "It was as if he were aiming for you."

A chill entered Keely's blood. "Honey, that's the last thing I wanted to hear." She winced as she straightened out her legs.

"Oh, Mom," Steffie whispered, staring with horrified fascination at Keely's legs, which were speckled with bits of gravel and blood.

"Just help me up, okay?"

Steffie grabbed Keely's arm and steadied her movements as she slowly got to her feet. She kept hold of her mother as they slowly rolled down the road.

By the time they reached the truck, Keely felt slightly nauseous from the burning pain running up her legs and along her arms.

"You have to see the doctor," Steffie insisted after helping Keely take her blades off and climb into the driver's seat. "You know, if you feel too bad, I could drive you."

Keely shot her an all-knowing look. "I'm only injured, Steffie. Not dying."

"Don't even say that!" She hopped into the passenger seat and quickly fastened her seat belt.

Keely swallowed a groan as she pulled out onto the road. The spots of blood on her arms and legs didn't help her peace of mind.

By the time they reached the medical clinic, her stomach was rolling over and over. With Steffie's help she was able to climb down and hobble into the clinic.

"What happened to you?" Allison asked, running over to take Keely's other arm.

"Skating accident," Keely explained.

"A truck sideswiped her!" Steffie said at the same time.

Allison's alarmed expression told Keely which statement she preferred to believe.

"It was an accident," she insisted. "The driver probably didn't see me." She allowed the receptionist to lead her into a back room and settle her on the examination table. Steffie followed her in.

"The doctor will be just a minute," Allison told them as she left, closing the door behind her.

A soft knock on the door alerted them to their impending visitor. Melanie stepped inside with a smile on her lips. Her smile dimmed when she noticed Keely's ragged condition.

"My, you did a good job on yourself," she observed, moving forward to better examine her injuries. "Allison said you were out in-line skating?'' She arched an eyebrow in question as she glanced up at Keely. ''Why?'' She looked as if she couldn't understand why anyone would do such a thing.

''It's great exercise,'' Keely explained. She let out a hiss when Melanie probed one of the wounds.

''Have you ever done this before?'' she asked.

Keely shook her head.

''Then I'm afraid you're not going to like the treatment I have to use for this.'' She walked over to the intercom and buzzed the office. ''I'm going to need the wire brush in room three.''

''Wire brush?'' Keely yelped, automatically drawing her legs up and wincing as pain shot up her calves.

Steffie turned green and stumbled to her feet. ''I think I'll wait outside,'' she announced, making an unsteady way to the door.

''Did you hear Keely Harper ended up taking a header while in-line skating?'' Rick stuck his head in Sam's door. ''I guess those cute little shorts of hers didn't cover enough skin so she ended up with a pretty bad case of road rash.''

Sam looked up. ''She fell?''

''Her kid says a truck sideswiped her.'' Rick shook his head. ''Man, a looker like her ending up on the road had to be a sorry sight.''

For a brief second Sam wondered what it would feel like to wipe that cocky grin off his deputy's face. He suspected the younger man didn't uphold the letter of the law the way he should, but so far, he hadn't been able to prove a thing. He knew the day he did was the day he'd kick that guy's butt out of a job.

''Maybe one of us should have a talk with her,'' he said slowly.

Rick shook his head. "The lady says it was an accident. It's the kid who disagrees."

"That kid has a pretty level head on her shoulders and I wouldn't discount anything she has to say," Sam said in a tight voice. "I suggest you stop by the Harpers and find out what happened."

Rick's handsome features were marred by his scowl. "Shouldn't we wait for someone to file charges?"

Sam chose to ignore his sarcasm. "I'd like to see some paper on this."

The deputy eyed Sam closely. "You got a reason for wanting this?"

Sam wanted to tell him better men than him had tried to stare him down and lost. But he knew the younger man still felt his oats too much. He figured his cocky swagger said it all.

"Since I'm the sheriff here, I don't need a reason," he said in a level voice that didn't quite disguise the steel in his tone. "Why don't you run out there now?"

Rick's expression was ugly as he turned away. "Yes, *sir!*"

Sam put down his pen before he gave in to his first inclination and threw it. He didn't want to admit he didn't like the idea of Keely being injured. Especially, if as Steffie said, it was deliberate. The Harpers hadn't lived here long enough to have any enemies. What could bring this about? He was determined to find out.

"Are you sure you don't need anything, Mom?" Steffie hovered over her mother.

Keely winced as she shifted her body. More aches and pains were making themselves known as the pain medication wore off.

"No, I'm fine." She cocked her head at the sound of a car driving up.

Steffie ran to the widow to peer out. "It's Sam!" Her smile just as quickly disappeared. "Oh, it's Rick. What does he want?" She walked to the door and opened it.

"Hey there, Steffie," he greeted her. "The sheriff asked me to come out and find out what happened."

"What happened was some idiot practically pushed Mom off the road," Steffie said with a scowl.

Without waiting for an invitation, he stepped inside and, seeing Keely in the family room, headed there.

"Heard you took a nasty spill," he said, taking a nearby chair. His eyes didn't leave her bare legs, which were peppered with raw skin and dots of medicated cream.

"It's one of the hazards of in-line skating." Keely shrugged it off. "I've been lucky before, so I guess it was just my turn."

"It wouldn't have been if it hadn't been for that truck that came racing down the road," Steffie blurted out, perching on the couch arm. "I don't care what Mom says, that truck driver tried to kill her!"

"Steffie, cut the dramatics, please." She gave a sigh. "Look, Rick, there was nothing more than a driver not watching what he was doing when he rounded a corner. I guess the residents aren't used to anyone skating on these roads."

"Did you see the truck?" he asked, pulling out a notebook.

"Just that it was big," she said dryly.

"It was dark blue and had orange flames painted on the hood," Steffie said promptly.

Rick sat up straighter at the description. "Are you sure?"

Keely smiled at Steffie's expression of outrage as if she silently demanded to know why he should discount her word.

"If I'd had a few seconds more I could have gotten the

license plate number,'' Steffie continued in a tight voice. "No offense, but this isn't exactly L.A., so I doubt there'd be all that many trucks around here with those kind of markings.''

Rick closed his notebook and slipped it back into his shirt pocket. "I already know whose truck you're talking about. And I don't like your idea of a joke.'' He stood up, deliberately towering over Steffie.

Keely straightened, fully prepared to protect her daughter.

"This is not a joke!'' Steffie shouted. "Look at my mom! Does she look as if it's a joke? If you know who owns the truck, then go arrest them and ask why they sideswiped her and didn't stop!''

"I own the truck, kid,'' he snarled, swiping the air with his hand. "And I wasn't anywhere near you or your mom.''

Keely stiffened while Steffie looked at him warily.

"You mean someone stole your truck?'' Steffie whispered.

"No one can steal my truck,'' he said between clenched teeth. "I just want to know why you described my truck. Why are you trying to make trouble for me?''

"All right, you two.'' Keely held up her hand to stave off further insults between them. "Sit down, Rick. I said *sit down.*'' This time he complied. "Steffie, you back off a little.'' She turned back to the deputy. "Whether you like it or not, Steffie described the truck she saw. Perhaps you should check on your truck. I have no desire to make a report about this.'' She sat back, fatigued by the angry emotion running so strong around her.

Rick stood up. Conflicting thoughts ran across his face. "I'll tell the sheriff then,'' he muttered, as he walked to the door.

Steffie scowled at his departing back. "Does he think

I'm some little kid who makes up something because I might not have seen the real thing?''

Keely closed her eyes. "Do me a favor," she murmured.

Steffie finally noticed her pale features and hovered over her. "What do you need?''

"Peace and quiet." She slowly rose to her feet. "I'm going to do something I haven't done in a long time. I'm going to take a nap." She carefully made her way down the hall.

"I'll make dinner," Steffie offered.

Keely waved her hand to indicate she heard her. Once inside her bedroom, she slipped off her clothing and slid into bed. Within seconds, she was fast asleep.

The voices are so loud! Why is Daddy shouting? Why is Mommy yelling? She was in the hallway, frightened because it was so dark, but even more scared to go back to her room just then. She inched her way toward the top of the stairs, so she could see. No! She didn't want to look! She didn't want to know! She didn't—

Keely shot up in bed, gasping for air that seemed to refuse to enter her lungs. Labored breaths caused black spots to dance before her eyes.

When she felt in more control of herself, she dropped back against her pillows. Why the dream? She couldn't remember ever having a recurring nightmare of this proportion until she moved here. One thing was coming to mind and she didn't like what it meant. That she just might be that little girl in the dream.

Chapter 8

Keely couldn't work. She could only sit there and stare at the computer screen as the cursor blinked a silent message for her to get cracking.

She hadn't had the dream for more than a week, but that didn't stop it from haunting her every waking hour. Voices echoed in her head and a child's cry entered her mind at odd times.

In a fit of temper, she threw a small stuffed animal she kept on her desk across the room. She wished her grandmother was still alive. Perhaps she could have answered some questions for her. Or at least assured her she wasn't going insane. Then the lightbulb clicked on in her brain.

"Someone here has to know something," she exclaimed, quickly shutting down her computer and jumping to her feet. Now was as good a time as any to do a little sleuthing.

"Why don't you get some lunch?" Fredda stormed into Sam's office.

He looked up, stunned by her abrupt order. "Why?"

"Because you've been a little cranky all morning and maybe a good meal will calm you down," she told him.

Sam knew there was another reason for her suggestion but doubted he'd get a logical answer out of her. Long experience had taught him it was much easier to just go along with whatever she said.

The minute he stepped outside the sheriff's office and saw a familiar figure on the sidewalk across the street he knew why the dispatcher had practically tossed him out of the building. He stifled a grin and crossed the road.

"Glad to see you're up and about," he greeted Keely with a brief nod of the head.

Her expression wasn't as pleasant.

"I did not appreciate your deciding a report needed to be filed on an accident that was nothing more than that, an accident," she said in a low voice.

Sam took her arm. "Have you had lunch yet?"

Her "No, but—" was blatantly ignored as he led her toward the coffee shop.

"Good, I haven't either."

Since the lunch hour was long past, there were few people around. Sam took a rear booth and gestured for Keely to take the opposite bench.

"What'll you have?" he asked.

"A hamburger and fries," she said grudgingly. "And a diet soda."

"Hey, can we have a hamburger with fries, bowl of chili, one diet soda and a coffee over here," he called out.

"Coming up, Sam."

He turned back to Keely. "When Rick got back to the station, he checked on his truck. It was missing and not found until much later that night."

She shrugged it off. "Some kids stole his truck for some joyriding."

"I can't see that happening during the day. And Steffie does talk a lot about where you two go skating." He glanced up and smiled at the waitress as she deposited their drinks in front of them. His smile faded when he saw the shock written on Keely's face.

She leaned forward, keeping her voice low. "I don't like this, Sam. There's no reason for someone to want to frighten me. It's not as if I've lived here long enough to make any enemies. I left this town when I was a little girl." For a moment, she froze as if something occurred to her.

"What?"

She shook her head. "Nothing. Just a crazy idea that really doesn't make any sense."

When their food arrived, Keely bit into her hamburger and chewed, but at the moment she didn't feel very hungry. When Sam told her Rick's truck had been stolen, she suddenly thought of the menacing note she'd received, then her nightmares and the sense she was being watched late at night. The only problem was, she couldn't understand why someone would show that kind of sick anger toward her. She could feel Sam's eyes on her as she sorted through her thoughts.

"Well, if it makes any sense, you make sure to let me know," he said.

She nodded.

"Hey, Sam, I see you have our lovely newcomer all to yourself." John stopped by the booth and clapped him on the back. "Must be the uniform," he joked.

Keely's smile wasn't as forthcoming as it should have been as she looked up and greeted the pharmacist. And she had an idea that Sam noticed that. She doubted the man missed very much.

"Heard you had an accident on those in-line skates," John said, turning to Keely. "How are you feeling now?"

"A lot better, thank you. I'm used to falling down when I'm skating," she replied.

"John, here's your coffee!" came a call from the front counter.

He nodded. "I guess I'll see you at the Pioneer Days Picnic," he said to her before walking off.

Sam turned back to Keely. "Not your type?" He grinned.

She rolled her eyes, looking like her daughter. "Very definitely not my type."

She thought for sure he would ask her what her type was, but he didn't. She told herself it was just as well, because right now she wasn't sure she had a type.

"I gather the Pioneer Days Picnic is a big deal around here?"

He nodded. "It's our annual celebration to honor the town's founders. We have it in the park with food booths and carnival rides. I know it sounds like small-town fun, but we enjoy it."

"Sam, you don't have to defend anything to me," she chided. "Believe me, I didn't spend all my time in night-clubs. For a while the high spot of my life was Steffie's dance recitals. I was never so glad as when she decided dance wasn't one of her strengths."

"Must have been something like Lisa's clarinet lessons. It came to the point her teacher begged her to quit."

Sam ate his chili but he was more aware of the woman sitting across from him. Keely always looked like a breath of spring. And smelled like it, too. He knew he'd been without a woman for too long, but it wasn't just that where she was concerned. Still, he wasn't about to get involved with her, even though she'd fascinated him from that first moment he'd laid eyes on her. He still had trouble believing she was willing to stay in Echo Ridge and he had to wonder what would happen if she ever remembered the reason why she left here thirty years ago. He couldn't imagine she would want to stay then.

"We really should embarrass them one day and drag out the baby pictures," she suggested.

"Sounds good to me."

When the bill came, Sam snatched it up before Keely could reach for it.

"No arguments," he said sternly, reaching into his pants pocket for his wallet.

A hint of a smile curved her lips. "I would never argue with a law officer," she said demurely, but a hint of mischief sparkled in her eyes.

Sam walked Keely outside, automatically glancing both ways. There was no missing Chloe watching them from the front window of her store. Or John standing in the drugstore doorway talking to Mrs. Morrison. Or Rainey just coming out of the barbershop and sending a dark glare in their direction. Sam doubted there could be any other man angrier at the world than Rainey. That was when he noticed Melanie stepping into the post office. He wondered if half the town was there at that moment just to watch them walk out of the coffee shop.

At the same time, he wondered if anyone out there now was the one who had stolen Rick's truck and tried to run down Keely. No matter what she thought, he had a sick suspicion that someone did have it in for her. Worse yet, it would be for something she didn't even remember.

"You're not really going to dance with that geek, are you?" Steffie asked as Keely parked the truck several blocks from the park. She looked around. "Wow, it looks as if the whole town comes out for this thing."

"I'd say so." Keely climbed out and locked the door. Even though they were a few blocks from the park, she could smell the zesty aroma of barbecuing meat. "Are you meeting Lisa?"

Steffie nodded. "Her dad is on duty today, so she came to the park early. She said the rides seem kinda dinky but there's usually an awesome haunted tower to walk through."

Keely shuddered. "Better you than me."

"Cotton candy first." Steffie grabbed her mother's hand and pulled her down the sidewalk.

"A real junk food day," she groaned, allowing her daughter to drag her along.

As they wandered among the food booths enjoying their sugary treat, Keely kept a covert lookout for Sam. While she saw several men in khaki uniforms, none of them was the man she was looking for.

"Well, look at you," Chloe said, coming up to them. She made a comical face at Keely. "Damn, you got that at one of those pricey boutiques in L.A., didn't you?"

Keely looked at her blue chambray vest embroidered with tiny yellow, pink and white flowers across the front. Her full denim skirt fluttered around her calves with the front partially unbuttoned to reveal a white ruffled petticoat. She had let Steffie pull back her hair into one of the intricate braids the girl enjoyed doing and wore denim flats to complete the outfit.

"Actually, I found it at an outlet mall," she replied. "Steffie and I used to enjoy roaming through the outlet malls more than the regular ones."

Chloe shook her head. "I must go shopping with you, too."

"I don't see where you need to worry." Keely openly admired her peach walking shorts and matching vest with a cream-colored T-shirt under the vest.

Chloe struck a model's pose. "With just about everyone here, I'm hoping for a good-looking male who will appre-

way Keely's hand shook. "Hon, you've been doing too much. You better just concentrate on relaxing today and having fun. There's dancing later on this evening."

"I just didn't sleep well last night," Keely said. "Stayed up too late finishing a book," she lied.

"Done that. Been there."

Keely had just turned around, lifting her cup to her lips when she saw Sam standing over by the bandstand talking to an elderly woman. She froze when he looked up and stared at her. With a cream-colored Stetson tipped a bit low over his brow and his sunglasses on, there was no way she could read his expression. The woman standing next to him also turned her head. Keely wasn't sure why the woman's face took on an expression akin to pain when she looked her way. And she wasn't sure she wanted to know why.

Sam turned back to the woman, said something with a brief smile and headed in Keely's direction.

"Well, I can see you'll be well taken care of," Chloe commented, as she took off in another direction. "And I'm sure the good lawman wouldn't want me around."

"Chloe!" Keely could feel herself turning red and silently damned herself for blushing like a teenager.

"If I had to lose out, I'm glad I lost out to someone nice." She patted Keely on her shoulder and sauntered off.

Keely was barely aware of her friend's exit since her gaze was locked with Sam's as he walked a straight line toward her.

"Mrs. Harper," he murmured, inclining his head in her direction.

A tiny smiled tipped up the corners of her lips. "Sheriff Barkley. It's nice to know the picnic is under the all-seeing eye of our local law."

His smile was just as small as hers, but she had a pretty

good idea his brown eyes were twinkling behind the dark lenses of his sunglasses.

"We aim to serve, ma'am," he said with the solemnness of a true peace officer bent on assuring the public of his trustworthiness. "How much of the festivities have you taken in so far?"

"Steffie let me get as far as the cotton candy booth before Chloe could rescue me."

His gaze seemed to center on her mouth. "Yes, I can see that."

Keely self-consciously touched each corner of her mouth with her fingertips and found the sticky substance. "It tends to get messy." She took a deep breath and decided to just go ahead and say it. "Are you on duty?"

"Not officially. Even my men who are officially off-duty are wearing their uniforms today so the kids don't have a prayer in thinking they can get away with anything when there's so many of us hanging around. Luckily, it's never cramped anyone's style, but it has cut down on fights."

"Then why don't you show me around?" she requested, tucking her arm in his. She looked up at him with a coy smile that she ordinarily would have hated herself for using. Still, it hadn't taken her long to realize that Sam was the slow-and-easy type and would need a bit of a push. While she declared loud and clear the last thing she wanted was a man in her life, that didn't mean she wouldn't mind having some male company for part of the day.

"What first?" Sam asked.

She looked around. "What would you suggest?"

"You'd probably enjoy looking at the craft booths," he suggested. "Of course, many of the good ladies will be trying to talk you out of money."

Keely smiled. "I've never been known as a soft touch, so I think I'll be safe as a window shopper."

Sam knew they were in trouble the minute they walked over to craft booths where the ladies could see them together and speculate to their heart's content. For once, he decided he shouldn't mind when Keely asked him to escort her. Also, his cop's nose was twitching more than a little after her skating accident. He hated to think it was deliberate, but right now that wasn't what his gut was telling him.

And if that was the case, it most likely meant something even more sinister. It meant that someone from Willis's past was in town and wanted to make Keely pay for her part in the man's murder conviction thirty years ago.

"These afghans are lovely!" Keely enthused, picking up one done in soft pastel shades. "A friend is having a baby soon and this would be perfect for her."

Sam wisely didn't say anything about her assuring him she wasn't a soft touch.

"If you'd prefer another color, I have a variety," Gladys Fitzgerald, a spritely woman in her eighties, told her. The gleam in her eye was more than enough proof she knew she was selling one of her treasured afghans.

Sam studied the intricate designs, amazed at what the older woman could do in spite of her arthritis. She had always told him it helped her keep her fingers nimble. He had one of her afghans decorating the bed in the guest room. She had given it to him after he found the kids who had been creeping into her yard at night and making noises like ghosts. Their punishment was spending the summer doing her yard work.

"This one," Keely said finally, holding up one that was an intricate design in pale blue, soft green, yellow and pink.

Gladys peered closely at her through her thick bifocals.

"You look very much like your mother," she said in her soft voice.

Keely immediately brightened. "You knew my mother?"

"Oh, yes, dear, she used to help out with the meals-on-wheels for the infirm." She sighed and shook her head. "Such a waste." She suddenly straightened up and managed a wobbling smile. "Enjoy your afghan."

Keely started to open her mouth to question the elderly woman further, but Sam took the afghan out of her hands and draped it over his arm, steering her away before she could say anything.

"I wanted to ask her about my mother," she protested.

"Gladys would only start detailing everyone's secrets," he said, relieved she hadn't seen his warning shake of the head to the other woman. He was grateful Gladys had understood right away.

The story of Keely's parents' deaths was probably the only secret left in Echo Ridge. For Keely's sake, Sam meant to do what he could to ensure that secret was kept.

Chapter 9

"**H**ow can they go on that again and again?" Keely commented, watching Steffie and Lisa hop out of a roller coaster car and get back in line.

"They have cast-iron stomachs," Sam told her. "They also noticed that one of the boys in their class is in line just in front of them."

She watched the girls posture and giggle and she could only heave a sigh. "Being a mother is hell."

"Being a dad isn't much better." He looked over toward the food booths. "Getting hungry?"

She lifted her face and sniffed the air, fragrant with the spicy aroma of roasting meat and barbecue sauce.

"Only if the food is as good as it smells."

"It's even better." He led her over to the booths. "Why don't you find a table while I get us something to eat? Soda or beer?"

"Beer."

He watched her head for the grouping of picnic tables

under nearby trees before heading for one of the booths. "Hey, Marie, how about two sandwiches?" he asked.

"So, Sheriff, who's the lady?" the young woman asked coyly.

He frowned at someone he'd known since she was a toddler. "Shouldn't you be worrying more about college than speculating about my so-called love life?"

"Sheriff, you haven't had a love life any of us have been able to talk about. And here you are walking around with some pretty lady," she said cheekily. "Besides, I figured you'd be willing to wait for me to graduate."

"Somehow I can't see Scott letting me horn in on his territory," he teased, accepting the waxed paper wrapped sandwiches.

She flushed prettily at the mention of her boyfriend's name. "I had to console myself with someone, didn't I?" she teased back as she accepted his money.

Sam received more kidding when he purchased their drinks and he deflected it the same way. He knew there would be gossip. It was inevitable. Still, he kind of liked it. As he walked toward Keely with their food, he noticed her bright smile and realized he wanted to see more of that.

Another thing he started to realize was that he wanted to see even more of Keely and was eager to find out just how her lips tasted.

"You expect me to eat all of that?" Keely asked, stunned by the huge sandwich he set in front of her. "I doubt I could eat even half of that if I was starving." She sipped her beer and nibbled on her sandwich. "Mm, I just might be able to make an exception this one time." She took a bigger bite.

Sam chuckled. "Red Whittaker firmly believes barbecue isn't any good unless it's slow-cooked for at least two days. Everyone looks forward to town gatherings just so they can have one of his sandwiches.''

With Keely's mouth filled with beef, she could only nod with enthusiasm.

"Think you're going to be able to finish it?" he joked.

"Mmmf," she mumbled then swallowed and took a sip of her beer. "Definitely, so don't even think about trying to steal any of this," she warned.

As Keely chewed her sandwich, she noticed elderly Gladys walking across the grass.

"You said you've lived here all your life." She waited as he nodded. "Did you know my parents?"

If Keely had thought about it, she would have realized that he hesitated just a second too long.

"I was a kid more interested in Little League and building the ultimate tree house," he replied.

"I wouldn't have expected you to remember me since I was so young, but I would think you might have remembered my parents," she pressed. "After all, my dad did run a nursery here."

Sam silently cursed. He'd forgotten her father had owned a local business at that time. At least she didn't know he'd worked for her dad that last summer. And when he thought about it, he could vaguely recall a big-eyed little girl with pigtails running around the trees and bushes.

"As I mentioned, back then I had my own interests," he said with a finality he hoped she would pick up on and leave the topic alone. He should have known better.

She idly twirled her beer bottle between her fingers. "Something is wrong here," she mused. "Both of my parents grew up here. I was born here, but it's as if people don't want to talk about them. I feel as if there's a secret about them no one wants to tell me."

Sam mentally uttered a few more choice curses. He should have known she was quick enough to catch on. He thought of all the years the truth about the Davises' deaths had been kept under wraps. How everyone living here at that time had been so shocked by the first violent crime committed in the town for more than fifty years and saddened that an innocent little girl had had the misfortune to be the only witness. After her illness that left her with the memory block regarding the murders, it was easy to manufacture a fiction about her parents being killed in an auto accident and in all these years that story had never been disputed.

"You're talking about something that happened thirty years ago," he said finally. "Some of the people who lived here back then have either moved or have passed away. Others have grown to the age where the memory isn't what it used to be and they'd hate to admit it."

Keely set down her sandwich and half turned on the bench so she could faced him. "Gladys didn't look feebleminded to me." A trace of alarm crossed her features. "What is it that no one will tell me?" she demanded.

Sam was hard-pressed for an answer and could only thank the fates when two whirlwinds descended on them.

"Oh, good, you're almost finished." Steffie plopped down next to her mother and picked up her sandwich. Two bites had it gone. "Actually, now you're finished." She presented Keely with her most blissful smile. "Do you know what we're missing?"

Keely looked instantly wary. "To be honest, I don't think we're missing anything."

"You're going to feed me, aren't you?" Lisa asked with hand outstretched.

Sam sighed and pulled out his wallet. "I pity the man you marry." He handed her several bills.

Lisa hopped up and ran off to the food booths.

"Lisa and I met this very nice man named Howard,"

Steffie said. She frowned at Sam when he covered his face with his hand and groaned loudly.

"Don't listen to her," he warned.

"Give Mom a chance," Steffie ordered then turned back to her mother. "Anyway, Howard has the answer to what we truly need at the house." She looked up and smiled when Lisa set half of her sandwich and a soda in front of her.

"You'll be sorry," Sam said.

"Not fair, Dad," Lisa scolded.

"You won't talk me into this," he replied.

Steffie threw up her hands. "Mo—ther." She drew out the word in two syllables.

Keely nodded. "Unfortunately, that is my name. All right, I'll bite. What does Howard have that we absolutely need."

"I can't just tell you. You have to see." She picked up her sandwich and happily munched away. "We'll take you over there after we finish eating."

"And here I thought it was all-important," Keely remarked.

"You'll be sorry," Sam told her, pity coupled with amusement coloring his voice.

Steffie shot him a quelling look. "She is an adult, you know."

Sam's gaze lingered over Keely's form. "Yes, I can tell."

Keely turned away before he saw her damning flush, but his quiet chuckle told her he hadn't missed it at all.

As soon as the girls finished eating, Steffie grabbed Keely's hand and pulled her to her feet. "All right, let's go."

Keely pulled back forcing the girl to halt. She turned back to Sam. "Would you excuse me? My daughter has something vitally important to show me."

"Are you kidding?" He rose to his feet. "I plan to watch this." He and Lisa walked behind them. "Just as long as my darling daughter understands I will say no right now."

"I wasn't going to ask," she said with a resigned sigh. "Good idea."

The moment Keely saw the enclosure made up of portable fencing and puppies sleeping on the grass within its protection, she had a sinking feeling she knew what her daughter was up to.

"Oh, please no," she protested even as Steffie pulled her toward the puppies.

"Aren't they adorable?" the girl said enthusiastically, dropping to her knees by the enclosure. She reached over the fence and picked up one of the black puppies, who immediately began licking her face. "You said we need a dog."

Keely stared at paws that were already the size of saucers. "I was talking about a cute little terrier," she retorted.

"We need a watchdog." Steffie plopped the puppy in Keely's arms.

The man standing nearby grinned. "Hi, Sam."

"Howard." Sam nodded. "Are these Lady Joy's pups?"

"Yep. She had some real beauties this time. I thought this would be a good time to find them homes. The price is reasonable," he added.

"Not in our household," he said fervently.

"Same here," Keely told Steffie.

"They're a shepherd-lab mix," the girl explained. "Ten weeks old and they're pretty much housebroken."

"Pretty much?"

"All right, close to it, but they make great watchdogs,"

she said with enthusiasm. "And with our living so far out, it might be a good idea to have one."

Keely took a deep breath. She had a sinking feeling this was one battle she could very well lose. She dreaded to think how much it would cost to feed a dog who would grow up to be the size of a small horse.

"Right now, they're still puppies and won't be eligible for watchdog status for almost a year," she said. "Until then, a puppy will be doing nothing but eating and piddling on the carpet, which I'm sure I'll be the lucky person to clean up."

"I'll take care of her." Steffie reached over and stroked another puppy's back.

"Not a female. Males are cheaper to neuter," Keely said, then groaned as she realized her statement only meant she'd somehow been conned into accepting a puppy into her home. As if he understood what had just happened, the puppy raised his head and licked her face with his tiny sandpapery tongue. She laughed at the enthusiastic face washing as the puppy strained to reach all of her face.

Sam squatted down behind her and whispered in her ear, "Congratulations, you're the mother of a fine bouncing baby boy."

At that moment, the warm slightly musky smell a puppy gives off blended very nicely with Sam's spicy cologne. She felt a brief urge to reach behind her and tug his face down to hers. Now, wouldn't that give something meaty for the gossips to latch on to?

Instead, Steffie's squeal of delight took away any further thoughts she had regarding the good sheriff.

"I mean it, a male puppy," Keely stressed as Steffie threw her arms around her neck and hugged her as tightly as the squirming puppy would allow.

"I'll throw in a twenty-pound bag of kibble," Howard offered.

"Great." Keely smiled gamely. "He'll have enough food for the first few days."

She looked at the hand stretched out in front of her and placed her own in it. Sam pulled her and the puppy she still held in one arm up.

"Is that the one you want?" Howard asked, gesturing to the puppy Keely held. His gaze flickered in Steffie's direction. She was holding another puppy. For a second she looked hopeful.

Keely efficiently checked both puppies. "This one is a male. This is the one we'll take," she announced.

"I will take full responsibility," Steffie vowed.

"Good, then you can pay the man," Keely said as pleasantly as possible.

She decided the stunned look on her daughter's face was worth it. But in the end, she was the surprised one when Steffie pulled out her wallet and handed Howard the money.

Keely turned to Sam.

"It's happened. My little girl has grown up." She looked as if she wasn't sure whether to laugh or cry.

"Don't worry, I'll probably be next." He gave her a brief hug.

"Dad?" Lisa turned her pleading gaze on him.

He slowly shook his head back and forth. "Not just yet."

"Ted's Ramona is due to have her puppies in a couple weeks," Howard volunteered.

"Shut up, Howard," Sam said without malice. "Ramona is a Great Dane," he explained for Keely's benefit.

"I guess I should consider myself lucky then." Keely allowed Steffie to take the puppy out of her arms. She couldn't believe that she already missed the warm armful.

"You can leave the pup here until you're ready to go home," Howard offered. He held up a ribbon. "I'll just write your name on the ribbon and tie it around the little guy's neck.''

Steffie looked torn at the idea of leaving her new baby, but the prospect of an evening at the midway beckoned. She slowly relinquished her bundle.

"How late are you staying?" she asked.

"Until closing."

"I'm not sure whether to thank you or not," Keely quipped before walking away with Sam.

"You'll feel safer with a big dog around," Howard assured her.

"He probably has a good point there," Sam said as they walked toward the midway.

"Yes, but he won't be responsible for food and vet bills for the next ten to fifteen years, either." She paused. "Still, Steffie's always wanted a dog and her father refused to have one. He said they were too much trouble. And it's not as if she's six years old and doesn't understand what responsibility is."

"This only means I'll have to give in sooner or later," Sam lamented. He steered her toward the carnival rides.

"Then I suggest you wait until Ramona has her puppies," she laughed.

If Sam was honest with himself he would have said he couldn't remember the last time he'd had so much fun. Keely's sense of humor and way of looking at things was infectious. She obediently laughed and squealed on the roller coaster and the Tilt-A-Whirl. She cheered Sam on while he threw baseballs at milk bottles and offered him a coy smile when he won a large panda bear, which he handed over to her with great ceremony.

"I keep this up and I'll feel as if I'm back in high school again," he said.

"Oh, my, am I dating the high school quarterback?" Keely cooed, fluttering her eyelashes at him.

He shot her a quelling look. "Can it, Harper."

"Oh, was it halfback instead?" she teased. "I never could keep all those positions straight. But then," she paused, pursing her lips and making a production of looking behind him. "Perhaps it was tight end."

Sam growled something deep in his throat as he grasped her arm and propelled her toward the sheltering trees.

Before Keely could ask him what he was doing, she had her back against a tree that effectively hid them from the festivities and Sam's mouth was covering hers.

He should have known she would taste like this—tangled sheets, the sweetness of sin and the heady spice of pure woman. She fit in his arms as if she had been fashioned expressly for him and her lips molded under his in the same way.

There were a million reasons running through Sam's head why he shouldn't be doing this. And a million more why he should.

His tongue swept through the dark cavern of her mouth, shuddering when her tongue curled around his, enticing him deeper as he angled himself even closer against hers. The warmth of her body had him thinking about pulling her down onto the grass and finding out how the rest of her felt. His hands swept up and down her back, urging her to shape her body against his aroused form. She murmured several incoherent words against his parted lips.

"If we get routed out of here by any of your deputies, I will never forgive you," she whispered, tipping her head back.

The faint lights from beyond highlighted her face. Her eyes were wide, lips shiny with moisture and swollen from his kisses. In his eyes, she never looked more beautiful.

"If any of my deputies dares to come over here and

disturb us, I will personally shoot the guy,'' he murmured before capturing her mouth again. He could feel her smile against his lips.

As they stood among the shelter of the trees, they were unaware of two teenagers watching them with very satisfied expressions on their faces. But there was someone else watching them, someone even further back among the trees, and that person's expression wasn't the least bit happy about the scene.

Keely still felt a little shell-shocked when she and Sam came out from behind the safety of the woods. She knew it was time to go home.

"There they are," Sam said, pointing off to the side.

"Let's gather up our newest kid and head for home," Keely said once she caught up with Steffie and Lisa.

For a moment, Steffie looked as if she were going to protest, but it subsided before it began.

"Did you two have fun?" she asked.

"Your mother enjoyed the rides," Sam replied.

The two girls exchanged a secret look.

"I'll call you tomorrow," Lisa told Steffie.

"We're going to walk them to their truck," Sam said.

The adults chose to wait in the background as the girls collected the puppy and Sam picked up the bag of kibble.

"I thought the town was safe at night," Keely said archly as they walked to her truck.

"It is, but it doesn't hurt for me to look around out here, too."

Sam stowed the bag of kibble in the back of the Blazer while Lisa held the puppy then handed him up to Steffie after she was settled in the passenger seat,

Keely stood by the open driver's door looking up at Sam

"I must say it was an interesting evening, Sheriff," she murmured.

A hint of a smile tugged at the corner of his lips. "Very informative, Mrs. Harper. I'm glad you enjoyed it."

She let her fingertip trail along his waistband. "Let me put it this way. If there weren't two impressionable teenagers on the other side of this truck, I would show you just how much I enjoyed it. Good night, Sam." She climbed up into the driver's seat and switched on the engine.

Sam blew out a deep breath as he watched the truck drive off.

"I'm glad you two guys had fun, Dad," Lisa said, walking over to him.

"Yeah, so am I," he said more to himself.

But Lisa caught his meaning and merely smiled.

It wasn't until they arrived home and Keely climbed out of the truck that she saw the creased sheet of paper on the driver's seat. She couldn't understand why she hadn't seen it before unless it was because her attention had been more focused on Sam.

Her blood ran cold when she read the crudely printed words: Get out, witch, while you still can. Otherwise, you could end up like your parents.

Chapter 10

"**I** want to know what the hell is going on here."

Sam knuckled his eyes open to better see the sheet of paper thrust in front of his face.

"Is this a test?" he asked in a raspy voice.

Without waiting for an invitation, Keely marched past him and continued walking until she reached the kitchen.

Sam groggily turned around and walked back the same way. He winced every time he heard a cabinet door slam.

"Where's your damn coffee?" He winced again at her shout.

"In the refrigerator." He lowered himself gingerly into a chair. "Do you mind my asking what's going on?"

Keely spun around. He was stunned to see her wild-eyed and features pulled tight. She spun back around and quickly prepared the coffee. She stood there, hands gripping the side of the counter as she stared at the coffee-maker as if willing the dark liquid to drip faster. He noted her spine was rigid with tension. The paper she had held out to him was crushed in one hand. He settled back, knowing she wouldn't tell him what was going on until she was good and ready. He would just have to wait.

He stifled a yawn. He just wished he'd had more sleep before this surprise visit had been sprung on him. Getting a police call three a.m. and not getting back until an hour ago had completely fuzzed up his brain. It was eleven a.m. now, but Sam felt as if it was the middle of the night.

He rubbed his hand over his face, grimacing at the bristly feel of his morning beard against his palm. He already sensed he wouldn't get in a quick shave and shower first.

The moment there was enough coffee in the pot, Keely poured out two cups and carried them over to the table. She set one cup in front of Sam along with the piece of paper, then sat down in the chair to his right.

"So tell me, noble sheriff, what do you think this means?" she asked with a sarcastic edge to her voice that could have cut steel.

Sam's blood ran cold the moment he read the words. Now he knew for sure the incident when she and Steffie were skating hadn't been an accident. It wasn't kids who'd boosted Rick's truck for a joyride. It was someone who was thumbing his nose at the law by stealing a law officer's vehicle and trying to run down an innocent person. Which could only mean one thing.

"Sam!" Her palm slapped down on the table in front of him. "I want to know what the hell this means?"

He looked up. There was fury in her gaze but also a hint of fear. He hated to think that no matter what he said, he could only compound that fear. He picked up his cup and drank deeply. The scalding hot liquid helped clear his head. He doubted there would be any chance of lifting prints off the note other than Keely's.

"Where did you find this?" he asked, gesturing toward the paper.

Incredibly, her face turned a pale pink.

"It was on the seat to my truck," she replied. "I didn't notice it until we got home last night." She cradled her cup between her palms as if she needed the heat to warm hands that looked oh-so-cold. "I didn't tell Steffie. I didn't want to frighten her."

Sam frowned. "Your truck was locked." He made it a statement since he remembered seeing her disarm the lock.

She nodded. "I didn't set the alarm only because I didn't see any need to. When I arrived home, I found it on the seat." When she picked up her cup, her hands trembled so violently she tightened her hold. The cup rattled against her teeth as she drank. "Who could hate me this much?" she whispered, once she'd set the cup back down.

Sam sighed. "I wish I knew."

Something about his tone caught her attention.

"But you have an idea why, don't you?" she said sharply. She leaned forward and grasped his arm that had been resting on the tabletop. *"Don't you?"*

The tension in the room was thick enough to qualify as a fog. Keely's face was so taut, she resembled a marble statue. Her gaze didn't leave his face as she seemed to search for the answer there.

Now, more than ever, Sam wished he'd had a decent night's sleep, so his brain wouldn't feel so fuzzy that it seemed as if he had to scramble for an answer that *would* satisfy her. As it was, he had a hunch the only answer that would satisfy her would be the truth. He leaned back in his chair and combed his fingers through his hair.

"Yes."

Keely straightened up. "Tell me."

He knew he couldn't lie to her. Lies would only put off the inevitable.

"I think someone has a major grudge against you, but I have no idea who." That was true. He didn't know who.

But he was going to check on old Willis and see if he was still in prison or if he was out. Sam would prefer the old man was dead.

Keely stood up and walked over to the coffeemaker. She refilled her cup and carried the pot over to the table, refilling Sam's cup also.

"A grudge? Against me? I haven't lived here long enough to make any enemies! Why would someone hate me so much?" she wondered, after she'd sat back down.

He didn't dare tell her. He had no idea what it would do to her, to discover something she'd locked away in the back of her mind for so many years.

"There could be any number of reasons," he said evasively, hating himself for putting her off with a cop's stock answer. "What I can do is look into this. Talk to people. See if anyone saw someone lurking by your truck last night. This kind of sloppy printing makes it difficult to recognize a person's handwriting. It doesn't look familiar to me." He flicked the edge of the paper with his fingertip.

Keely's fury seemed to leave her body at the same time as her bones did. She collapsed back in her chair. She placed her hands together, the fingertips touching in steeple fashion, and rested them against her lips.

"Does it have something to do with my parents?" she asked in a soft voice.

Sam squeezed his eyes shut, more because he couldn't bear to see the pain in her face than because weariness was still riding over him in waves.

"I will see what I can find out," he said finally.

That was when Keely had a good look at him and realized he wasn't wearing anything more than a pair of white briefs. His chest had the breadth of a mature man, a faint sprinkling of gray among the darker brown hair dusting the tanned skin. A round puckered scar marred one shoulder and several white lines scored his skin just under his armpit and across one nipple. Her mouth grew very dry. That was when she realized that they were alone in the house. She should know. Lisa had stopped by and picked up Steffie, so they could attend a baseball game at the park. It was so quiet in the room the wall clock ticking was the only sound.

How foolish could she have been? As it was, she'd paced her room most of the night as the words from the note echoed in her head. She lost count of the number of times she'd stood at the window looking out. She wondered if the person who wrote it was out there watching her, knowing the note had upset her. The moment Steffie left the house, Keely had grabbed her keys and run into the garage. A stop at the sheriff's station alerted her that Sam was at home, so she sped out here. She just hadn't expected to find him looking sleepy and tousled. And incredibly sexy.

She wasn't sure whether to feel embarrassed or aroused.

If she was smart, she'd make as graceful, and swift, an exit as possible.

"Did I come at a bad time?"

Sam's shoulders shook with laughter. "Nice time to ask that." He sipped his coffee.

She fidgeted in her seat. "It might have something to do with it being eleven o'clock in the morning and I obviously got you out of bed," she said nervously. She wanted to look anywhere but his chest, but her eyes refused to leave such a lovely view.

"I guess this is when I should apologize for intruding so abruptly," she said with hesitation hitching her voice. She thought about standing up, but she wasn't sure her legs would support her.

Sam shrugged. While his near naked form bothered her it didn't bother him. "No problem. I was called out last night because of a fight at the tavern. Only got back to bed about an hour ago.''

Which meant his sheets were rumpled on his bed. She quickly shifted her errant thoughts back to the subject at hand.

''It's just that note had me so upset that I couldn't even think straight.'' She didn't think she was babbling. Oh, God, she hoped she wasn't babbling.

Sam shook his head. ''I'm hungry. You up to eating something?'' He stood up and headed for the refrigerator.

Keely could only see a very firm male butt encased in white cotton. Her mouth was watering but not for eggs and bacon.

''I really should go.'' Did her voice honestly sound that faint?

''Don't worry. I haven't burned anything in a few weeks.'' He pulled out a carton of eggs and a package of bacon.

Keely jumped to her feet and walked over to him. ''Tell you what. I'll do the cooking while you shower.'' She nudged him to one side with her hip.

Sam grinned as if he guessed her suggestion was more for him to dress than to shower.

''Yes ma'am.'' He sketched a salute and ambled out of the room.

It took all of Keely's willpower but she didn't watch him leave the kitchen. She figured she'd already seen enough and what she saw was definitely all man.

She would have tried to be a little fancy and whip up an omelette but it didn't take long for her to realize scrambled eggs would be all she could handle.

By the time Sam returned with damp hair and cheeks freshly shaved, she had eggs and bacon ready and bread in the toaster. She nodded for him to sit while she set the filled plate in front of him.

"I couldn't find any juice," she told him.

He grimaced. "Lisa probably finished the last of it this morning. She's supposed to leave a note when she does, but she never remembers." He dug hungrily into his food.

"Do you get called out in the middle of the night often?" she asked, reclaiming her chair. She rested her chin on her palm as she waited for his answer.

"Not too often." He slathered raspberry jam on his toast. "But I was on call last night. As soon as I felt Lisa was old enough to be left alone at night, I put myself on the call board for nights. I never believed in having my men do anything I wouldn't do. When I got down there Fergus was on a roll and not about to be hauled in for the usual drunk and disorderly charge."

"Fergus?" she repeated.

He nodded. "Fergus is a retired logger and he looks like a Sherman tank. He can break a man's jaw by barely tapping it and he's broken more than his share of other mens' bones. Essentially he's harmless, but about once a month he remembers Gina, who left him fifteen years ago, and he drowns his sorrows in a few beers too many. He'll start a fight and we get called in. Right now, he's sleeping it off in a cell and once he wakes up, we'll let him out and he'll go down to the tavern and pay damages."

"That's it? No fine? No jail time?" Keely asked

Sam shook his head. "No, not as long as he pays for damages. That's the difference in a small town. We juggle the law a little more out here and take things into account that wouldn't be considered in the city."

She shook her head in wonderment. "I like that idea."

"So do I."

Keely sipped her coffee as Sam finished his meal.

"That was great," he told her as he pushed his plate to one side and reached for his coffee cup.

She shrugged. "No problem. Steffie's into cereal bars right now, so breakfast isn't hot food as much anymore."

"And around here cereal bars and cereal period are a fact of life if we want breakfast." He grinned.

Keely stood up. "And now I am leaving. I left the puppy in the laundry room because there wasn't much there he could destroy."

"How's he doing?"

"He cried all night. Steffie finally took him to bed with her and he stopped crying. I'm sure that dog will be spoiled before the week is over." She pulled her keys out of her jeans front pocket.

"Leave the letter with me," he advised, also getting to his feet. He followed her to the door. He kept his voice matter-of-fact, but there was no way he could completely hide his concern for her.

Keely was in the process of pulling the door open when Sam grasped her arm and turned her to face him. His mouth brushed across hers in the lightest of kisses but was felt strongly by both.

"I will ask around and see what I can find out."

For a moment, her gaze was shadowed with uncertainty. There was no denying she wanted to learn the truth. But at what price and to whom?

Chapter 11

*The little girl was so afraid she didn't dare cry. If she
cried, the bad man would hear her and know she was out
of bed and saw everything. He would hurt her next. Why
did he hurt her mommy and daddy?*

Keely was jerked awake as the fear flooded her veins.
She should have known better than to curl up with a book
when she felt so tired. She hadn't anticipated falling asleep
and worse, she hadn't anticipated the dream haunting her
during the daytime.

She rubbed her face with her hands to dislodge any lingering sleep. She jumped when something cold and wet
nudged her bare leg. Then laughed when she realized it
was the puppy.

"Poor guy, did I scare you?" she crooned, picking him
up and setting him on her lap.

She sat there for the longest time, holding the puppy as
if he could keep away the demon that stole in and so violently invaded her dreams.

The longer she sat there, the angrier she became.

"Enough," she stated, jumping to her feet and picking up her phone. She quickly punched out a number. "It's Keely," she said before Sam could get out a hello. "If you're going to question people living on that street, I'm going with you."

"Civilians do not accompany peace officers when they're on an investigation."

She blithely ignored his clipped tone. "I'm part of that investigation and I might pick up on something you won't."

"Keely, I am trained for this kind of work and you're not," he reminded her.

"And I'm a woman who still might pick up on something you don't," she argued. "Men don't have that famous intuition we women do."

His sigh was audible over the phone. "Keely, this isn't a good idea."

"When are you going?"

"I mean it."

"I'll go by myself." She turned away from the large picture window as if by doing that she could hide from anyone who might be lurking out there. She sternly resisted closing the drapes.

"If you think that threat will work, it won't." Her silence sent her reply loud and clear. He swore fluently. "All right, you can go only because if I don't let you, you'll do this on your own. But I want you to remain in the background and not open your mouth."

"I'll be good, Sam," she promised.

"You damn well better be or we'll both be sorry. Be down to the station at ten in the morning," he ordered.

She glanced at the clock. "Why can't we go this afternoon?"

"Because, Mrs. Harper, the person we need to see is

out of town today,'' he stated in slow, sure tones. ''I'm going to make some notes so we ask all the right questions tomorrow. Now, is there anything else.''

Keely opened her mouth, ready to tell him about her dreams. She felt the need to share them with someone and she felt if anyone would understand and assure her she wasn't going crazy, he would.

''Keely?'' His voice sharpened.

''No, nothing else,'' she said softly. ''I'll be there at ten. Thank you.'' She hung up, but her fingers rested across the back of the receiver, slowly sliding across the plastic as she stepped back.

She turned away just in time to catch an anxious-looking puppy hopping around on his oversize paws.

''Oh, no, big guy. Outside with you!'' For now her attention was diverted from darker thoughts.

''Let's go play miniature golf,'' Steffie suggested after they'd finished dinner. Without prompting she had picked up the dishes, rinsed them off and loaded them in the dishwasher.

''Where did all this energy of yours come from?'' Keely asked. The nap she'd taken earlier had only left her feeling more tired rather than refreshed. By the time Steffie came home, Keely had applied enough makeup so she didn't look as drawn as she felt.

Steffie shrugged. ''They have an awesome course and it would be fun.''

Keely noticed that Steffie even remembered to put powdered soap in the dispenser. If she didn't feel so worn-out she would be suspicious of her daughter's unusually helpful behavior.

''Could we put it off until tomorrow night?''

Steffie shook her head. ''Oh, come on, it will do you good to get out.'' She sat down on the floor and pulled the puppy into her lap. She giggled as he eagerly licked her face.

"I don't think we should leave him alone for the evening," Keely said.

"A couple hours wouldn't hurt, would it?" she asked. "Just one of those mother-daughter things."

Keely did find the idea appealing. "All right," she conceded. "Take the puppy outside for a while and make sure he does everything he should while I freshen up."

"I wish you could go with us, baby." Steffie held the puppy up and nuzzled his face. "But I don't think they'll let you in, so let's go outside so you can do all those gross things a puppy should do outside." She jumped up and went out, still holding the puppy in her arms.

Keely went into her bedroom long enough to apply blusher and lipstick and spritz on cologne. She tucked a few stray tendrils back into her ponytail and stared into the mirror.

She wasn't sure what she thought she'd see, but she knew what she did see. A thirty-five-year-old woman who had survived a bad marriage and gone on to make a new life for herself and her child.

For a brief second she imagined the reflection in the glass wavered until a little girl's face looked back at her.

Keely leapt back. She knew it was her imagination, but the image was just a little too startling since she knew the little girl's face she thought she saw was her own.

The miniature golf course was busy that evening but not so busy that too many people had to wait to play. While Keely paid and retrieved clubs, balls and scorecards, Steffie fidgeted and looked around.

"There are days when you're worse than a five-year-old," Keely said, handing her a club and ball. "Do you want to go first?"

"Sure." Steffie still glanced around.

"Then go," she suggested in a level voice.

Steffie grinned sheepishly and set her ball down. Within seconds, the bright blue ball was rolling down toward the hole and rolling right past it.

"Concentrate on the ball and not who's here and you'll do better," Keely advised, setting her green ball down next. "If I find out we're here because you're hoping to run into a boy, I will let you clean the bathrooms for the next month."

"So far I haven't seen any boys I'd want to run after," she said with a sniff.

"We'll see."

"Hey, Steffie!"

Keely's head snapped up the same time as Steffie's. Mother looked at daughter with that expression that told her the jig was up. Father and daughter walked up with daughter having the same look of surprise on her face and father having the same expression mother wore. Sam cocked an eyebrow at Keely.

"Fancy meeting you here," he drawled.

"Yes, amazing, isn't it?" she returned. "Did Lisa happen to have the same uncontrollable urge to play golf as Steffie did?"

"She suddenly decided she couldn't manage to spend the evening at home with her old man," he replied dryly.

Both girls sported smiles of innocence as they gazed up at their parents.

"Funny we all showed up here, isn't it?" Steffie chirped. "Why don't Lisa and I play ahead of you two? You adults would probably have more fun playing each other than with us anyway."

"Oh, but Steffie, I thought it was a mother-daughter thing," Keely said pleasantly with just a hint of hurt in her tone.

Steffie wiggled under her mother's gaze. "I'm thinking of you, Mother."

"Of course you are, dear."

"Go," Sam said, letting the two of them off the hook. "While you two play, I'll buy Keely a cup of coffee." He moved over to stand next to Keely and rested his hand against the small of her back.

He barely got the words out and the girls were moving on to the second hole.

"We were set up," Keely said, watching the two girls with their heads together.

"I know."

She looked up, curious to see his reaction and was surprised to see him grinning.

"Come on, Mrs. Harper." He steered her in the other direction. "You can tell me about some of those uncontrollable urges of yours."

The moment they stepped into the snack bar, they were both aware they were under scrutiny of the other patrons. Most just nodded while a few tried to make conversation. Sam, politely but firmly, cut it short and headed for the end booth.

"Small towns love to have something to talk about," he said. "Coffee all right with you?"

Bemused, she could only nod.

Keely watched Sam stand at the counter and give their order. He was dressed casually in jeans and an oatmeal-colored T-shirt, but all she could think about was seeing him sleepy-eyed and wearing nothing but a pair of white cotton briefs. She quickly looked away as if her thoughts could be heard by everyone else there. When he returned with the coffee, she managed a smile and a murmured thank-you.

"So," he said, taking the seat across from her, "do you

want to tell me what got you going that you had to call me this afternoon and demand to play junior sheriff?''

She wished she used cream or sugar in her coffee so she would have something to do to put off answering his question.

''How long has the golf course been here?'' she asked brightly, as if he hadn't already asked her a question.

''Two years. What upset you enough you felt you had to call me?'' His eyes bored into hers. ''Did you get another note? A phone call?'' Something about her posture must have alerted her he was on the right track.

Keely looked furtively around the brightly lit snack bar with its vivid orange plastic tables and blue molded plastic booths. The chattering was noisy and enthusiastic. Not exactly the right place to talk about nightmares even if she didn't have to worry about anyone overhearing her.

''It's the idea that someone would plant such a hateful note in my truck,'' she said in a low voice. ''I've thought so much about it that I feel very strongly that I need to search out the truth myself.''

He stared at her for several moments. She forced herself not to fidget under his gaze. She sensed he didn't believe her and she was preparing herself to spout more lies when he slowly nodded.

''That's understandable as long as you realize that you might not like the answers you get,'' he told her.

''Well, well, look who's here.''

Keely silently cursed before she mustered up a smile and lifted her head.

''Hello, John.''

While the pharmacist was smiling, his eyes appeared ice-cold as he looked down at them.

''Playing some miniature golf?'' he asked pleasantly.

''Just waiting for the kids to finish,'' Sam replied. ''The last thing they wanted was the old folks horning in, so we agreed to wait for them here. I guess they're afraid we'll ruin any chance they have of attracting admirers out there. Admirers for their golf skills, of course.''

John just kept smiling. ''Yes, of course.'' He glanced again at Keely. ''I'm glad to see you're doing so well, Keely.''

''Thank you.''

''Yes, those kind of accidents can be pretty nasty.'' He lightly tapped the top of the table with his fingertips as if to punctate his words, then he moved on.

''Is it my imagination or did the temperature just drop a good fifty degrees?'' Keely murmured.

''A rejected suitor, perhaps?'' he quipped.

''He's a nice man, but...'' She shook her head.

''But what?'' Sam leaned forward.

''I don't know.'' Her brow furrowed in thought as she tried to put her feelings into words, but it wasn't proving easy. ''There's just something about him that bothers me and I can't figure out why.''

''I wouldn't worry,'' he soothed.

''True, why should I when there's so much else going on in my life?'' She picked up her coffee and sipped the hot brew. ''But I don't like hurting anyone's feelings.''

''Considering the number of widows in the area who have their eye on John, you don't have to think he'll be pining away for your company. I can think of four offhand who wouldn't mind getting their manicured little claws into him.''

Keely shook her head in wonderment. ''I swear this town is better than a soap opera.''

Lines crinkled around his eyes as he grinned at her. ''Honey, soap operas are based on this town. You're just the new face for this season. Don't worry unless someone talks about comas.''

"Sheriff, are you telling me you watch soap operas?" she teased.

"Our dispatcher does. She has a small TV in the back room where she takes her lunch break and catches up on her favorite show. No one is allowed to disturb her during that hour if they want to live. We tease her a lot about it, but we find ourselves wandering through there to see what's going on." He looked a little sheepish about his confession. "Steve, one of my deputies, was pretty upset when Lorraine discovered that Carlos was only seeing her because he was secretly in love with her twin sister, Lorna."

Keely rolled her eyes. "Wrong!" she sang out. "Carlos is actually Lorraine's illegitimate child from her college days, but he's been cautious about telling her the truth."

Sam's face broke into a slow grin. "Well, damn. You watch 'Fall River Nights,' too."

She nodded. "Thanks to the magic of VCRs, I haven't missed an episode since the first day. Steffie went to school with Veronica Blake's daughter." She named the star of the show.

Sam let out a low whistle. "Your kid ran with fancy company."

"Along with the son of a computer company CEO, the daughter of an international banker, a son and daughter of a retired diplomat and the daughter of a Secret Service agent," she told him. "Ironically, they were all perfectly normal kids without a shred of egotism. They used to spend a lot of time at our house emptying the kitchen cabinets of food, splashing water out of the pool and playing the stereo full blast."

"I'm surprised she doesn't feel as if she's come down in the world," Sam said.

"Steffie's never been class-conscious. I've always been

proud of her ability to look within a person instead of considering what they have materially."

"Thing is, she and Lisa act as if they were twins separated at birth."

Keely nodded. "They do tend to think alike." She looked out over the course and could see the two girls giggling as Steffie attempted to hit her ball into a dragon's open mouth. When her ball finally rolled through, red and orange lights lit up and a roar sounded from the dragon. The girls jumped up and slapped a high five.

"Which may not make it safe for us." Sam glanced around. Luckily, no one was in their area, but he still lowered his voice. "How do you feel about that?"

She didn't turn away or act coy because that wasn't her style. Keely had always prided herself on her directness with others. She wasn't about to change her ways now. She looked at him straight on, unblinking, no delicate flush of the cheeks.

"When I moved up here, I was still smarting over a nasty divorce and had no plans to become involved with anyone," she said quietly. If she hadn't been watching him so intently she wouldn't have noticed the faint flicker of light in his eyes die. "But then, I hadn't planned on meeting you, either." The light just as quickly reappeared. She smiled. "Besides, it already seems we have a seal of approval from our children."

He grinned back. "But do we want them to know about this too quickly?"

She gave him a mock frown. "Of course not! Their puberty is making us crazy. The least we can do is make them a little crazy as they try to figure out what's going on."

He lifted his coffee cup in a silent toast. "I'm always for that."

Keely lifted her cup and tapped his with it. "I still want

to take things slow," she warned him. "I don't believe in taking chances."

"Does that mean I can't ask you about those uncontrollable urges you happened to mention earlier?" he whispered.

Now she did blush. "I think that's a subject better left for another time."

"Too bad. I was interested in hearing your ideas on the subject."

"Finish your coffee, Sheriff. We have two girls to chaperon." She smiled.

"Just remember they won't always be with us."

Keely knew that. In fact, she was beginning to look forward to a time the girls weren't around.

Sam didn't believe in watching the clock. He always felt it didn't accomplish anything. And it hadn't. Not until he knew Keely Harper was showing up that morning at ten to accompany him. He had a hunch she was the prompt type and her appearing before Fredda's desk at ten sharp told him he was right. She stood out there looking lovely in a navy-and-cream plaid skirt that brushed against her calves and a dark indigo denim shirt with the tails tied just above her waist. She had piled her hair on top of her head in a careless twist. His fingers itched to release the pins holding her hair in order to watch it tumble down around the silver earrings that dangled by the side of her neck. He regretted he was on duty.

"Mrs. Harper." He greeted her with a pleasant smile that showed nothing more than an official meeting one of the people he protects.

"Sheriff." She inclined her head in his direction. "You said to be here at ten."

"That I did. I'll be with you in just a moment." He returned to his office to get his hat and immediately wished he'd been faster as Fredda crowded in and closed the door behind her.

"And you claim there's nothing going on?" she scoffed. "When are you going to learn to tell me the truth?"

"There is nothing going on, Fredda," he informed her, as he snagged his hat off the coatrack. "I'm merely helping Mrs. Harper with a problem."

She narrowed her eyes with a suspicious glare Sam always hated seeing. The woman was just too damn smart for her own good!

"No woman in here on official business wears the perfume she's wearing," she argued.

Sam ducked his head to whisper in her ear, "I promise to be careful and keep my handcuffs out of her reach."

She frowned and swatted at him. "Maybe you'd be better off giving her the handcuffs and seeing what she'll do with them."

Sam was chuckling as he walked out of his office. A chuckle that almost dried up when he saw Keely standing near Fredda's desk. He gestured for him to precede her and they exited the front door under the curious gaze of two deputies and Fredda.

"Perhaps my coming in wasn't such a good idea," Keely commented as Sam led her over to his truck emblazoned with the sheriff's seal. "I seemed to give your staff a bit of excitement in there."

"It's not often we get lovely ladies visit us," he told her.

Within minutes, they were driving away, and Sam realized Fredda as right. Keely's perfume was most definitely something to remember. He felt as if the fragrance were already permeating the air and would never dissipate.

"We'll visit Nan Cooper first," Sam said. "You were parked in front of her house and I know for a fact she hasn't attended the picnic for the last fifteen years."

"Is she an invalid?"

"No, just someone who had a fight with Wendy O'Connell, who's in charge of the craft booths and declared she wouldn't step foot on the park grounds if Wendy was there." Sam turned right at the stop sign and cruised. He occasionally raised a hand in an answering wave when someone shouted his name, and he was amused by the curious looks his passenger received. "But that doesn't mean she misses anything else that goes on outside her living room window. That means you will remain in the background and not say a word."

She arched an eyebrow. "So, I'm to act the part of the good little woman and stay out of the way?" she cooed.

He knew he was treading on dangerous ground. "That's right."

"We'll see."

Sam would have dearly loved to argue with that comment, but they had already arrived at Nan's house. He parked in front and walked around the truck to help Keely out. When she stepped down, he noticed her toes were painted the same coral as her lips. The woman definitely had the gift to send his senses reeling.

He kept a respectable distance as they walked up the concrete pathway edged with a brick border and colorful flowers. Window boxes lined both front windows with even more color.

"Her garden is her pride and joy," he explained as he advanced the three steps leading to the front porch and rapped his knuckles against the screen door. "Miz Nan," he called out. "It's Sheriff Barkley."

"Heaven's sake, Samuel." A tiny voice was heard just before an even tinier figure appeared at the door. "What brings you out here?"

Silver hair was braided into a coronet on top of her head and her blue-flowered housedress looked as if a wrinkle wouldn't dare mar the fabric. Faded blue eyes viewed Keely from behind a pair of spectacles.

He instantly took off his hat and held it between his hands. "We were hoping we could ask you a few questions."

"No use in you two standing out there when you can come in," she told them, although it had the sound of an imperial command. "Have a seat. Would you care for some iced tea?"

"That would be very nice, Miz Nan," he replied.

She frowned at him. "Why haven't you introduced me to the young lady, Samuel? You were taught better manners than that."

Keely hid her smile at Sam's chagrined look.

"Miz Nan, this is Keely Harper. She moved to Echo Ridge a few months ago," he explained. "Keely, Miz Nan Cooper is one of our leading residents. She taught school for more than forty years and was our principal during her last ten years with the school district."

"Would have been longer if that blasted school board hadn't stepped in and said I was too old," she huffed. "I always knew Darren would be a pain once he got on the school board, and I was right." She turned to Keely. "The boy was nothing but trouble in school. He would have flunked English if his father hadn't done most of his homework. You were Charles and Alice Davis's daughter, weren't you?" She nodded decisively. "Yes, I can see the resemblance to Alice and Evelyn."

Keely perked up. "You knew my parents?"

"Of course, I did, dear. I taught both of them, although your father was a much better student than your mother. She tended to daydream too much." She glanced at Sam and smiled as if receiving a silent message from him. "Now, you two have a seat while I get our tea." She bustled out of the room, leaving behind the old-fashioned scent of lavender.

Keely looked around at the highly polished but shabby furniture brightened by intricately tatted lace doilies. Crystal bowls filled with fragrant potpourri were scattered on various small tables. A wall covered with photographs captured her interest and she wandered over there to study them. They turned out to be group class photographs with the year and class grade neatly printed underneath. She did a quick mental calculation in her head and finally located the appropriate photo. She traced her forefinger across the rows of smiling children until she discovered the one she was looking for. She suddenly giggled.

"No offense, but you were a very homely kid," she blurted out, pointing to one of the photos.

"Samuel was a late bloomer, but a sweet boy from the first day I knew him," Miz Nan explained as she stepped into the room carrying a silver tray. Sam quickly rose to his feet and took it from her. She sat on the couch and picked up the crystal pitcher, pouring golden tea into three ice-filled glasses. A plate covered with cookies was also set out along with three coasters. She beamed at Sam. "And he turned into a very nice-looking man and has a heart of gold."

Sam shifted uncomfortably in his chair and looked as if he wanted to be anywhere but there.

"We're hoping you can help us with a problem, Miz Nan," he said, accepting the glass she handed him.

"What kind of student was Sam?" Keely asked at the same time.

"A very good one, attentive, finished his assignments," the older woman said. "But once he started noticing girls—" she shook her head in exasperation "—he turned into a regular dreamer. After more than a few afternoons in detention, he soon came up to mark."

Keely walked over to take the chair next to Sam. "What was his best subject?" She picked up her glass and drank the contents.

"We're here to get some answers," he growled in an undertone.

Keely smiled at him and patted his arm as if he was ten years old. "It's always best to start out with a pleasant conversation," she explained.

"Samuel always had excellent communications skills," Miz Nan replied. "That's what makes him such a good lawman. He knows enough to listen when it's applicable."

Sam sighed and sat through ten more minutes of Miz Nan reminiscing about his much younger self. Now he really wished he hadn't brought Keely along. She was sitting there looking so damn beautiful and sincerely enjoying herself. He wasn't sure whether to wring her neck for prompting Miz Nan's stories or kiss her senseless for being so kind to a lady he'd admired ever since he could remember.

"Miz Nan, I'm sorry," he interrupted without an apology in his heart, "but we actually came here to see if you might be able to help us. Mrs. Harper parked in front of your house the day of the Pioneer Days Picnic. It seems someone broke into her truck."

"Oh, my dear!" Miz Nan covered Keely's hand with her own tiny one. "I sorely miss the days when the worst crime we had was boys stealing fruit off trees. I do hope nothing important was taken."

"No, she was lucky." Sam spoke before Keely could. "Maybe someone came by before they could steal anything. But we were wondering if you happened to see anything that night. Anyone lurking around the truck. Anything suspicious going on."

The older woman tapped her forefinger against her chin as she looked thoughtfully into space.

"I do remember seeing a truck parked in front and people stopping by it, either to talk to someone or by themselves. Of course, if they looked as if they were going to try some mischief I would have called your office immediately," she assured him.

"Do you happen to remember who you saw out there?" he pressed.

She looked down her nose with the stern expression he uncomfortably remembered from school. Only Miz Nan could take him back to feeling like a ten-year-old again.

"Young man, my memory has not failed me yet." Her lips pursed together. "I recall John by the truck for several moments. He appeared to be lighting a cigarette. Also the doctor. She also stood there for some time." She thought for a moment. "And there was that rude Mr. Rainey standing around. Let me see. Your deputy. The young one who acts like a cock of the walk."

"Rick," Sam interjected.

She nodded. "I also recall that lovely Chloe who owns the bookstore standing there for some time. I thought she was waiting for someone, but no one else approached her." She shook her head. "I do believe they were the only ones who stood there for more than a moment."

Sam silently cursed. He received a list he didn't expect. He shared a glance with Keely and guessed by the expression on her face she hadn't expected this, either.

Chapter 12

"At the rate she was going, I thought she was going to name half the townspeople by the time she finished," Keely said with a dejected sigh when they left the house a half hour later. Miz Nan wasn't about to allow them to leave too soon and she even extracted a promise from Keely to bring Steffie by for a visit.

"If she'd seen them there she would have named them," he said, climbing into the truck. "Miz Nan might be ninety-three, but she has a mind sharp as a tack." He chuckled. "When she was my teacher, I thought she was older than dirt, but none of us boys ever got anything past her."

"I liked her." She cast him a sideways glance. "I just bet she has some interesting stories about her teaching days."

"I wouldn't suggest you ask her about those days," he warned.

She leaned back and smiled. "Then I'll just let her talk."

Sam put the truck in gear. "I'm sorry she couldn't help you more."

"She gave you something to work with, didn't she?" she asked hopefully.

"I have a place to start," he replied.

Keely slumped down in her seat. "I just wish I knew who would leave such a horrible note." As she said the words, her mind suddenly backtracked to the note she'd received when she first moved here.

"Sam," she said hesitantly. "Not long after we moved up here, I received another note like that one."

His head whipped around then he quickly turned back to watch the road. "And you didn't remember until now? Why didn't you tell me about it when you first got it?"

"I told you. It happened when we first moved here and I just thought it was someone playing a nasty trick on me," she explained.

He let out a heavy sigh. "Okay, that's it." He jerked the wheel and made a hard right turn.

"What are you doing?" Keely asked, holding on to the door handle to keep her balance in the seat.

"We're going somewhere for a talk where there are no ears," he said grimly, making several more turns until they were headed out of town.

Keely felt uncomfortable at the idea of Sam's idea of a talk. She didn't need to be psychic to figure out he was going to demand answers to questions she wasn't going to like to hear and others she might not even know the answers to.

Sam drove several miles out of town then turned onto a dirt road. By the time he stopped his vehicle, they were parked alongside a lake.

"A popular fishing spot come next month," he explained, climbing out.

She didn't wait for him to come around to her side. She

got out on her own and followed him toward a splintery-looking picnic table. She wrinkled her nose in distaste at the idea of sitting down on it. Splinters in her behind weren't her idea of fun. She opted for standing.

Sam walked down to the water's edge and looked out. One hand was wrapped around the back of his neck, massaging the area. He spun around.

"Just how bad was your divorce?" he asked in clipped tones.

She was surprised by his question, although she told herself she shouldn't have been.

"It was nasty. I want to think he wouldn't send me threatening letters and drive all the way up here to leave a note inside my truck, but it's not easy. But as it happened more, I decided he wouldn't go to all this bother."

"Why did you divorce him?"

Keely took a deep breath. She knew if she was to get involved with Sam, the subject would come up, but it didn't make it any easier.

"He was unfaithful," she said quietly.

"Did you consider counseling?"

Her smile held no humor, only remembered pain. "Jay was unfaithful many times and when he finally got a case of the guilts he decided he wanted to shift the blame over to me," she said, clasping her hands tightly in front of her. "The best way to do that was to claim Steffie wasn't his."

Sam looked stunned by her reply. "So he accused you of having an affair."

Keely nodded. "I threw his affairs at him, he threw Steffie's parentage back at me. It didn't matter that she is his mirror image and that she looks just like his sister at that age. He decided she wasn't his and that was that. During the divorce proceedings, he declared he would not pay child support for a child that was not his. My attorney assured me a blood test would prove him wrong, but I told him I didn't care.''

Sam shook his head violently, unprepared to accept such a thing. ''My God, what kind of man had you married?''

''One who didn't grow up,'' she said bluntly. ''He hurt his only child in a way that will never go away. Steffie flat out told him as far as she was concerned, she preferred he wasn't her father because his genes were not something she'd care to share. After that, she never called him by anything but his first name. Daddy's little girl grew up very quickly as she realized just how human he was,'' she said softly. Her eyes were shadowed with the pain from those days. She mustered up a smile. ''But she's come a long way since then and I'm proud of her.''

''And what about you?'' he asked.

She lifted her head, hearing the challenge in his question. ''Jay lost my love and my respect when I learned he was unfaithful,'' she said candidly. ''If he couldn't keep his pants zipped when he was around other women, I knew I didn't want him around me. He fought back with the accusations I'd had affairs also and that Steffie wasn't his. I told him what a fool he was and that I only hoped he could live with his lies. But he'd rather convince himself how much of a fool I was for moving up here than try to frighten me. Believe me, he wouldn't consider that kind of harassment.'' She sank down onto the bench with her hands clasped in front of her. She lifted her head. Her lips trembled as the enormity of what was going on finally hit her full force. ''Why is someone doing this to me?''

Sam had a vague idea why it was happening, but he didn't dare say it aloud. Not just yet. He'd have to have a talk with Melanie. See if she had any answers for him.

''Has there been anything else?'' He had to remind himself he was a cop first. He couldn't help her unless he kept his mind on his work.

Keely hesitated. "Feelings," she said reluctantly. "Just a sense of someone outside late at night watching the house. Some nights I think I smell cigar smoke and I feel as if someone's at the edge of the woods watching the house. I get up in the middle of the night and look out my window and imagine I can see a shadow among the trees beyond the house. And I've gotten phone calls."

"Why didn't you call the station? Have it checked out?" he demanded.

Her lips twitched in a wry smile. "Because I was afraid it was nothing and I'd be branded a hysterical female."

"Next time you feel someone's out there you don't hesitate in calling me," Sam ordered. "I don't care what time it is."

Keely shook her head as if the action would banish it all. "I also have these horrible dreams about a child who is so afraid," she murmured. "Sam, I'm so terrified that I'm that child."

He looked at her downcast head wishing he could offer more than words. In the end, he walked over to her and lightly placed his hand on her hair. She looked up, then stood, moving so close to him he could feel the rise and fall of her breasts brushing against his chest. He put his arms around her at the same time her arms circled his waist. Sam wasn't content with that. He rested his head against her head as her cheek lingered against his shirt-front.

"I'm not a coward, Sam," Keely whispered. "I don't believe in the bogeyman and I don't look under my bed at night because I think someone might be hiding there. I came up here because I wanted peace."

"You'll have that peace, Keely. I promise," he said in a low voice.

Except they both sensed that peace just might come at a high price.

* * *

Sam watched Keely drive away from the station parking lot. So many questions filled his mind and he wasn't sure where to begin.

"You wanted to see me?" Rick appeared at his side.

Sam nodded. "I want you to schedule drive-bys several times a night for the Harper house," he ordered. "Mrs. Harper feels kids have been hanging out around there. Let's deter anyone from making mischief."

The deputy looked as if he had questions, but the implacable expression on his boss's face suggested they wouldn't be welcomed right now. He settled for a nod.

"Will do." He looked off. "You know, it might be someone older than kids."

Sam whipped around. "Why would you say that?"

He shrugged. "She's a good-looking woman. Some of the men around here might be hanging around hoping they can get lucky."

"What exactly do you mean by that?" he asked in a tight voice, not wanting to have it spelled out but needing to hear it.

Rick was surprised by the darkening of Sam's features. The anger in them. "What I mean is, anything can happen. There hasn't been a rape in this area for almost three years. But we've had some new people move in, some so-called hermits high up in the woods who might have decided they're in need of feminine company."

Sam felt the chill run through him at Rick's words. Only because they could be true. So far, things had been kept quiet in town. The hermits were survivors of wars who returned only to discover they couldn't live in a civilized world again. They refused to live in civilization and came into a town only a few times a year for staples. They were usually quiet, wary of any human, and didn't appear to relax until they were on their way out of town.

"I just want the drive-bys," he said quietly. "And if anyone sees anything suspicious, I want it followed up on. Get me?"

"Loud and clear," Rick drawled sarcastically. "Wouldn't it be easier if you just screwed the lady and spent your nights in her bed?" He stepped back at the fury emanating from Sam's eyes. He held up his hands in mock surrender. "Hey, you can't kill me for making a suggestion that you've probably been thinking about for a while."

"Take a suggestion from me, Deputy," Sam said in a low voice that fairly throbbed with anger. "Don't make that suggestion again." As he walked away, Rick noticed his hands were clenched at his sides. The younger man knew he had come very close to being a victim of Sam's fist planted in his face.

"Hi, Allison, is Melanie busy?" Sam greeted the nurse as he stepped into the medical center.

"She's finishing up with her last patient before lunch," she replied. "Did you need to speak to her?"

"I'll even go one better and take the lady to lunch if she doesn't have prior plans."

"Well, I did expect Harrison Ford to drop by and whisk me off, but I guess I can settle for you," the doctor teased as she walked out of the examination room in time to hear Sam's offer.

"Good enough."

"So what's up? I thought you were making time with our newest resident," Melanie quipped as they made their way to the coffee shop.

"Everyone's a matchmaker," he grumbled good-naturedly as he walked alongside her.

"It's natural when you haven't shown much interest in anyone since you moved back here." She waited as he pushed open the door and preceded him inside.

Sam chose his regular booth in the back and waited until Melanie was seated. He suffered curious glances from all around and quickly ordered. Throughout the meal, they made light conversation. Since they had dated a few times, they were familiar with each other's likes and dislikes. It hadn't taken long to realize they were better off as friends rather than lovers.

"All right, you've lulled my senses with a fine meal," she said wryly. She clasped her hands and placed them on the table. "So, why don't you tell me why you really wanted to have lunch."

Sam grimaced. "No secrets, huh?"

Melanie smiled and nodded.

He took a deep breath. "All right, what can you tell me about blocked memories?"

"Blocked memories?" she repeated. "Such as?"

"Such as a kid who suffered through a horrible trauma and blocked that trauma from her mind."

"Amnesia then," she clarified.

Sam shook his head. "Whatever. Trauma from severe illness."

Melanie picked up her glass and sipped her soda. She rolled the carbonated beverage around in her mouth as she ruminated.

"Illness can affect the memory," she replied. "Especially if there are memories that one wants to forget. What else can you tell me?"

He hesitated. "A small child suffers through a personal horror that destroys the life she had once known. Manages to keep it in perspective for a certain length of time then falls very ill. During the recovery period, it's discovered the child doesn't remember anything of that horror."

Melanie stared at him for several moments. "You're talking about Keely Harper, aren't you? I saw her medical records when we bought the practice," she explained at

Sam's look of surprise. "Her family doctor extensively charted her trauma, illness and loss of memory. Has she started to remember what happened to her parents? Is that why you're asking me about this?"

"She's just had dreams about a little girl," he said in a low voice. "But I don't know what to do. How to handle it if she starts asking questions about her parents. I've heard you can create emotional problems if you talk about something a person is not ready to remember yet."

"These are questions you should ask a psychiatrist, not me," she explained. "I can only tell you that if she isn't ready to confront those memories, she shouldn't be forced to. Coming back here might be releasing some of the memories she's buried and maybe it's time for them to surface. But they need to surface at her speed. No one else's."

Sam nodded. "She's scared, Mel. Really scared."

"Then be there for her when she needs you. For now, that's all you can do." She reached across the table and covered his hand with hers. "Now it's time for me to get back to the clinic."

"Thanks, friend."

Melanie smiled back. "At least the woman who caught you is someone who deserves you."

"Hey, I'm not caught yet," he protested.

Her expression said otherwise. "Trust me, Sam. You don't have eyes for anyone else but her. Talk about falling fast. I guess we all should have known you'd fall hard when the right one came along." She slid out of the booth and stood up. She leaned down to brush a kiss across his cheek and walked away.

Sam remained at the table for a few more moments as he thought over what Melanie said. From what Keely said, she was remembering what had happened thirty years ago. He wished he could put her out of her misery and tell her the truth. The trouble was, he had no idea what the truth would do to her.

Sam had to be watched. There was no reason for him and the witch to stop by the old lady's house. It was easy to figure out why they had. She had parked her truck in front of the old lady's house and they hoped she had seen something. No problem there. She wouldn't have seen anything that looked funny. Nothing out of the way. Just a bunch of the town's residents walking past. Some stopping to talk.

That was the best part. Knowing there was no worry about getting caught. Of being under suspicion.

Good thing he was so visible. He'd be easy to keep tabs on. As for the witch, it would be even easier since she had stopped at the hardware store today to pick up some supplies and mentioned she was going out to her family home to do some work there.

And while she was there, there was no reason why a little surprise couldn't be arranged for her at the other house.

Surprises were a speciality.

Chapter 13

Keely hadn't completely mastered her anxiety while spending time in her childhood home, but she forced herself to put her fears at bay while she finished cleaning the kitchen and then went on to scrub the downstairs bathroom. As she moved though the downstairs rooms she mentally placed her furniture in what she felt were the most advantageous spots.

She knew her furniture would fit in after the walls were painted and the floors sanded and varnished. The chimney would be cleaned and a fire burning merrily in the fireplace to warm the room. So why did she still feel it would be best to sell the house?

With bones aching and muscles crying for a hot bath, she packed up her cleaning supplies and headed out to her truck. She'd completely lost track of time and realized it was starting to grow dark. She had no idea she'd stayed there so late. Out of habit she glanced at her watch, wondering about Steffie, then laughed.

"That's right. Steffie's at a slumber party," she reminded herself out loud. "I'll have the house to myself. I can do whatever I want without my darling daughter asking why I can't act like an adult."

She sped home in anticipation of an evening to herself and relaxing with a good book and a glass of wine.

Keely parked in the garage and entered through the kitchen door. She flipped the light switch in the dim room then swore when nothing happened.

"Just what I need," she muttered, blindly seeking the drawer that held the flashlight. "Hopefully, it's a burned-out bulb and not a blown fuse. I'm coming, puppy," she called out when she heard the pup scratching at the laundry room door and crying piteously. She felt guilty that she hadn't thought of taking him with her while she cleaned. It would have been better than his being locked up in the laundry room with his toys and plenty of papers laid on the floor for accidents.

Keely barely had the correct drawer pulled open when soft strains of music drifted in from the family room. She was hearing music she knew she didn't own and she sensed it wasn't coming from the radio that might have been mistakenly left on.

She froze as the haunting lyrics about pills and a white rabbit invaded her brain with frightening images. A man and woman freeze-framed in her mind's eye. Mouths open as if they were screaming. The color red everywhere.

She forced herself to move. She scrambled for the drawer, but the flashlight eluded her frantic pawing though the contents. A sob broke from her lips when she finally realized the flashlight wasn't there.

"Does the music make you remember, Keely?" a whispery voice echoed throughout the house. "Does it frighten you?"

Her eyes darted everywhere, but with the room so dark

she couldn't see anything. Even though they were adjusting to the darkness, she could see little but outlines of furniture. She crept along the wall, her hands splayed out at her sides. *Where was the damn phone?* She suddenly couldn't remember.

"You made a lot of people suffer, Keely," the voice taunted. "Did you know that? Do you know what you did long ago? How many lives you ruined?"

She breathed shallowly through her mouth, so she couldn't be heard. She wanted to scream, to demand the music be turned off. The images that flashed inside her head were just as frightening as the dreams she'd had.

"Keely," the whispering voice sang out. "Do you want to play hide-and-seek? You hide and I'll find you."

All she could think of was she wanted Sam. He would protect her. He would keep her safe. Except for now, it was up to her. What did this person want from her? The question screamed inside her head, but her lips couldn't form the words. She found her way into the living room. No matter where her eyes darted, she couldn't see anyone in the corners or long shadows slicing across the large room. She focused on getting to the bedroom. There, she could lock her door and call Sam.

"Do you like the song, Keely?"

She jammed her hand in her mouth to keep from crying out. By now, she'd reached the hallway opening. All it would take was a run to the other end.

"Oh, Keely, pretty Keely."

Keely cried out when a hand touched her shoulder. She started to run, but the hand held on to her tightly. She sobbed, jerking around to strike out with her fists. She heard a soft grunt and a curse when she hit a soft area and the hold was loosened.

"*Witch!*" Cursing followed her flight.

She had just reached her bedroom doorway when her

feet seemed to fly out from under her. Keely fell hard on her front, momentarily knocking the wind out of her. She tried to scramble to her feet, but hands held tightly on to her ankles.

"You can't escape me, Keely. I watch you at night. But you knew that, didn't you?" the asexual voice whispered. "You knew I was out there watching you. You know everything, don't you?"

Keely tried to claw her attacker, but the figure evaded her attempts. At the same time, hands touched her here and there. She battled ineffectually as they teasingly patted her neck, stroked her breast, her upper thigh and along her waist. Sobbing louder, she tried to kick and bite, but she couldn't connect. She crab-walked backward in an attempt to get away but the taunting voice and hands merely followed her.

"Get away! *Get away!*" she screamed. "I don't know why you're doing this, but leave me alone!" She sobbed with frustration when her back hit the side of the bed and she found herself in the room's corner.

"I was tired of watching you from afar, Keely," the voice went on at the same time the touching continued. "I wanted you to know I'm here for you. I want you to remember."

Her head whipped back and forth. "I don't know what you're talking about!"

"You will, Keely. You will. You will know everything and you will suffer for what you did. You were a bad girl, Keely, and you need to be punished."

Keely was past hearing. She screamed and kept on screaming until her throat was raw. By now, she was huddled in a corner of the bedroom, her body curled up tight against the enemy.

"Oh, my God! Keely!"

The moment hands touched her she screamed until her

throat was hoarse. Her eyes were wild and unseeing, her hair damp around her face as she swung her head back and forth.

"Keely!" Hands planted themselves on her shoulders and shook her so hard her head snapped forward and backward.

She blinked several times until Sam's face came into focus.

"He touched me," she said in a voice still raspy from her screams. "He played music. He touched me." She kept saying the two lines over and over again as Sam hauled her into his arms and held on tight.

His chest rose and fell with labored breaths. "Honey, do you need to see a doctor?" he asked in a raw voice. "Do you want me to take you see Melanie?"

It took a moment for her to understand his meaning. She still refused to let go of him. She shook her head.

"He—only—touched—me," she whispered.

Sam rose to his feet while keeping a strong hold on Keely.

"I want the entire house dusted for prints!" he shouted.

Rick appeared in the doorway. "Wow," he muttered.

Keely turned her head just enough to see her dresser drawers open and the contents pulled out. Every piece of lingerie had been scattered about with spots of red marring the exquisite silk pieces. She started shaking violently.

"It's red nail polish." Sam read her mind. "A scare tactic."

"It's working." Her teeth chattered.

"She's going into shock." Sam started to pull away, but she only tightened her hold. He looked at Rick. "You're in charge. I'm taking her to my place."

"What about her kid?" the deputy asked.

Keely clutched Sam's shoulders. "No, I can't let her see

me like this," she pleaded. "She's at that slumber party. She doesn't need to know."

Sam wasn't about to argue. Not when she was right. Keely looked as if she'd been through a war.

"Call me as soon as you have something," he ordered, guiding Keely out of the room.

"I'll go ahead and take the pup home with me," Rick offered.

Sam almost forgot about the dog. "Thanks. I'll pick him up tomorrow."

Keely trembled violently in Sam's arms as he practically carried her out of the house. She whimpered when she saw deputies wearing latex gloves as they checked out the living room, one was in the kitchen.

Sam wasted no time in bundling her into his truck.

"Sweetheart, I need to get around to the other side of the truck and get in," he said gently as he tried to disentangle himself from her stranglehold.

She watched him with wide eyes as he quickly walked around the front of his vehicle and climbed in. He reached over and fastened her seat belt.

His brain cursed long and hard as he stared at her white features. Her eyes were dark with shock against her pale skin. Her arms were tightly wrapped around her middle as she rocked back and forth in her seat. Someone had frightened the hell out of her and he vowed to make sure that person paid for this crime.

He switched on the engine and drove down the driveway.

Sam had no idea how to handle the situation. Should he talk to her? Assure her she was all right? He had a sick feeling he would have to treat her the same way he would treat a rape victim. Because, unhappily, she had been raped, even though it had been her mind that had been violated and not her body.

As Sam parked in his garage, he was grateful Lisa wasn't home and Steffie wasn't around to see her mother so distraught. Speaking softly, he guided Keely into the house, being careful not to touch her.

She stood in the middle of the kitchen looking around as if she'd never seen the room before. Her body still shook and her teeth chattered.

"I'm so cold," she whispered, wrapping her arms around her body.

Sam didn't waste any time. He hustled her through the house to his bedroom and into his bathroom. He turned on the shower full blast and once the water was warm enough, gently pushed her into the cubicle, not hesitating to step in after her.

"It's okay, Keely," he soothed, running his hands up and down her arms, then pulling her against his chest so he could stroke her back. "You're safe now."

"No!" Her head whipped back and forth in argument. "I'll never be safe again." She buried her face against his shoulder.

She didn't protest when he grasped the hem of her T-shirt and pulled upward, tossing it down to the shower floor. He unzipped her shorts and pushed them down. Her bra and panties soon followed.

Keely stood still as Sam soaped her down then shampooed and rinsed her hair. His deduction that she needed to be scrupulously clean was obviously correct. After he finished, he grabbed a towel off the rack and wrapped it around her. Once they were out of the cubicle, he stripped off his own soaking wet clothing and snatched up a second towel, draping it around his hips.

Keely ran her fingers through her dripping hair, pushing it ruthlessly away from her face. Devoid of makeup and with wet hair, she should have looked haggard instead of a stark beauty that Sam couldn't miss if he tried. But she also looked like a lost child.

Sam gently brushed her cheek with his fingertips. "I'll be right back," he promised.

Luckily, Lisa had left her hair dryer behind and he was able to sit Keely down on the commode lid and dry her hair without any regard to style. For now, he wanted her to rest. He knew a statement had to be made. Sam Barkley the sheriff demanded one now. Sam Barkley the man knew it would have to wait.

"How did he get into my house?" Keely whispered as Sam helped her into his bed, carefully covering her up. "I always lock up. How did he know I wouldn't be there?"

"Let me get you something to drink," Sam said, starting to move away, but she gripped his arm.

"No, I need you," she told him, tears filming her eyes. "Don't leave me. Please."

Sam moved away just long enough to don a fresh pair of briefs then he climbed into bed and gathered her into his arms. It wasn't until she was warmly cradled against his chest that he realized she was crying. Not hysterically. Not loud, but silently, with only the feel of her tears on his bare chest alerting him. All he could do was hold her and let her know she wasn't alone.

He was touching her with hands that were cold and odd feeling. Taunting her with those hateful words. The song played in the background over and over again until the words were branded in her mind. She tossed and turned, trying to evade him. Wanting to get away, but she was cornered. She couldn't escape.

"No!" she screamed, bolting upright.

"Keely. Keely, you're all right. You're having a bad dream." Warm hands covered her shoulders. Turning her until her face rested against a hair-dusted chest. "I won't let anyone get you."

She wiped her cheeks with her fingers, feeling the dampness of tears on them. "Those horrible things he said to me," she said in a choked voice. "The way he touched me." She shuddered. She wrapped her arms around him, feeling protected in his embrace. Keely's emotions were running high. Adrenaline raced through her veins and her heart refused to slow down. She needed something to calm her. A reassurance she was all right. She raised her hands to rest on his shoulders at the same time she raised her head. "I need you, Sam," she murmured, pressing frantic kisses against his mouth. "I need you so much."

He was stunned by the frenetic motions of her hands and lips as she reached down to his lap. His erection sprang into her hand.

"Keely," he started to protest, fearing she wasn't fully awake and had no idea what she was doing.

She shook her head and kissed him, thrusting her tongue into his mouth.

"Love me. Love me," she chanted, stripping off his briefs, straddling his lap and lowering herself onto him.

Sam sucked a deep breath as he felt her moist walls embrace him. Her inner muscles contracted, caressing him in a way he couldn't remember ever experiencing before. He might have dreamed about this, but reality was a far cry from any fantasy that ran through his mind.

She moved in a rhythm set in her mind and it was surely driving Sam crazy. He knew this was purely for her, but there was no doubt he was feeling it, too. He could feel himself tightening, the desire rising in a furious spurt to claw at him. When he climaxed, he bucked up and held on fast as she ground herself against him.

Sam could feel rivulets of sweat trickle down his chest as Keely collapsed against him. He rested his cheek against the top of her head as he tried to regain his breath. It took him several moments to realize she'd fallen into a deep sleep. He groaned as he carefully lifted her off him and placed her to one side. Still asleep, she curled up into a ball with the pillow bunched up under her head. He slid down under the covers and slipped her back into his arms. It was a long time before he closed his eyes.

When Sam awoke some time later, he realized he was alone in bed. For a moment, he panicked, thinking the previous night had been a dream, until he smelled her scent on his skin. He started to get up when he heard the drumming sound of the shower in the bathroom. He lay back down.

Keely walked out of the bathroom with a towel wrapped around her body and a second towel wrapped in a turban around her hair. Droplets of water still glistened on her bare shoulders. She stopped short when she noticed Sam was awake. She offered him a faltering smile.

"I'm not sure whether to apologize or just slink away," she said in a low voice, refusing to look at him.

He sat up with his back braced against his pillows. "There's nothing to apologize for."

Keely's face was a bright red. "Let me just say that last night wasn't my usual style."

"You won't hear me complaining." He could tell by her hunched shoulders and refusal to look at him that he should drop the subject. "How about some breakfast?"

"I made coffee." She slowly turned to look at him.

Sam climbed out of bed. He figured his best bet was to act as natural as possible. And if he didn't stop to think that she wore nothing beneath that towel, he just might make it to the bathroom without embarrassing them both.

While he stood in the shower with his face upraised against the streaming hot water, his mind replayed the previous night in stunning detail. He groaned and tried to concentrate on anything but the way Keely's naked body felt against his. By the time he finished with his shower, he felt almost human again.

Enticing smells from the kitchen lured him there after he put on a pair of sweatpants.

Keely was in the process of slipping an omelette onto a plate as he walked in. She glanced up and returned to her task.

"Toast will be done in a minute," she said, as she then poured grapefruit juice into two glasses and carried them to the table.

Sam waited to pick up his fork until Keely sat down. He dug in hungrily.

"This is great," he said sincerely.

"Maybe it's because you worked up an appetite," she replied.

He looked up in time to see her face turn a becoming pink. She wrinkled her nose.

"That didn't come out right," she muttered with a self-deprecating smile, as she busied herself with her food.

For a while, they were both silent as they ate.

"That was great," Sam complimented as he enjoyed another cup of coffee after he'd finished his meal. He looked up guiltily when she rose to her feet and gathered up the plates. "It's only fair I do the dishes."

Keely shook her head. "It doesn't take long to rinse them off and put them in the dishwasher." She soon proved herself right while Sam relaxed with his coffee and enjoyed watching Keely bustle around the kitchen. Now he realized he should have thought to bring some additional clothing for her with them last night. While her wearing the same clothes didn't bother him, he felt it probably bothered her.

She seemed to take an inordinate amount of time cleaning the counters and stove.

"If you rub the surface any harder nothing will be left," he said quietly.

Her back was still to him. She slowly put the cloth down and turned around.

"I should apologize for last night."

Sam gently twisted his finger in his ear as if he were checking his hearing. "Excuse me?"

Keely seemed to have to force herself to look directly at him. "For last night," she said haltingly. "I mean, I practically ravished you." The expression on her face was embarrassed at the very least.

"Did you hear me protesting?" He grinned. He had to grin at her apology. "I was just sorry you didn't attack me again."

Keely opened her mouth to say more then snapped it shut again. She eyed him with a predatory gaze.

"Perhaps I didn't think you could survive another encounter," she said huskily.

Sam would have enjoyed continuing this sensual banter, but his cop half was kicking in and he had to get ready to go to the station and see if they'd found anything.

"As much as I hate to bring in reality, I guess I should let you know I'm going to need a statement," he said quietly.

As quickly as the blink of an eye, the mood was broken. Keely's smile disappeared and her eyes were flat as glass.

"When do you want me at the station?"

"I don't want you to leave the house just yet. I'll stop off at your place and pick up some clothing for you, then come back here." He continued. "I don't want you staying there, Keely. Steffie can use Lisa's other bed and there's a guest room for you."

"I can't hide!"

"It's called protective custody," he corrected her. "And you two will be staying here. I'll pick the girls up at noon and explain the circumstances to Steffie. I'll take her by your house to pick up clothing.''

"Sam, I cannot stay here!" Keely argued.

"Protective custody," he said firmly. "And yes, you will." He got up and headed for the hall. "I've got to get ready for work."

She was fast on his heels. "Will you let me know what they found?"

"Yes. Rick took the puppy, but I'm sure he'll have brought the little guy in today."

"I want to argue more, but you're walking away from me," she said, still following him.

Sam stopped in the doorway to the bedroom. "The last thing I want to do is argue with you. I have to get dressed." He paused. "Make use of the washer and dryer. You can borrow one of my T-shirts." He carefully closed the door.

Keely stood for a moment, staring at the door.

She couldn't stay here! Not after last night. The memory of making love to Sam was vivid in her mind. Even more vivid in certain parts of her body. She had woken up that morning feeling like a new woman. When she walked into the bedroom after her shower and saw him looking so sleepy and adorable, she wanted to jump his bones again. Then she remembered why she was there and her desire swiftly waned.

Two showers hadn't erased her tormentor's touch. She imagined she could still feel his hands on her body. She was only grateful he hadn't tried to rape her. She knew she wouldn't have given in easily, but the idea was still horrifying.

In desperation, she escaped to the family room and the television.

When Sam walked in, now dressed in his khaki shirt, badge and jeans, Keely was curled up on the couch, her eyes glued to the television screen.

"It's that good, is it?" he asked.

"They're talking about how to get along with your neighbors," she said in a monotone. "I thought I might pick up some helpful hints."

"That couldn't have been the only thing on."

Keely shook her head. "It was either this or watching Jeannie prance around in her harem costume or 'Muppet Babies.' I'm opting for this."

"Considering I'm your neighbor, I wouldn't worry." Sam stood behind the couch and spread his arms on the back. "I'll be back after I pick up the girls. Is there anything special you want from the house?"

"You're really going to make me stay here?" she demanded.

"Yep."

"Then you'll have to bring my computer and my files." She hoped that would change his mind.

"Fine. I'm sure Steffie will know which things you'll need. Be a good girl and don't open the door for anyone but me." He dropped a kiss on top of her head.

"Tough guy."

"You betcha."

Keely remained on the couch, listening to the sound of Sam's truck diminish as he drove off. Her lips slowly curved in a smile that said it all. She was most definitely reliving last night.

Chapter 14

"Nothing?" Sam threw the file folder down onto his desk.

"Not a thing," Rick replied. "Didn't she say something about the guy's hands feeling weird? He was obviously wearing gloves. The only room tossed was her bedroom and a lot of her clothing was covered with red nail polish. Fredda saw what we brought in as evidence and told us color name and brand. It's pretty common."

Sam shook his head in frustration. "How did he get in?"

"Broken window in Steffie's room." Rick eyed his boss. "How was Mrs. Harper last night?"

"Scared spitless. She worked out her fear with tears and seems to be handling it well. But I told her I don't want her staying there. After this attack, she should be in a protected environment. I'm going to have her and Steffie stay with Lisa and me. If that bastard got in their place once, he can do it again, and next time Keely and maybe even Steffie might not be so lucky."

"Are you sure that's a good idea?" Rick asked.

This was a blunt question that Sam would have normally jumped on the younger man for with both feet. But today, he was tired and still feeling pretty damn good about the previous night.

"The girls will probably enjoy it since they're practically joined at the hip anyway. I'll even have unlimited use of my phone," he said lightly.

"Okay, boss." Rick started to get up, then stopped. "Anything else?"

Sam thought for a moment. "Nothing I can think of. I guess we should have known we wouldn't get lucky with fingerprints, but I can always hope."

"Why would anyone want to terrorize her anyway?" the deputy asked. "It's not as if she's lived here long enough to make any enemies."

Sam took a deep breath. "Ask Fredda for the Davis file from thirty years back. It was before your time and to be honest, no one around here talks about it. After you read it, you might come up with some ideas. All I ask is that you don't talk about it."

Rick nodded as he stood up. He looked a little puzzled, but he seemed to sense his boss wasn't going to answer any more questions until he'd done as Sam asked.

Sam leaned back in his chair and stared up at the ceiling. Unhappily, there were no answers written there. This was something he was going to have to do all by himself.

Someone had been out here.

Remembering something Keely had said, Sam drove out to her house and walked around back. With head downcast, he walked in a straight line back and forth just in front of the woods, looking for something, anything.

It wasn't until he was about a hundred yards among the trees that a speck of color attracted his eye. He crouched down and combed through the twigs, dirt and leaves until he uncovered the rest of it. The color he spied turned out to be a cigar band. He dug into his pocket for his pen and slid the barrel under the top part of the wrapper while he pulled an evidence envelope out of his jeans pocket. Within seconds the band was slipped into the envelope. Further searching uncovered several more cigar bands.

"I don't like this at all," he muttered with grim menace as he made his way back to his truck.

"What's wrong with Mom?" Steffie demanded before she climbed into Sam's truck. Lisa stood next to her, also looking worried.

"Now why would you ask that?" he asked hoping to inject a little lightness in the mood.

"Because I feel it."

Sam muttered a few uncomplimentary words about intuition. "Get in," he ordered. "We're stopping at your place for you to pick up clothes and your mom's computer. You're going to be staying with Lisa and me."

The two girls exchanged looks then, as if strings directed their action, turned their heads at the same time to face him.

"I'll explain when we get back to the house," he said with a long-suffering sigh. "Just get in please. After we get the clothing, we'll pick up the puppy. Rick took him for the night."

The girls climbed into the back and Sam drove away, not bothering to listen to their frenzied whispers from the back seat.

When they reached the house, Sam instructed them to wait while he went through the house first. After a quick inspection he gestured to them that it was safe to enter.

"Wow, what a mess!" Steffie muttered, wrinkling her nose at the fingerprint powder dusting the furniture surfaces. She suddenly grabbed his arm. "Mom's all right, isn't she?"

"She's fine," he assured her. "But I'm sure she'd like a change of clothes."

Sam remained behind the girls as they tentatively walked down the hallway. Steffie entered her room first and pulled out an overnight bag and began piling clothes into it.

"Mom's suitcase is in the hall closet," she told Sam.

He nodded and retrieved the suitcase and carried it into Keely's bedroom. He winced at the sight of clothing strewn everywhere. He hadn't realized Steffie had entered the room until he heard her gasp.

"Why would someone do something this horrible?" she cried.

"Hard to say," he muttered.

Steffie uttered soft cries of distress as she picked through her mother's clothing to find suitable items. While she packed, Sam dismantled Keely's computer and carried the equipment and file of disks out to the truck.

The threesome was quiet as Sam drove back to the station, where Rick was waiting with the puppy. The expression on the deputy's face was more than a little disgruntled.

"He chewed my boots," he complained.

"They'll be replaced," Sam promised, taking the leash. "Got something for the file." He handed him the evidence envelope. "I found these out by the house. See who in town sells these and if it's remembered who buys them."

Rick nodded. "I'll get right on it."

"So Mom stayed at your house last night?" Steffie asked once Sam had returned to the truck and bundled the pup into the back seat where he bounced happily between the two girls.

"That's right." He hoped his face didn't turn red.

The girls exchanged a telling look.

"I didn't realize the sheets for the guest room bed were clean," Lisa commented.

"Washed them last week," Sam lied, fervently wishing he didn't have such a smart daughter.

When they walked into the house, an appetizing aroma was coming from the kitchen.

"Mom's stew," Steffie said with reverence.

"Something edible," Lisa said, racing after her friend.

Sam followed them after making sure the puppy did his business outside. He walked into the kitchen finding Keely wearing one of his T-shirts with her shorts. He instantly decided he liked the combination.

"You had the ingredients for stew and we all needed to eat," Keely told him.

"I'll put your suitcase in the guest room," he offered.

"Oh, we'll take it in." Steffie took it out of his hand. Before he could protest, she and Lisa were out of the kitchen.

"We're in trouble," he muttered.

"Why?" Keely's eyes danced with amusement.

Sam wiped his forehead with the back of his hand, not surprised to find it damp. "They're putting your suitcase in the guest room and the first thing they'll check is the bed."

"So?"

"So, they'll find the bed doesn't have any sheets on it since they weren't clean."

"Sam." She touched his arm. "They'll find sheets on the bed because I put them on this morning. I had very little to do and the last thing I wanted to do was watch a talk show on kids who believe their parents came from another planet and are now afraid the mother ship will show up and take them away to another galaxy." She took a deep breath. "You looked around the house, didn't you?"

He nodded. "And found cigar bands among the trees. They hadn't been there all that long either."

She looked relieved. "It wasn't my imagination then."

"Not at all." He traced the back of her hand with his fingertip. "Too bad I had to pick up the girls. We could have had a quiet lunch."

The gleam in Keely's eyes told him she knew he was trying to get her mind off the seriousness behind her staying here—along with giving her a less than subtle reminder of the previous night. She inserted her fingers just behind his belt buckle and wiggled them against his shirtfront.

"Ah, but that would take all the fun out of it, wouldn't it?" she murmured.

Obviously, her hearing was better than his at the moment since she was two feet away when the girls bounced back into the kitchen with the puppy following them with his ungainly gait.

"When will lunch be ready?" Steffie asked.

"No 'Hi, Mom, I'm glad to see you're all right.'?" Keely mocked.

"You're with Sam, so I know you're fine and I figured you didn't want to talk about it."

"True, but remember it's nice to say something. Lunch will be in about fifteen minutes." Keely inserted a tray of rolls into the oven.

"Then I'm going to unpack."

"This is going to be so neat!" Lisa enthused as the girls disappeared again.

"They bounce back better than a rubber band," Sam groused.

"I'm glad they do," she said quietly. "What now?"

He shook his head. "You won't like it, but when I'm not here, there will be a deputy in the driveway. You're not to go anywhere by yourself and neither are the girls.''

Alarm flared in her eyes. "Do you think—?" She stopped, afraid to voice the worst.

"I just want to take precautions," he explained.

Keely turned back to stir the stew. "This isn't good, Sam. You have Lisa to worry about."

"I'll feel better with you here. Besides, I'm holding your computer equipment hostage. I'll set it up on the dining room table if that's okay with you. And we can have your phone calls forwarded over here."

She nodded. "I just hope I can work."

"I'm going to find him, Keely," he vowed.

Keely smiled and walked over, looping her arms around his waist and hugging him. "I know you will, Sam," she said quietly. "That's the only reason I'm staying here."

"That's the only reason?"

She grinned. "We can discuss the other reasons later on."

"I'm holding you to that."

"You two can find something to do while Keely and I take care of business, can't you?" Sam said, after they finished lunch. "After you've done the dishes, that is."

"Dishes?" Lisa repeated.

He nodded. "Wash and dry. By hand, no less. It will be good practice for you when you live in a place without a dishwasher."

A crestfallen Lisa looked at Steffie. "You are not company. You have to help."

"Fine, as long as I don't have to wash."

Sam and Keely went into the family room where Sam had already laid out a pad of paper and a tape recorder on the coffee table. She sat in one of the chairs, deliberately keeping her distance from him as he took his place on the couch by the pad and tape recorder.

"I want to record this so the facts will be straight," he explained. "Is that all right with you?"

She nodded jerkily.

Sam switched it on, then stated his name, title, date and time. "Please state your name and address," he said quietly.

Keely cleared her throat and gave the information in a near whisper.

"Now, Keely, I want you to tell me everything you did from the time you left the station yesterday," he said.

She clasped her hands tightly in her lap. "I stopped at the hardware store for some supplies," she said in a halting voice. "I had thought about going out to my parents' house and doing some more work. I went home, changed my clothes and went out there about one o'clock." He nodded for her to continue. "I was so focused in finishing the downstairs I didn't realize it was starting to get dark. I didn't worry about Steffie since I knew she was at a friend's house. I drove home from there and went in."

"By what door did you enter the house?" he asked.

"The kitchen door leading to the garage," she replied. "When I went inside, I heard the puppy crying and scratching the laundry room door. I tried to turn on the light, but it wouldn't come on. I thought it was a blown fuse or burned-out lightbulb, so I looked for the flashlight in one of the drawers. That's when I heard the music." She started shaking. "And someone calling me. Taunting me." In her agitation, her eyes turned glassy. "I couldn't find the flashlight and I just wanted to get away from the music and the voice. But wherever I went, I couldn't escape the voice and the music. Then he started touching me. Teasing me." She rubbed her hands up and down her arms as if she were chilly. "I ran into the bedroom so I could reach the phone, but he followed me and kept touching me.'' She shook her head. ''I don't know what happened then. I just blanked out until you showed up.'' She huddled in the chair. She blinked several times. ''Why did you come?''

''An anonymous phone call saying they heard screams coming from your place,'' he answered. ''The voice was disguised and the call made from the gas station pay phone so we have no idea who made the call, but it was obviously whoever had been out to your house. The perp knew he wouldn't get caught and probably hoped we'd find you an emotional wreck.''

Keely looked away. ''I learned something new last night, Sam. I learned that rape doesn't have to be physical,'' she said in a low voice throbbing with the emotional pain she'd been suffering. ''My home was violated. My life was violated and my mind, especially, was violated. That scum didn't want me to suffer physical pain. He wanted me to *suffer* and what better way than to scare the hell out of me, so my imagination can conjure up even more nightmares.'' She shifted her position and lifted her hand to brush a lock of hair away from her face, which was screwed up in thought. ''Nightmares,'' she murmured to herself. ''Nightmares.'' She looked up. ''The music! That song was always in my nightmare.''

Sam wanted nothing more than to switch off the tape recorder, but not when she might unwittingly come up with something important.

''Your nightmares played that same song?'' He wanted to clarify her statement.

She nodded then remembered the recorder was still running. ''Yes. In fact, the first time I heard it was at the bookstore. And it frightened me then. But why?''

''The music you heard in your house came from a CD. And you don't own it?''

"No." Keely uttered a soft sigh. "I must have heard that song before, but why would it suddenly frighten me now?"

Sam had an idea he had the answer, but he didn't know if it would be a good idea to bring it up just yet. He switched off the recorder.

"I'm afraid most of your clothes were ruined," he said quietly.

"I couldn't have worn them even if they had been cleaned," she said with distaste. "It will give me a good excuse to go shopping."

"I'm sure the girls will be only too happy to help you with that chore."

Keely pulled her legs up under her body and remained in that position as she stared at Sam.

"What?" he asked, confused by the intensity in her stare.

"You know something, don't you?" She leaned forward, bracing her arms on the chair. "What, Sam? Tell me what you know? Dammit, I need to know!"

He stared back at her. "There are some answers I'll need first before I'll know if I'm right."

"Why don't you tell me what you think you know and perhaps I'll have the answers for you," she bargained.

"No, Keely."

She reared back as if slapped. "You don't trust me."

"I don't trust *me* until I have the answers I need." He stood up. "I have to get back to the station. One of the deputies will be out front if you need anything. Let the machine pick up the calls. I'll have your calls transferred over here by the end of today."

Keely unwound herself and stood up. She looked tired and very unhappy. "The cop at work," she drawled.

A flash of emotion crossed his eyes then abruptly disappeared. "It's my job."

She sat back down looking as if all the bones in her body had suddenly dissolved. "I'm sorry. I'm being a witch and you don't deserve it. You're doing everything you can and all I'm doing is giving you more trouble."

"Hey." He pulled her up and into his arms. "I guess when you moved here, you didn't expect all of this."

Her face was pressed tightly against his shirtfront so she settled for a quick shake of the head.

"We're going to get this all sorted out, Keely. I promise." He caressed her hair in long soothing strokes.

"Sure, easy for you to say." Her grumbled words were muffled by her mouth still pressed against his chest. "You're not the one in protective custody."

"I figured you'd be happier staying with me than with Rick. I've seen his place and he's a regular slob," he said in an attempt to lighten the atmosphere.

Keely tipped back her head and wrinkled her nose. "Steffie wouldn't have been happy at all."

"Neither would I," Sam whispered in her ear before stepping back. "I've got to get in. I know it won't be easy, but try not to worry and if anything else comes to mind, write it down and we'll go over it tonight."

She nodded.

The moment Sam was out of the house, Keely felt forlorn. She could hear the faint sounds of music coming from Lisa's bedroom and bits and pieces of words. She would have dismissed it if she hadn't heard her name and Sam's. She crept down the hall and remained a few feet from the bedroom doorway.

"Maybe this isn't exactly the right mood, but it's great that they're sharing a house," Lisa said. "They'll get to know each other better. Dad can see how great your mom is and vice versa."

"At least we know your dad isn't slow on the uptake.

What a kiss at the picnic! Better than anything in the movies.'' Steffie giggled.

Keely could feel her face burning and knew she was probably a flaming red.

"Yeah, but you figured they slept together and we saw the sheets on the guest room bed. What made you think that?" Lisa asked.

"Just something about them. You know, intimate." Steffie emphasized the last word as if to give it special meaning. "You had to have felt it, too."

"I don't know. It's hard to think of my dad doing *it*," she confessed. "I mean, he's so old."

Keely covered her mouth with her hand to keep her laughter from spilling out.

"Yeah, well, Mom's not exactly young, but she'd tell me that while she's way over thirty, she can still boogie," Steffie declared.

Keely pressed her hand tighter against her mouth. The pressure in her stomach to hold back her laughter was increasing by the second. At the moment, she wasn't sure whether to go in and lecture the girls on their candid discussion or hug them for their idea of their parents making the perfect couple.

Except at the moment, she wasn't sure if she and Sam together was a good idea. She was positive he was keeping something back from her. And she meant to find out just what it was.

She silently crept back to the kitchen. The girls had done their job, leaving the room gleaming.

"May as well set up the computer and see if I can accomplish anything," she said to herself, heading for the dining room.

The moment Sam reached the station, he headed for his office and flipped through his card file. After finding the number he wanted, he picked up his phone.

"You're talking about someone who was put in here thirty years ago," one of his old contacts further north told him.

"All I need to know is if he was released," Sam explained. "He was given a life sentence, but we all know with good behavior he can be out by now."

"Be grateful for computer records, old buddy." The faint click of computer keys sounded over the receiver. "Okay, here we go. Yeah, Willis was released about six years ago. He'd been a good boy while he was in. He stayed out of trouble and earned a hell of a lot more credit than demerits. I can give you the address and phone number we have on record, but there's no guarantee he still lives there."

"I'll take it. Anything else you can give me on him? Maybe a picture?"

"I can do it, but it might not do you much good. The guy was roughed up pretty bad his second year in. Some guy didn't like the idea of his making a cute little girl an orphan and sliced his face up. He had some plastic surgery to correct the worst of the damage, but he still looked pretty bad. He might have been able to have more since then. He doesn't look anything like he did back in the sixties."

"Fax me the last photo you have, too."

"You know, the guy did his time, and since there hasn't been anything on him since he got out, you're not going to be able to just haul him in without a concrete beef."

"I have a beef. There's that orphaned little girl who's all grown-up and being terrorized by someone very familiar with what went on back then," Sam said grimly.

"Whoa. All right, I'll fax you everything. Get back to me once you hear something."

"I will. Thanks."

Sam sat back in his chair and stared unseeing at the wall as he tried to compute everything he'd learned so far.

If Willis didn't look anything like he did before, would he have had the guts to come back here? Sure, why not. Especially with Keely no longer living here. Then she came back and he felt his new life was threatened. That she might see him for who he really was. If it happened there'd be no doubt most of the town would come out for a lynching. Feelings still ran strong in regards to the Davis murder. One of the first violent crimes in years and there hadn't been one since.

He tried to think of anyone who had moved into the area in the last six years.

"Fredda!"

"Why do we have an intercom if you persist in shouting my name?" A cloud of heavy jasmine perfume preceded the clerk as she appeared in his doorway holding several sheets of paper. "This just came over the fax addressed to you."

"Thanks." He laid out the papers side by side. "Who do you remember moving in here in the last six years?"

She tapped her forefinger against her chin. "Let's see. Stan, who owns the gas station. That old codger who has the hardware store. Wilkes, who took over the dry cleaners when Leonard retired. The Hendersons. Miriam Rogers moved back here after her divorce."

"Okay." He held up his hand to halt her recitation. "Could you do me a favor and write out the names of anyone you remember."

She gave him a stern eye. "I have my duties, you know."

"And this is another one. It's in conjunction with the Harper attack."

Fredda hadn't been at her job for more than thirty years

for nothing. "Are you saying that bastard Willis might be back here?"

Sam nodded. "There's a good chance he is."

Fredda sat down. "But we'd all know him," she protested.

"He had his face cut up during a fight in prison and had to have corrective surgery. He doesn't look the same at all and it's guessed he had more surgery after he got out." He slid the fax with a photograph on it across his desk toward her.

Fredda picked it up and studied the black-and-white grainy likeness. "A lot of scars on his face," she murmured. "The idiot should have aimed for his black heart." She tossed it down. "Saved all of us a lot of trouble. All right, I'll see who I can come up with and I'll give Miz Nan a call. Anyone I don't remember, she will." She stood up and headed for the door then paused. "Does Keely remember anything from back then?"

Sam knew he could trust her. "Only a series of bad dreams that she doesn't realize has anything to do with her."

She tsked and shook her head in sympathy. "Poor girl. She had a lot on her plate back then and it seems she has even more now." She narrowed her eyes. "You find that man, Sam. You find him and I'll gut him like the animal he is." With that, she left.

Sam stared at the sheets of paper. "Whoever said men are more bloodthirsty than women hasn't met Fredda."

Chapter 15

Keely wasn't sure what was worse—being forced to stay in a house that wasn't hers or seeing the sheriff's car conspicuously parked in the driveway. The deputy was polite when she took him some coffee and explained if she wanted to go somewhere he was to go with her.

In the end, she did what she usually did when she felt out of sorts—she baked.

"Something smells good," Steffie commented, walking into the kitchen. Lisa was behind her and the puppy followed them.

"Go away, this is all mine." Keely pulled the square baking pan out of the oven.

"She made chocolate pudding cake," Steffie said with awe.

Lisa ran for a drawer and pulled out spoons.

Keely stared at the two expectant faces and sighed. "All right, sit down. But you better realize I intend to get more than my share."

"This is so good," Steffie told Lisa as they all sat around the table.

The three were soon enjoying the warm cake topped with the pudding mixture.

"I know this might sound kind of crass, but I like having you here," Lisa admitted shyly as she dipped her spoon into the pan.

Keely realized Lisa didn't need any signs of her bad mood. The girl had lost her mother when she was very young and with the age she was reaching, she probably felt the need for feminine comfort that her father wasn't able to provide. She leaned over and hugged her.

"If nothing else, I'll make sure to teach your father more dishes to cook," she promised.

Out of the corner of her eye she noticed the two girls exchange a secretive look.

Keely knew the last thing they needed to hear was that their parents had made love the night before. They'd probably gleefully run for the closest preacher!

Thoughts of Sam was enough to send warmth flooding through her veins. She knew she had made love with him because she needed to feel again, but it had turned into more. They had connected in so many complex ways she couldn't even count.

She only hoped it wasn't all due to the person after her. For someone who vowed she didn't want another man in her life, Keely was finding out that having someone like Sam around wasn't all that bad.

As if he'd followed the train of her thoughts, he called up on the phone.

"We're following a few leads," he said crisply. "Don't expect me back all that early, so don't worry about holding dinner for me. Is Joe out front?"

"He's not only out front, he's practically parked at the

front door. He also told me wherever I go, he goes." She took a deep breath. "Sam, how old is he?"

He chuckled. "He's old enough."

"When did he start shaving? This morning? This is nuts, Sam. If I'm cooped up here with Baby Face Badge Boy, I'm going to feel as if I'm protecting *him!*" she demanded.

"Are you sure you want him trying again when the girls are with you?"

Keely swore under her breath. "I didn't need to hear the voice of reason, even if you are right. What do you think will happen now?"

"Hopefully, nothing. With luck, he'll figure he has you pretty well spooked and you're hiding out at my place. He'll sit back and savor his victory and hope you'll be chewing your nails waiting for another attack. Once he feels you've relaxed enough, he'll probably strike again."

Keely tossed a crumpled piece of paper across the room. It wasn't as good as breaking something, but it helped lower her frustration level a little.

"All right. I'm relaxed. I'm happy. My nails are even starting to grow back," she snapped.

"Trust me, Keely, it won't be that easy," he said seriously. "With this type of situation, all you can do is sit and wait."

"I'm not a patient person," she explained.

"Then I guess we'll have to come up with a way for you to work off that frustration, won't we?" With those last words lingering in the air, he hung up.

Keely stood still, her hand frozen to the receiver.

"I'd be better off if I didn't have a vivid imagination," she whispered to herself, setting the receiver down.

As it grew late and shadows deepened around the house, Keely was grateful for the deputy out front. Joe had been replaced by Dave, who was thankful for the thermos of coffee and plate of food she brought out.

A tour of the house had her discover a deck off the master bedroom and Keely sat out there after dinner while Steffie and Lisa watched television. She was smart enough to keep the outdoor lights off so she couldn't be seen. Ignoring the two chairs out there, she opted for sitting on the step just outside the room where she could enjoy the clear evening sky.

But Keely couldn't remain lazy for long. She rested her elbows on her knees, her chin on her cupped hands as she cast her mind out over the past few months. Who could it be? Who would hate her so much?

The low rasp of the sliding door opening had her turning her head. Sam looked down on her.

"Are you sure it's a good idea for you to be out here?" he asked, stepping down beside her and sitting on the step.

Even in the dim light, Keely could see the lines of weariness on his face and tracked the way his hand rubbed the back of his neck in a tired gesture.

"I can heat something up for you if you're hungry," she offered.

He shook his head. "I ate at Sissy's earlier. Still feeling antsy?"

She shrugged. "I worked it off cooking dinner."

"Yeah, the girls said it was pretty awesome." He smiled. "You're spoiling my kid. She won't want to go back to my cooking."

"Don't worry, I made them help." She smiled back. "I told Lisa it was a good learning experience for her. She said she's afraid if you learn to cook, it will be all healthy food."

He leaned over and whispered in her ear, "I think I'd rather you tempt my taste buds."

She slanted him a look that fairly sizzled. "Really? I thought I'd already done that."

Sam took a deep breath and blew it out slowly. "You sure know how to go about it when you want to raise a guy's blood pressure."

Keely smiled, looking extremely pleased with herself. Her smile started to dim. "Did you find out anything?"

"Only that three stores in town carry that brand of cigar I found by your house. And no one can remember any one person buying them. I never knew so many people smoked them. Even women." He exhaled a heavy sigh. "No fingerprints were found in your house."

Keely narrowed in her eyes in thought. "Could he have been wearing gloves? His hands brushed against my bare skin a few times and they felt strange." She shuddered at the thought.

"It looked as if he was clever enough to do that. There was nothing on the CD he left in your system. No tags on the case to indicate where it had been bought."

"There's a reason why that song upsets me," she said softly, speaking to herself as much as to him. "And the house. Why would I become almost ill when I go inside?" She turned to him. "Sam, I want to go back to the house tomorrow."

"I don't want you staying there," he argued.

She shook her head. "No, I mean my parents' house."

He hesitated. "That might not be a good idea, either."

"I need to," Keely insisted. "I need to make myself remember why it all bothers me so much and what the nightmares mean."

Sam stared at her for a long time. He grimaced. "You won't go without me."

She laid her hand on his arm. "I'd appreciate that." Using him for balance, she stood up. "I need to know,

Sam. But I'm glad I won't have to be alone.'' She dropped a kiss on top of his head and walked back inside.

Sam remained out on the deck, allowing the quiet to seep into his pores and soothe a tired spirit. Today hadn't been a good day for him. Everything came up a blank. No fingerprints. Not one clue had been left behind except for the CD and that seemed to have been left there more as a taunt to everyone. Entry had been through Steffie's bedroom window, which had been broken and the screen had been propped up against the side of the house. All he had was a traumatized victim who couldn't give anyone a description of the intruder because it was dark.

He didn't like the idea of Keely going into her parents' house and fighting to bring her fears to the surface. But he knew if he had argued with her she would have gone without him and there was no way he was letting her go anywhere by herself.

He was still outside when he heard sounds of the girls getting ready for bed. The light in Lisa's room soon winked out, but their muted voices could still be heard from the open window. He smiled. He couldn't remember the last time he'd seen his daughter so animated and happy. She'd always had friends, but it seemed Steffie was someone special. It didn't surprise him. Not when the mother was pretty special to him.

That night Keely lay in bed, listening to the soft night sounds. She noticed Sam was still up when she went to bed. The faint aroma of cigarette smoke wafted in from his deck and she could hear sounds of him moving around. She knew the girls were asleep. She'd checked on them a few minutes ago when she went to the kitchen for a glass of water. Now she could hear sounds of Sam obviously getting ready for bed. Keely thought of the night before when he thrust her into the shower where she was able to warm the chill that had crept into her bones. The way he'd dried her and even made sure her hair was dry. She considered these thoughts the warm fuzzies. Then she thought of later on. Their lovemaking had been quick and explosive and she knew she wouldn't mind doing it again, but at a much slower pace. She smiled in the dark.

"Oh, Keely, what a bad girl you are," she murmured to herself as she sat up.

She crept down the hallway, holding her breath as she passed Lisa's room. She rested her fingers on the doorknob that would let her into Sam's bedroom, took a deep breath and carefully twisted it and pushed the door open. A faint slice of moonlight allowed her to see Sam lying in bed. Keeping hold of her courage, she stepped inside and closed the door behind her, resting back against the wood.

"It's about time you got here." His voice cut through the silence.

A smile curved her lips. "You had the gall to think I'd come in here?"

"No, I'd hoped." He raised himself up on one elbow. "Are you going to stand there all night?"

Keely pushed herself away from the door. She glided across the floor, raising her arms and pulling off her nightgown at the same time. When she reached the bed, the nightgown was on the floor and she was slowly slipping into bed.

Sam blew a low whistle of appreciation. "Very nice."

She smiled. "Honey, tonight, you're going to get something much better than nice," she purred, running her palm across the breadth of his chest, pausing to tease a coppercolored nipple with her fingertip. With her palm flat against his chest, she could feel the moan that began deep down and moved up his throat. "I always wanted to seduce a man, Sheriff," Keely whispered, caressing the hairroughened skin with slow circular motions that soon had him moving against her hand. "And there seems to be something sinful in the idea of seducing a man of the law. What do you think?"

He cleared his throat several times. "I think you're doing just fine," he finally rasped, trying to turn toward her, but she effectively kept him prone on the bed.

"I'm glad to hear that," Keely said throatily, looming over him looking like any red-blooded man's idea of a fantasy. She dipped her head and gently sucked on his earlobe. "You inspire me, Sam," she whispered in his ear as she delicately touched the inner shell with the tip of her tongue. "I think my ideas started the first time I saw you. A cop without an attitude. A cop who's obviously a good father and a cop who just happens to be extremely sexy." She twisted around to tease his other ear.

Sam drew in much needed air. "I never thought of myself as sexy."

She shifted so that she was straddling his hips while nibbling along his jaw.

"Trust me, you are," she said in a breathy voice. "I can feel it." She swept her hand down his side, lingering on his bare hip. "Oh, yes, I can feel a lot." She delicately licked the curve of his throat as her hand trailed down even further and encircled his heat.

Sam hissed a curse that could have been a prayer. He wasn't sure if she was a witch or an angel as she moved her hand in a leisurely manner that soon had his hips moving in the same rhythm. Her skin had been cool at first but quickly warmed as he swiveled his hips against hers. She enticed him with her body. Sang a siren's song with her lips and performed more magic with her hands.

He inhaled the languorous scent of her skin that brought to mind a wooden front porch with rockers, jasmine climbing up trellises and women wearing white cotton and lace gowns that brushed against their ankles. A woman who would smile demurely at her suitor and offer him her hand or cheek. And if he was lucky, she would prove to be a lusty lover in the bedroom. Keely Harper was very definitely a lusty lover.

When she settled herself over him and engulfed him, he felt as if he'd died and gone to heaven.

"Shall we dance, Sheriff?" she whispered, as her lips covered his, her tongue tracing the seam of his lips before slipping inside.

They were joined physically and mentally. It was as if their minds communicated to each other on another plane, telling the other what felt good.

Sam knew instinctively that suckling her breast would bring a gasp of pleasure to her lips. He knew that the line of her spine was ultrasensitive to his touch and as he reared up under her to fill her fully, she would moan his name.

As before, their climax was explosive, leaving both of them exhausted yet exhilarated. Keely nestled herself in Sam's arms after she adjusted his alarm clock.

"Why did you change the time?" he asked, content to have her curved against his side.

"I need to get out of here before the girls wake up," she replied, pressing a kiss against the curve of his shoulder. "Let's not give them any ideas, shall we?"

As far as Sam was concerned, he was more than willing to allow the girls to get any ideas they wanted. He also knew this wasn't the time to think about getting involved. There were too many dark clouds hovering overhead and he needed to clear them before they could think about themselves. For now, he'd be selfish and take what he could get.

"What perfume are you wearing?" he asked suddenly.

"I'm not." She yawned. "Just powder and body lotion called Southern Nights. Steffie gave it to me for Christmas last year."

He fell asleep realizing why the mental picture of Keely wearing nothing more than powder and baby lotion popped into his head. He made a mental note to buy several gallons of the lotion.

The alarm had barely begun to bleep when Keely shut it off. She had meant nothing more than to kiss Sam and sneak back to the guest room, but Sam soon showed her he had other ideas. Luckily, while it was some time later that a smiling and satisfied Keely made her quiet trek back to the guest room, the girls were still in bed sound asleep.

"We have to have a baby-sitter now?" Lisa burst out after her father explained she and Steffie could not leave the house without one of his deputies accompanying them.

"Until this is taken care of, yes," he said firmly. "I don't want to scare you girls, but this person might take it into his mind to grab one or both of you in order to get back at Keely. This guy is pretty sick in the head. We don't want to give him any more advantages than we have to."

Steffie leaned over and took Keely's hand. "Oh Mom," she said with a soft sigh. "You don't deserve junk like this."

She smiled and kissed her on the cheek. "Thank you, sweetheart. I don't want the two of you to feel as if you're prisoners kept in the house. As long as you make sure the deputy can see you, I would feel better. Or if you're with a group of friends, I would appreciate your not leaving that group with anyone but that same deputy. I don't care who the person who approaches you is or what they say."

Both girls looked at Sam who nodded his agreement.

"I know this is a lot to ask of you, but this person might be someone we all know," he said grimly. "Someone we wouldn't even suspect. We can't trust anyone right now. If I had my way, the two of you would be staying with someone out of town, but—'' he held up his hand as the two burst into argument "—I knew that was one option you wouldn't agree to. So you'll live by the rules we've set down. And if either of you veer from them, you'll both be packed off to Lisa's grandmother in Sacramento.''

"Gee, Dad, why don't you just send us to San Quentin,'' Lisa muttered before turning to her friend. "Grandma still lives in the dark ages when girls our age didn't wear makeup, didn't talk to boys and didn't wear shorts even in the house. She also has a nine o'clock bedtime we'd have to keep, too.''

"Gee, and I thought my grandmother was bad.''

"Louise isn't bad,'' Keely cut in. She glanced at Sam. "Jay's mother thinks she's a reincarnation of Auntie Mame. I won't even tell you what she served for dinner the last time we were there.''

"It was from Tibet and it was disgusting.'' Steffie made a face. She quickly sobered. "Okay, we'll live by whatever rules you guys put down because we know it's for our own good.''

"I worry when she's this agreeable,'' Keely said.

"They know that if they don't do what they're told, they're packed off to Grandma's, and if you knew this lady you'd walk the straight and narrow, too,'' Sam told her. "She was the reason they say someone has iron in their backbone.''

"Can we have friends here?'' Lisa asked.

Sam turned to Keely. "That's up to you, since you'd be the one to put up with them.''

"One apiece is fine, but no slumber parties for right now.''

They nodded.

"Keely and I need to go somewhere this afternoon, but someone will be here with the two of you.'' Sam stood up and walked over to the rack where he kept his hat. His weapon was already comfortably holstered at his side. He dropped a kiss on top of Lisa's head, ruffled Steffie's hair and touched the back of Keely's neck with his fingertips. A moment later he was gone.

As if planned, the moment Sam was out the door, two sets of eyes swiveled in Keely's direction.

"Mother, is there something we should know?" Keely asked archly.

Keely merely smiled as she refilled her coffee cup.

"Follow the rules or you get to visit Grandma" was all she'd say.

Chapter 16

"This is a good idea, right?" Keely appealed to Sam during the drive to her childhood home.

"You felt it was. If you don't, we can go back," he said agreeably, pulling the truck over to the side of the road and letting the engine idle.

She huffed several times. "If I don't go I'm a coward who's afraid to face the truth." She looked at him narrowly. "A truth I have a hunch you already know."

"I only knew your dad while I worked for him," he replied. "Back then, I was more concerned with my bike and not letting old lady Morrison catch me stealing apples from her tree."

She looked as if she wasn't sure whether to believe him and turned back around. She clasped her hands tightly in her lap.

"Let's go."

The moment Sam parked in front of the house, he sensed the tension coming from his passenger. He shut off the engine and turned in the seat. Keely sat stiffly, her hands clasped so tightly her knuckles were white. She stared straight ahead as if the windshield held all the answers for her.

"Are you sure?" he asked softly.

She nodded jerkily and reached for the door handle. She hopped out before he could come around to help her out. With her back ramrod stiff, she walked toward the front door and unlocked it. She pushed the door open, but she didn't enter immediately.

Sam remained behind her, letting her know he was there without her feeling he was pressuring her. A red-hot knot centered in his stomach as he stared at her back. When she finally walked inside, he stayed close by.

Keely walked around the living room, pausing at the wall not far from the fireplace. Her hand hovered in the air as her unfocused gaze stared at the same spot for some time.

"Mommy hated the couch and wanted a new one," she whispered. She shuddered and moved away. She headed for the stairs and slowly climbed upward.

Sam waited until she'd reached the top of the stairs before he switched on the portable cassette tape player he'd carried in with him. He'd kept it behind his back so Keely wouldn't see it. Now, he placed it on the floor and punched the Play button.

Keely froze at the top of the stairs the moment the haunting music echoed in the empty house. She dropped to her knees and clung to the bannister.

Sam moved up the stairs, but remained behind her.

"What do you see, Keely?" he asked softly.

"The loud voices woke me up," she said in a barely there whisper. Her eyes were glassy with terror. "Daddy was yelling a lot."

He dropped down behind her, but didn't touch her for fear of breaking the spell. "Was he yelling at your mom?"

She shook her head. "I wasn't supposed to get out of bed. But the night-light was off and I can't sleep without the night-light." She clutched the rungs with her fingers as she stared downstairs at a scene only she could see. "Daddy was yelling at Mr. Willis. He said he wasn't a nice man and did something really bad. Mr. Willis yelled back at Daddy. I didn't like them yelling." She started shivering violently. "And Mommy started yelling, too. She was really scared. I don't know why. Her favorite song was playing on the radio. I liked it cuz it had her name in it. Mom would laugh cuz when it played, I'd sing 'go ask Alice' and tell her we needed a white rabbit." Her voice was a monotone as if she were telling a story she wasn't part of. Sam wanted nothing more than to take her in his arms and spare her the horror she would soon relate, but he deliberately held himself back.

"So, Mr. Willis was mean to your mom?" he asked in a quiet voice.

Her head bobbed up and down. "He said Daddy owed him money, but Daddy said he didn't do what he was supposed to do. Mr. Willis had a toy gun with him and Mommy screamed like she does when she sees a spider." Her lower lip trembled and tears coated her voice. "Mr. Willis shot my daddy with the gun. Mommy screamed and called him names, but he shot her, too. There was a lot of red stuff on their clothes." She unhooked her fingers from the rungs and carefully crab-walked backward. "I don't want Mr. Willis to see me," she whispered. "He might do something bad to me." She kept up her stealthy retreat until she reached a door then she crept inside and carefully closed the door after her.

Sam took several deep breaths. He wasn't sure whether to shout or cry. But he knew one thing he was going to do. He slowly got to his feet and walked down the hall. He opened the door and looked in.

Keely was lying on the floor.

"If I keep my eyes closed, he'll think I'm asleep," she whispered. "I can hear him at the door and he's seeing if I'm asleep. So I'll hold my dog and pretend to be asleep."

Sam felt the chill invade his bones. Willis had come upstairs and actually checked on her? What if she hadn't had the presence of mind to pretend to be asleep? Would she have been a victim too? Perhaps Willis wouldn't even have been convicted, since she had been the prosecution's star witness.

"But you're safe now, Keely." He kept his voice low and nonthreatening. "Mr. Willis is gone."

She turned over and sat up, sliding backward until she reached the wall. "Why did he have to kill them, Sam?" she asked in a hoarse voice. "Was money that important to him?"

"He had a couple kids, so maybe that's why. But his wife left him before the trial started." He moved over and crouched down by her. "That's why the song affected you so much, although you've probably heard it many times before without even thinking about it. You were back up here where it all began. Somehow he knew the song would upset you."

"The first time I heard it was at the bookstore. I felt as if a fog surrounded me and I heard shouting. That's how my nightmare would start. With shouting," she mused. She combed her fingers though her hair, which hung loosely down to her shoulders. "A courtroom. People asking me questions. A man trying to say I didn't even know what I was talking about. I was only a little girl. I couldn't say the handyman killed my parents."

"But you did and he was convicted because of what you saw."

She raised her head. Eyes glimmering with tears looked at him. "You knew everything, didn't you? Why didn't you tell me? Why did you let me go through this?"

This time, he followed through on his wishes and pulled her into arms. "It wouldn't have been a good idea. You had blocked out that entire time. Your remembering couldn't be forced." He kissed her forehead and noticed her skin was icy to the touch. "I wasn't going to suggest you do something like this, but I knew if you were going to go through with it, I was going to be with you."

She clutched at him as if he were her lifeline. "The man committed two horrible murders. He's still in prison, right? Right, Sam?" Her voice sharpened when he hesitated.

"No, Keely, he's out. Has been for a few years," he said quietly. "He got out early for good behavior."

Her lips parted, her eyes dilated with shock as the words rocked her back and forth like a cold slap in the face.

"The man killed two people in cold blood and would have killed a child if I hadn't pretended to be asleep," she said in a low voice throbbing with fury. "Yet they let him out for good behavior? What does this say about our justice system?"

"Prisons are overcrowded. If someone keeps his act together while inside, he has a chance of getting out. My dad was in charge then and I don't even know if he heard about it when it happened, but he probably did and purposely kept it quiet. I'm sure he knew if there was a chance Willis would come back here, there would be a lynching party waiting for him."

Keely kept shaking her head, unable to believe all she was hearing. The chilling memory of how her parents were killed in such a violent manner was now a recent memory for her. And the man who had destroyed a little girl's life had been set free because he behaved himself in prison. She rubbed her hands over her face.

"Why didn't anyone ever say anything to me about this?" she demanded. "I can't believe everyone who lived here back then is gone now. This must have been the biggest thing to happen up here since the Gold Rush."

He tightened his hold, pressing her cheek against his shirtfront. "That was a decision made thirty years ago. After the trial ended, you got very sick. There was a time the doctors weren't sure you'd survive. When you did and it was learned that you'd forgotten everything about the murder, your grandmother decided it was a sign. She sold her house and moved the two of you out of here. She didn't want you to ever remember the truth behind your parents' death. Your grandmother was a much loved woman in this town and it seemed to be an unspoken agreement that the murder wouldn't be mentioned around you back then. When you came back it was pretty obvious you hadn't remembered what happened and no one felt it was right to bring it up first."

Keely assimilated his words. She was stunned people would care so deeply about a person's feelings that they were willing to do such a thing for someone they hadn't truly known.

She disengaged herself from his arms and stood up. She didn't bother brushing the dust from her jeans as she walked out of the room. Sam followed more slowly. By the time he reached the top of the stairs, she was standing by the cassette recorder. She had stopped the tape and pulled it out of the machine. She held the tape up and carefully unwound it until ribbons lay in a brown shiny pool around her feet. She didn't turn around as she spoke.

"I need to go into town," she said in a voice that gave no indication what her mood was.

By the time Sam was downstairs, Keely was out in his truck. He paused long enough to pick up the cassette recorder, and on his way out he flipped the lock and closed the door.

"I want to go to the newspaper office," she said in a monotone.

Sam stifled a deep sigh. "Are you sure that's a good idea?"

She turned her head. The blank expression on her face was chilling Sam's soul.

"Was playing that song to help jog my memory a good idea?" she asked. "I guess in your mind it was. Now I have to do something to finish the process which means I need to read some old articles. Where else will I learn besides the newspaper office?"

He didn't bother to argue with her. He figured he'd lose anyway. Keely was right. He'd made the judgment call in playing the song while she was in the house and it had worked. He wasn't sure if she hated him or not for what he'd done. So far, she hadn't shown much in the way of emotion. He switched on the ignition and drove down the driveway. Instead of turning toward his house, he turned toward town. If she was going to find any articles on the murders, he preferred to be present.

"Hey there, Sam," the man at the front desk in the small local paper's office greeted him. He nodded toward Keely.

"George, this is Keely Harper," Sam said. "Keely, George Weaver has been the newspaper's owner, editor in chief, head reporter for the last forty years."

George nodded a head covered with snowy white hair that was pulled back into a ponytail. With his faded jeans, tie-dyed T-shirt and sandals he looked like a refugee from the sixties. His dark eyes were keen as he offered Keely his hand.

"Mr. Weaver, do you have the back issues for nineteen sixty-seven?" Keely asked.

He glanced at Sam, who nodded and mouthed the words "She knows."

"I've kept up with the times and they're all on microfilm," he replied, sliding out from behind his desk and heading for the back of the room. "Why not come on back here and I'll get out what you need."

"So you know, too," she said, the lack of tone in her voice making it impossible to tell if it was a threat or statement.

George turned around. "Yes, Keely, I know. You were a very brave girl back then. Have a seat here."

Keely followed him to the desk and sat down in front of the microfilm machine. George came back with a spool of film and quickly threaded it through. He turned it on and leaned over, scanning it in bits and pieces until he came to the front page he wanted.

"Everything you'll need to see is on this spool," he said quietly. He glanced over at Sam. "Take all the time you want."

"Thank you." Keely's eyes were already focused on the screen.

Brutal Double Homicide Rocks Echo Ridge!
This morning, the bodies of Charles and Alice Davis were discovered in their home, victims of bullet wounds to the heart and lungs. Alice's mother, Evelyn Stuart, discovered the bodies when she stopped by to pick up her granddaughter, Keely. Luckily, the five-year-old child had been sleeping upstairs and was unharmed. Police are conducting an intensive investigation to learn the reason for the killings and bring the murderer to justice.

Keely reached out with her fingertip, gently tracing the

grainy photograph of a man and woman smiling at the camera.

"I've never seen them before now," she whispered. "Grandma said there weren't any pictures. I guess she thought if I saw a picture of them I might remember." She moved the tape a little further ahead then stopped.

Edgar Willis Arrested for the Murder of Alice and Charles Davis!

Due to Keely Davis's testimony, Edgar Willis was arrested for the murder that shocked our small town. She told Sheriff Fred Barkley that the family handyman had been arguing with her parents and shot them. She had gone back to her bed and pretended to be asleep because she was afraid the bad man would hurt her, too. Fingerprints found at the scene matched Willis's. Due to the heinous nature of the crimes, there is no bail set.

Keely stared at a photograph of a man in his thirties who stared sullenly at the camera. Underneath his chin was a jail identification number.

"What do you remember about him?" she asked softly.

He thought for a moment. "Good worker, but had a bad temper." He winced at his bad choice of words. "He had two kids, a wife who was afraid of him but never said anything negative about him. No one else complained about him because he was always on time for his jobs, drank only on the weekends and stayed out of people's way."

Keely continued staring at the picture. "He built the back porch," she said to herself. "But afterward, he wanted more money even though the price had already been agreed on. My dad told him he was paid and he wouldn't get any more. That's why he came back that night. He wanted more."

As if she couldn't bear to look at it anymore, she scanned forward. She read every word regarding the trial. Arguments made by both sides and a story about a little girl who told a story about the family handyman shooting a gun at her parents and now her mommy and daddy were in heaven and how much she missed them. The defense tried every trick in the book to trip up her testimony, but for a five-year-old she was very self-contained and answered in a clear piping voice. There was no doubt when the guilty verdict was unanimous.

Edgar Willis was given a life sentence in prison. People declared they wanted him to die there. His wife had divorced him before the trial began and moved herself and their two children out of the state.

"Why was he so angry?" Keely asked, turning around to Sam. "Why would he do something so vile when he had to know he'd be caught?"

He shook his head. "I remember overhearing my dad talking about it. Edgar had been drinking and could be a mean drunk at times."

"Did he start fights? Did anyone ever press charges against him?"

He shook his head. "His wife had it rough enough and he always paid the damages. No one had any idea he would go as far as he did. No warning."

She stared at him, her face pale as if it were carved in marble. "Wonderful. No warning, a man who must have been troubled and people felt sorry for his wife, so no one ever intervened. During this time, Edgar Willis's anger must have been building up until all it could do was explode. Unfortunately, my parents were in the way when it happened." She pushed back the chair and stood up. "I can't do this anymore." She walked swiftly toward the front, her sandals making barely there taps on the wooden floor. She paused by George's desk. "Thank you, Mr. Weaver. It's been enlightening." She pushed open the door and walked outside.

Sam cursed under his breath as he hurried after her.

"It's better she knows all of it, Sam," George called after him. "It's the only way she can get on with her life."

"Not if someone is trying to end that life," he muttered, pushing open the door with a heavy hand.

As he stepped onto the sidewalk, he felt a prickling sensation tickle the back of his neck. He remembered the last time he'd felt that. A coked-out kid carrying a sawed-off shotgun had been training his sights on Sam. Sam had ducked just in time.

Without appearing as if anything was seriously wrong, he glanced around. All he saw were the usual residents out shopping or local business owners returning from lunch or standing in a doorway talking to a customer or friend.

Could it be one of them? Could one of these people be in contact with Edgar Willis giving him information about Keely?

He only wished he knew what he could do to stop this here and now.

He walked over to Keely, who was standing by his truck's passenger door.

"Home?" he asked.

"Not just yet." She looked at a point just past his shoulder. "I want to stop by the Realtor's first."

"The Realtor's?"

She nodded. "I'm going to put the house up for sale."

Sam opened his mouth, ready to ask why she was making this impulsive decision, but he wasn't sure he wanted to know. Because if Keely put the house up for sale, she would have no reason to stay here and he wasn't about to let her go.

Chapter 17

Keely was in pain. Remembering the night of her parents' murders was bad enough, but reading the objective newspaper accounts of the crime and trial that followed tore her apart inside.

She knew she could never live in the house. The memories would now be too strong.

She spoke to the Realtor, explained she wanted the house listed for sale as is and then asked Sam to drive her back to his house.

Steffie and Lisa were anxious for their return. She gently put off their questions and explained she was tired.

"I'm going to take a nap," she said quietly, pausing to hug each girl before walking to the guest room.

"Dad?" Lisa looked at her father.

"Sam?" Steffie asked at the same time.

"I can't tell you all of it," he said, after herding them into the family room. "That's up to Keely, but she had a great shock today and she needs to work it through before she can talk about it, so how about giving her a break, okay?''

They both nodded. They then looked at each other and turned back to him.

''We know you and Mom are sleeping together,'' Steffie said without preamble, ''and it's okay with us. We know you didn't want us to know since it's something you wouldn't want us to do, but don't worry. We just wanted you to know we're all right with it.''

Sam had been floored before but never by two teenage girls.

''Thank you,'' he said for lack of anything else.

Steffie grinned cheekily. ''You do make a cute couple.'' She giggled as they bounced back to Lisa's room.

Sam sat there for a long time. After shaking his head at the memory of what he'd just been told, he stood up and headed for the guest room. He eased the door open and found Keely curled up on the bed. He walked over to the side of the bed and carefully sat down. He brushed his knuckles across her cheek.

''Had a talk with the girls,'' he said softly. ''They wanted to give us their seal of approval.''

She looked up questioningly.

''They said they know we're sleeping together and that it's okay and they don't plan to do it themselves.''

A watery chuckle erupted from Keely's lips as if she wasn't sure whether to laugh or cry. She sat up, punching her pillow behind her back.

''What are they trying to do?''

''I think it's pretty obvious.'' He kept his hand near her shoulder. ''It has been from the beginning.''

Keely didn't look at him. ''If you don't mind, Sam, I'd like to be alone.''

He wanted to be angry with her. He wanted to demand she open her eyes and realize what was important; that *they* were important. Then he wanted to make slow sweet love to her and take all her pain away by taking it inside him. He wanted her to know just how important she was to him and that he couldn't let her go now.

Instead, Sam edged away and stood up.

"Just remember it was done for your good," he reminded her. "A lot of people kept quiet about this because they didn't want you hurt. Now it's best if you try to go on."

"Considering that there's a good chance this Edgar Willis is after me, I can't imagine that happening," she said bitterly. "I don't see why you can't find him. Doesn't the prison have any more recent pictures of him? Or even age that mug shot you have of him?"

"Since he isn't accused of a crime, I can't do anything about it. Plus, that old picture won't do any good. He had to have plastic surgery since then and he doesn't look the same," he admitted.

"Why am I not surprised?" she muttered, looking away.

"You're safer here than you would be in a big city," he offered.

"They'd lie to me there, too."

Stung by her reply, he walked out.

Keely curled up in bed in the fetal position. She couldn't understand the pain and confusion racing through her mind. One more problem piled on top of the others.

Was this Edgar Willis trying to hurt her now? Why? He had served his time in prison. While she hated the idea he'd been set free, she couldn't imagine his bitterness would be so strong he'd risk another prison sentence. The newspaper picture still stuck in her mind. Especially his sullen expression on his face and the dark secrets in his gaze. He would be thirty years older now. Hair would be gray or white. Lines in the face, but even if he'd had plastic surgery she couldn't imagine the angry eyes would change. She rolled over onto her back and tried to envision the face thirty years older.

Instead, her mind veered off and the face in her mind changed into Sam's. Sam who had stood by her. Who held her while she cried and relived an old pain. Sam who vowed to protect her with his own life. She knew it would take time for her to come to terms with what had happened today, but it wasn't something she needed to worry about right away. The last thing she should do is punish him for helping her.

"Be a grown-up, Keely," she told herself. "Don't do anything that might make you lose what's turned out to be the best thing to come into your life since Steffie was born."

Sam was relieved to see Keely had pretty much returned to her old self when she came out of the guest room an hour later. There were still some shadows in her eyes but nothing like before.

"It's just going to take time," she admitted to him, as she walked past him toward the family room, where Steffie and Lisa were watching television.

She asked Steffie to come with her and they walked outside to the patio table. Steffie looked apprehensively at her mother.

"Is everything okay?" she asked. "Sam wouldn't say anything after you guys came back."

Keely took a deep breath. "This won't be easy for me to say, so I hope you'll stay quiet until I finish. If you stop me to ask questions, I may not be able to go on."

Steffie nodded, but her gaze was still troubled.

"It has to do with my parents' deaths and why I got so upset the first time I walked into their house." Sometimes Keely's words were halting, sometimes she had to stop and shore up her inner strength to go on, but she managed until she finished the story.

Steffie sat across from her, tears running down her face. "Oh, Mom," she sobbed, grabbing hold of her mother's hands. "How sad for them! But I'm so glad nothing happened to you. No wonder you seemed to hate the house."

"That's why I think I'll put it up for sale."

She stilled. "But you said the owners we're leasing from don't want to sell their house. What are we going to do?" She suddenly brightened. "Stay here?"

"Don't go there, Steff," Keely warned.

"I think Sam's in love with you," she confided.

"I mean it, Stefanie. Don't try anything."

Steffie jumped up and ran around the table to throw her arms around Keely's shoulders.

"Oh, Mom, no wonder you had those horrible nightmares," she consoled. "Still, people up here must be really nice if they kept this all a secret. It's nothing like L.A., where people don't seem to care as much. We did right in coming up here." She kissed her on the cheek and ran back to the house.

Keely closed her eyes. She felt so drained she wasn't sure she could move. When she looked around she noticed Sam standing at the door. She felt bereft when he turned away and didn't come outside to join her.

She told herself she shouldn't have been surprised. He was going to leave it all up to her. She would have to make the next move. She just hoped she would make the right decision.

Sam was hazily aware of Keely slipping into his bed much later that night. She curled up against his side while he put his arm around her shoulders. She rested her cheek against his chest.

"Just sleep," she whispered after pressing her lips against the skin covering his heart.

Feeling easier in his mind, he drifted back to sleep. But he was aware of her wakefulness. He finally felt her ease her way from his arms and heard the soft slide of the glass door opening then closing. He opened his eyes and watched Keely sitting on the step just outside the door. He climbed out of bed and wrapped the blanket around his shoulders before walking outside.

"Hey," he said softly, sitting down with a leg on either side of her hips. He opened the blanket and wrapped it around her. She leaned back against his chest, resting her hands on top of his.

"It's so peaceful here." She sighed. "No cigar smoke, either."

"It's supposed to be nonsmoking in these woods anyway, but there shouldn't be any of those worries," he said, resting his chin on top of her head.

"Sam."

"Hm?"

"I love you." She could feel the tension in his arms surrounding her.

"I loved you first," he whispered against her hair.

She wondered if he could sense her smile. "I love you more."

"I'll love you forever."

She turned around in his arms, kneeling on the step and looping her arms around his neck.

"Are we crazy?" she whispered. "Does this have something to do with all the hell going on in my life? Or can we trust ourselves for knowing what's real and what isn't?"

Sam kissed her forehead. "You feel real to me. What I feel *for* you is very real. What was going on between us started even before the other stuff began. We'll finish it together and go on from there.''

Her expression was hopeful. The expectancy seemed to sparkle in her eyes as the moonlight bathed her face in a pearly glow.

"We will?" she asked.

"We have to," Sam said with a teasing lilt in his voice. "The girls gave us their seal of approval, remember?"

Keely laughed as she hadn't laughed in a long time. She hugged Sam tightly.

"I'm afraid to hope," she confessed.

"Then just remember that as long as I'm with you, you can hope all you want to." Sam pressed butterfly kisses against her closed eyelids. "But what starts out as hope will soon turn into reality."

He stood up, easily picking her up with him, her legs wrapped around his hips.

"I think what comes next should go on behind closed doors," he muttered. "No use in letting the bears find out what we humans do."

"Lions and tigers and—" She nibbled on his ear. "If I'm going to confess any of my uncontrollable urges to you, I'd rather do it in private."

Sam took a deep breath. "I'm sure glad I take my vitamins," he said as he closed the sliding glass door behind them.

A figure stood down among the trees looking up at the couple as they sat on the deck and as they returned to the house's interior. This time there was no cigar smoked.

She had been out to her parents' house today. Then she had gone to the newspaper office. She would only have gone there if she remembered everything. That wasn't good news. That also meant she'd have to be watched more.

It was more than clear they were lovers. Perhaps the

best way to get to her was through him, but Sam wasn't any small-town sheriff who was given the job because everyone liked him. He had been a big city cop in Homicide. He'd worked some major league cases and had plenty of contacts if he wanted information. Information was the last thing that should be retrieved right now. So it was a question of watching and waiting until the time was just right.

"What shall we do today?" Steffie asked, collapsing in a chair and swinging her leg over the arm. She quickly straightened up when she noticed the warning light in her mother's eye.

"I realize this is more than a little boring," Keely apologized. She was sitting at the dining room table, with her computer in front of her. The cursor had been blinking at her as she tried to concentrate on a new sales pamphlet for a candy company. Usually the idea of making the delicious confections had her imagination running overtime.

Not today. Enforced confinement for the past week had been slowly wearing and tearing on everyone's nerves. Sam had tried to console Keely by saying it was a good way to see if the two girls could handle it. She reminded him he wasn't the one spending the days with them.

Keely wondered what a chocolate drop would look like wearing a sun hat, sunglasses and lounging on a beach chair.

"Can we go to Connie's this afternoon?" Lisa asked. She had been lying on the floor with a book in front of her. She hadn't turned a page for the past half hour.

"I had no idea my company was so boring," Keely said drily.

"Connie is having some friends over for a barbecue. Couldn't our baby-sitter drive us over then pick us up later?'' Steffie asked. ''You need to get your work done and maybe it would be easier if we weren't around.''

Keely settled back in her chair. ''Your concern is gratifying,'' she teased. ''All right, you can go, but you do not leave Connie's house for any reason or with anyone but Rob, me or Sam. Understood?''

Both heads bobbed up and down before they jumped up and ran back to the bedroom. Within ten minutes they were gone, promising to remember every one of Keely's warnings.

''Peace and quiet is perfect for me,'' Keely said to herself, returning to the keyboard and the idea of mocha chocolates hanging on a coffee tree.

She started the design when the phone rang. She stiffened at first even though she hadn't received any more calls. She had hoped that meant her tormentor was deciding to leave her alone.

''Hey there,'' John greeted her. ''How about coming into town for lunch? You've been hiding out so much that we rarely see you around here.''

Keely made a face. ''I'm sorry, John, but I'm working on an important project I need to finish today.''

''I had hoped you'd give me a chance before deciding to hook up with the sheriff,'' he joked, but it fell false on her ears.

''Please don't take this the wrong way, John, but I don't think it was meant to be,'' she said gently.

''How can you say that when you never gave me a chance?''

She could feel the trembling start deep down inside her as his anger lashed out at her. Was he the one after all? Was it nothing more than a man who felt she was for him? It wouldn't be the first time. She licked her dry lips.

''John, please don't say anything like that,'' she suggested, keeping her voice even. "I hope we'll still be friends."

"I wanted more than your friendship, Keely," he snarled in a low tone still vibrating with anger. "Just don't come crying to me when he dumps you." He slammed the phone down.

Keely winced at the loud sound in her ear. She started to punch out the sheriff's station phone number, then stopped. What could she tell Sam? That John acted like a rejected suitor? No, she'd wait until he got home.

She returned to her work, but trying to make chocolates look festive for the summer wasn't as easy now as it was before.

"I want a raise," Fredda declared, striding into Sam's office.

"You do, huh?" He grinned. "For what?"

"For coming up with more than your damned deputies did." She plopped down in the chair and tossed two sheets of paper in front of him. "In fact, I probably came up with a few goodies none of us would have thought of." She smiled, sure of herself.

He picked up the first paper and studied names typed neatly on the white surface, with penned-in notations next to each name.

A couple of lines furrowed between his brows when he looked up. "What exactly are we talking about here?"

Fredda rolled her eyes at what she considered the innate stupidity of the male.

"You wanted to know who remembered Edgar Willis," she stated. "I figured if we needed to find out about Edgar, we might as well find out about his wife and children, too. After the divorce, she moved to Utah. Kids had some trouble there. Oh, if a Detective Vetter ever calls for Samantha Barkley, it's only because it was easier to use your name."

"Fredda!" He threw up his hands. "You represented yourself as a peace officer?"

"You weren't here, it was easier and he was ready to talk."

"There are deputies who could have talked to him," Sam reminded her.

She snorted her opinion of that. "It was much easier this way. You'll see my notes about my talk with him on the second page." She tapped the paper with a lavender-tinted fingernail.

Sam picked up the sheet and read. The more he read, the more clouds of anger darkened his face. "There was no way we could have known this before," he said, crumpling the paper in his fist.

She shook her head. "No way at all. It was pure luck I happened to talk to this guy. He remembers the family pretty well. Kids were in and out of trouble from high school on and they blamed Keely for every misfortune they had. Edgar's ex-wife died ten years ago and the kids had already left home."

Sam smoothed out the crumpled sheet of paper and re-read it.

"I had no idea," he murmured. "There isn't any resemblance."

"Read on," she urged. "I think you'll find that part pretty interesting, too."

As Sam's eyes wandered down the page, his blood chilled.

"I've got some questions to ask," he muttered, standing up. He grabbed his hat and started out of the office. He stopped when he reached her chair. He pulled her out of the chair and planted a smacking kiss on her lips. "You've got the raise."

Fredda's squeal of delight was the last thing Sam heard as he stormed out of the office.

Chapter 18

Keely stared at the computer monitor. She was almost finished. She felt it didn't have the sparkle previous brochures had, but it was better than she expected.

She glanced at the clock as she stretched the kinks out of her back. It was as she turned to look at the time that she noticed something seemed different on one of the walls. She stood up and walked over.

"Oh, my," she whispered, tracing the edge of two photographs that had been added to the collage. One had been taken of Lisa and Steffie the afternoon Keely and Steffie had tried to teach Lisa how to in-line skate. She had started to fall and Steffie reached out to grab her, only to fall with her. Keely had grabbed a camera and snapped the moment. The other photograph was a complete surprise to her. She and Sam had been sitting on the deck, each holding a glass of wine. Keely was seated on the deck floor with her legs propped up on the railing while Sam sat against the railing facing her. What hit her hard was the expression on his face. He hadn't said he'd loved her when that picture had been taken, but the expression on his face had said it all. She traced the line of his lips and face.

"Oh, Sam," she said in a breathy voice. "It was all meant to be, wasn't it?"

She had no idea how long she stood there until the telephone rang. Still thinking about the man in the picture, she picked up the receiver.

"Hello?"

"Keely." The whispery voice sent ice sliding down her spine.

She clutched the receiver tightly. "What do you want?"

"I really want you, but I have something almost as good. Something very dear to you. Can you guess what that is?"

"Oh my God, you can't." For a moment, she forgot to breathe. "There's no way. You're playing mind games with me."

"No mind games, Keely. Denim shorts, a red T-shirt and a denim vest with red patchwork on it. Does that sound familiar?"

Keely's fingers touched her lips as if to hold back her cries of anger.

"There's more. Green shorts and a green-and-white T-shirt."

Keely slowly lowered herself to the floor.

"Let them go. They have nothing to do with this."

"Oh, but they do. After all, you care for them a great deal, don't you? By my having them, I know you will come to me. I haven't liked you staying with the sheriff. I haven't been able to see you as much that way. So I'll make a bargain with you. You come to me. Don't call the sheriff, don't alert the deputy parked out front. You come by yourself."

Keely almost crawled to her computer. She pulled herself into the chair and sat at the keyboard.

"I will. Where am I supposed to go?" As the whispery voice gave her directions, she typed them out and pressed the print button.

"Don't tell anyone, Keely or something very bad will happen to them," the voice warned.

"If you hurt one hair on either of their heads, I will kill you."

Laughter was the answer to her cold threat.

"We'll see who will die first. Don't be late, Keely."

It was a few moments before Keely realized she was listening to a dial tone. With her back stiff with resolve, she stood up and headed for the kitchen. With a broad smile, she took a glass of soda out to the deputy and a piece of cake.

When she returned to the house, she headed straight for Sam's gun cabinet. She knew where he kept the key and soon had it unlocked. She chose a weapon, loaded it and locked the cabinet back up. She figured she'd seen enough cop shows on TV to know what to do with it. Afterward, she quickly changed into jeans and a loose cotton shirt to hide the gun nestled against her back, and pulled her hair back in a ponytail. She was going to be ready for a fight.

Sam soon had more answers. As he drove down the street, his mind was racing with thoughts. As the radio crackled and his name was spoken, he picked up the microphone.

"Yeah, Fredda?"

"Sam, Rob hasn't checked in and when I tried to reach him, he didn't answer," Fredda told him.

That was all he needed to hear. "I'm on my way. Keep trying to reach him."

As Sam sped toward his house, horrifying pictures kept

intruding. He didn't dare think of the worst as he kept increasing the speed, even going so far as to turn on his siren. If anyone hadn't pulled over in time, he would have driven over them without a second thought.

When he saw his deputy's body collapsed on the front seat, he did fear the worst, until a further check showed him the young man was sound asleep. The empty glass and plate showing only a few cake crumbs gave him the idea what might have happened. Sam raced inside the house.

"Keely!" The moment he was inside, he knew there was no one there. "Dammit!" He saw the weapon missing from his gun cabinet and knew only one person could have taken it. He started for the kitchen in hopes Keely had left him a clue when he noticed her computer was still on. He glanced at the screensaver characters dancing across the screen and tapped a key. There was his clue in neatly printed letters detailing the message and the directions Keely had been given by the caller.

"Oh, damn," he muttered, before hitting the print screen button. As the printer spit out the paper, he returned to the gun cabinet. Within seconds, he had a high-powered rifle with scope and his favorite handgun.

With a grim expression marring his face, Sam was soon on the road, traveling at high speed. He only wished he knew how long it had been since Keely had left, but he couldn't imagine it had been very long. As he drove, his mind raced with ideas on how to sneak up without being seen. He glanced at the radio. Would backup be a good idea or not? Keely and the kids were involved. Dammit! His hands tightened on the steering wheel so hard it almost seemed to crack under his grip.

Keely had had only herself for protection thirty years ago and somehow survived. He wasn't about to let her take that chance this time.

* * *

When Keely parked her truck in the dirt parking area, she noticed no other vehicles around. As she slowly climbed out, she tried to reach out with all her senses to see who might be there.

"Mom!"

"Keely!"

The two young voices galvanized her to action. She ran down to the lakeshore. What she saw took her breath away. Steffie and Lisa were tied together and sitting in the middle of a rowboat that looked as if it could fall apart at any moment. And if it did.... She forced herself not to think of what might happen.

"We're sorry!" Steffie shouted. "You told us to be careful, but we didn't know!"

"Hello, Keely." The disembodied voice called out.

She spun around but only saw the empty picnic tables and trees.

"Why are you doing this?" she shouted. "You said they would be safe."

"And they will. As long as they don't rock the boat." The chuckle sent chills down Keely's back.

She resisted the urge to reach for her gun. She didn't want him to know she had it yet.

"You've been a coward hiding behind a phone and in shadows. Why not step out here and show yourself," she challenged.

"Oh, Keely, do you think you can anger me with puny words like that? I know better. But I will be showing myself."

As she heard the rustle of bushes to her right, Keely quickly spun in that direction.

"Mom, be careful!" Steffie shouted.

Keely understood what she meant when a figure stepped out into the open.

"Not you!" She couldn't stop staring, not even noticing the weapon pointed directly at her.

"Amazing what a voice changer can do, isn't it, Keely?" Chloe asked, holding up a small black box in her free hand. "I must admit it's been amusing tormenting you all this time, but now it's time for you to pay up."

"But the cigars," she stumbled over the words.

Chloe looked proud of herself. "A nice trick, wasn't it? I wanted you to think it was a man. I wanted you to think Edgar Willis had come back to kill you. You thought you were going to die that night in your house, didn't you? Perhaps I should have killed you then, but it was more fun to frighten you. And I did frighten you, didn't I?"

"But why would you do all of this?" she asked, still confused.

Chloe's face hardened. "Because you ruined my family. Because of you my father was sent to prison and my mother took us away from all we'd ever known. I loved this town. It was like something out of a book or a movie. Everyone helped each other. I felt safe here even if my father didn't always make me feel safe. But then my father was stupid enough to kill your parents and people looked at me as if I were something they'd wipe off the bottom of their shoes." She sneered. "So we ended up in some stupid town where my mom worked as a waitress and brought home men. My brother left home as soon as he was old enough and I wanted to do the same. I wanted to come back here. But not as Carole Willis. So I gave myself a whole new life." She straightened up, although the frightening light in her eyes never dimmed. "I was welcome here. I was treated like someone important." She glanced quickly behind her and shouted. "Come on out and see what I have for you."

Keely wasn't sure what to expect when a bearded man walked slowly out and stood beside Chloe. She hadn't expected to see Mr. Rainey, who owned the hardware store, staring back at her.

"You're Edgar Willis," she whispered.

He shifted uneasily, but didn't answer her. He turned to Chloe. "Why are you doing this?"

"Why am I doing this? I'm doing this for you. For all of us." She waved her gun around. "She ruined our lives. She sent you to prison. Mom took us away from the only home we knew!" she shrieked.

Edgar-Rainey reached out to her. "I did something wrong. I paid for it. Don't do what I did, Carole."

"My name is Chloe! I don't go by that other name anymore!"

Keely felt as if she'd stepped into a horror movie. Sam had mentioned Willis had had plastic surgery in prison and thought he'd had more when he'd gotten out. Obviously, he hadn't. Instead, he'd grown a beard to hide the scars. Just as Chloe had returned, so had he. And now so had she. As if they were all meant to finish what had started thirty years ago.

"Chloe." She purposely kept her voice low and even, nonthreatening. She didn't want to give her any reason to fire the gun. Keely was afraid she was the girls' only hope. "I was a small child back then. I only answered questions and told the truth. You lost your father, but I lost both of my parents. And I lost my memories of them."

"You were the poor little girl who suffered," she snarled. "I was the murderer's brat." Her face was a tight mask of fury. "You were adored. I was hated."

"Chloe, you'll only ruin your life the way I did," Rainey implored, reaching out to touch her arm. "Honey, please don't do this."

"Stop it!" She shook him off. "She deserves it. I could have run you down that day in Rick's truck. The bastard forgets that many times he leaves his keys in the ignition."

She smirked. "And then that day in your house. You were scared spitless, weren't you? You were scared of me and I was glad. Every other time I saw you and had to be your friend only made me sick to my stomach." She glanced at the lake. "I guess you didn't warn the girls very well, did you? It was easy to lure them away from their friend's house. Good ole Chloe doing Sam a favor by picking them up because they'd caught the intruder."

Sam stood back among the trees listening to Chloe's story. Here he'd been looking for a man and it turned out to be a woman creating hell for Keely. He'd always thought of Rainey as a cantankerous old man. He'd had no idea he was actually Willis.

He fitted the rifle stock snugly against his shoulder. All he wanted was one clear shot. Except, the way Chloe was standing, if he missed her he could accidentally hit Keely. He couldn't afford to take that chance.

He felt the sweat pouring down his forehead into his eyes. He wiped it away with his sleeve and peered through the scope again. He feared he would have only one shot and he would have to make it good.

"Mom, the boat is filling with water!" Steffie cried out with panic in her voice. She and Lisa struggled against their bonds.

"Don't move!" Keely ordered. "You might tip your-selves over." She looked back at the couple. "Why did you do it? Why did you kill them?"

The old man shook his head. "I've had thirty years to think about it, dream about it, and I can't give you an answer. They said I would have killed you if you had been awake." His face twisted in sorrow and old regrets. "I wouldn't have hurt you. I couldn't."

"Then why are you allowing her to do all this?" Keely

demanded, waving her hand to encompass Steffie and Lisa. "Why did you let her put me through hell all these months?"

"I didn't know," he explained. "I didn't even know Carole was here until she came to me. Somehow she figured out who I was. She brought me out here today saying she had something special to show me. I had no idea it had to do with you. I just wanted to be left alone."

"You need to finish this!" Chloe screeched, looking put out she had been ignored this long. "She destroyed our family. We'll destroy hers." She lifted her gun, pointing it at the boat.

Keely guessed her intention the moment the gun swung away from her.

"No!" She reached behind her but before she could pull the gun out of her waistband, a rifle shot rang out and with a cry of pain, Chloe dropped her gun and grasped her shoulder. Red dripped down her fingers. She fell to her knees, crying and cursing.

"*Mom!*"

Keely didn't think twice. She was barely aware of Sam walking out of the woods as she ran to the water's edge, toed off her shoes and made a shallow dive. The cold water hit her like a shock wave, but she didn't stop keeping a steady pace toward the rowboat that was listing dangerously.

"Listen to me," she panted. "We have to keep the weight as balanced as possible to avoid tipping while I try to untie you." They shifted over slowly while Keely carefully pulled herself up on the side of the small boat. She gave a sigh of relief that the knots weren't too difficult to loosen. Just as the rope dropped off the girls, the boat started to tip dangerously. "Jump out!" she screamed.

Both girls dove over the other side at the same time that

the boat rolled over. They swam around to Keely and awkwardly hugged her.

"You said not to trust anyone and you were right," Steffie sniffed.

"We're sorry," Lisa also sniffed.

"Let's just get back to shore," she said, wanting nothing more than to haul them into her arms and never let them go.

By the time they reached the shore, Sam had Chloe's uninjured arm handcuffed to a post and Rainey squatting down beside her, patting her hand in a clumsy manner. The woman's tears had left makeup smears along her cheeks and under her eyes. Her gaze fell on Keely, who walked up to her. Keely had an arm around each girl.

"It isn't fair!" she screeched, jerking at her handcuff. "Why should you win this time, too?"

Keely could only feel pity as she looked down at her. Even looking at Rainey and realizing who he was didn't inspire any anger in her. She felt past that now.

"Did all of this make your world any better, Chloe?" she asked softly. "Did it?"

"It would have if you were dead! And don't look at me that way! I don't need your damn pity."

"No, I guess you wouldn't want it." She turned to Sam, who reached out for all three of them.

"Do not ever scare me like that again," he said hoarsely, hugging them tightly. "I'm too old for this."

"You saw the note," she murmured. "You saw it." Her shoulders shook as she broke down in tears. "I was so afraid."

"You weren't the only one." He kissed the top of Lisa's then Steffie's head. "I'm calling someone else out to pick Chloe up."

"What about Rainey?" Keely asked.

"He hasn't done anything wrong."

"Miss Keely."

She turned her head but remained in Sam's arms. Rainey stood nearby, looking uncertain of her reception.

"I was an angry man back then," he said in halting words. "And I hurt people. I'm sorry I hurt you."

Keely managed a tentative smile. "Thank you, Mr. Rainey."

It took a moment for him to realize she hadn't used his real name. His shoulders seemed to slump with relief.

"I came up here to start over," she said. "You came back because it was all you knew. I won't tell anyone. As far as I'm concerned, Chloe tried to drag you into her scheme because she thought it would upset me." She looked past him at the woman who still pulled vainly at the handcuff. "No one will believe her."

Rainey looked to Sam, who nodded.

"I'll be getting back to my store then. That Dunlap boy has a habit of putting the nails in the wrong bins." He walked off, limping slightly. He looked over his shoulder a few times, as if he couldn't believe what just happened.

"Whoever said small-town life was boring had no idea," Keely said in a choked voice.

By the time reports had been filed and Chloe booked and jailed, Keely and Sam were exhausted. Steffie and Lisa ate fast-food hamburgers and dragged themselves off to bed. Keely changed into a nightgown and walked out onto the deck.

"It's just me," Sam said, coming out holding two glasses of wine.

She turned her head and smiled. "Hey, just you." She accepted the glass he held out.

"How do you feel now that it's over?"

"Relieved, sad, tired," she confessed. "I had no idea it was Chloe. All this time I thought it was a man."

"I did, too. She covered her tracks pretty well." He sat down beside her. "She's not talking now. Rainey called and said if she didn't have money for a lawyer, he'd pay for one. He also said he hopes some therapy will be suggested. I told him I'd see what I could do."

"So many twists and turns," she mused.

"What now?"

Keely looked at Sam. She could swear he looked as if he were steeling himself for the worst.

"I was thinking that if I sell the house we could use the money to add on a few rooms here," she said. "The girls aren't going to want to share a room full-time. And we could expand the master bedroom into a suite. I've always had a hankering for one of those big sunken tubs with Jacuzzi jets. A tub big enough for two." She set her wineglass down and looped her arms around his neck. "What do you think?"

"If you're thinking that way, we better also think about getting married."

She lifted her lips to his. "I thought you'd never ask."

The heat flared up between them like a rocket.

"I wish you had been the first," she confided. "But then I wouldn't have Steffie and you wouldn't have Lisa."

He chuckled. "No, we'd probably have a combination of both, Lord help us."

"So, I gather you like my idea?" she teased.

"Come on in and I'll show you how much."

She allowed herself to be pulled to her feet. "An even better idea."

Epilogue

Two years later

"Smile!"

Flashbulbs went off with blinding light.

"Okay, Mom, enough pictures," Steffie begged.

"Keely, we're almost blind!" Lisa protested.

At age eighteen, both girls were taller, losing the awkwardness of youth and showing the beginning bloom of womanhood. Dressed in formal gowns, they stood next to their prom dates as Keely snapped pictures.

"I have some good ones," she declared, setting the camera on the table.

"Tell Sam not to scare the boys," Steffie whispered as she hugged Keely. She grinned and patted her mother's protruding abdomen. "No more candy bars for you."

"Watch it or I'll insist curfew be at ten," Sam told her.

Steffie wrinkled her nose at him. "Such a horror you are."

The boys smiled uncertainly at Sam as they ushered their dates out. The night of the senior prom was not one to be missed.

"Did you really threaten them?" Keely asked as Sam held her hand while she almost fell back onto the couch.

"Hell, yes, I did!"

"Are you going to be that bad with the new one?" she asked, keeping her hand on her belly.

He sat down next to her and leaned over to kiss her tummy. "Worse. Especially if it's a boy." Because of Keely's age she'd had amniocentesis, but they insisted they wanted to be surprised about the sex of their child.

Keely noticed a few more lines around his eyes and additional silver in the brown hair, but otherwise Sam was the same man. With Chloe in a psychiatric institution and Rainey keeping to himself, the secrets had been kept. As she'd been taken away, Chloe had screamed Rainey's name as her father, Edgar Willis, but she sounded so distraught no one believed her.

Keely placed her cupped palm against Sam's cheek feeling the roughness of his skin against hers.

"I love you," she said, letting all her love and passion for him show in her eyes.

He grinned. "I loved you first."

"I love you more," she continued in what had become a tradition between them.

"I'll love you forever."

Of that, Keely had no doubt.

* * * * *